NOLAN

A DARK IRISH MAFIA ROMANCE

JANE HENRY

D1607676

J. HENRY PUBLICATIONS

FREE BOOK

Would you like to read *Island Captive: A Dark Romance* totally free? Sign up HERE for my newsletter, and grab your freebie!

SYNOPSIS

She's my nemesis.

My prisoner.

I'll make her beg for mercy.

I'll make her scream my name.

I'll make her mine.

Sheena Hurston's been a thorn in my side for years.

But when she tries to bring my family to ruin, I'm done playing games.

She will pay for what she's done.

No one comes before my family.

S*HEENA BELONGS TO ME*.

READING ORDER

Though each book in the Dangerous Doms series is a stand-alone, the chronological order is as follows:

Keenan

Cormac

Nolan

Carson (late July 2020)

Chapter 1

Nolan

I WALK along the rocky cliffs that overlook the Irish Sea, the most beautiful view in all of Ballyhock. Seems my brothers find solace here, so why can't I? But I don't. Every step I take makes me more restless, more antsy.

Today's the second year anniversary of my father's death.

I kick a rock with the toe of my boot and watch it tumble downward until it splashes in the sea below, quickly swallowed up. Gone. A hard, dangerous weapon one second, forgotten the next. An omen? I'm feeling melancholy tonight.

Up until a year or so ago, I reckon I was the one no one really respected in The Clan, the class clown. And hell, I earned that title, drinking myself to damn near death before I'd hit my twenty-fifth birthday.

But that was the old me. Before my father died. Before my brother Keenan took the throne as Chief and I moved up in rank. Before I kicked alcohol and took hold of my own life.

I take a smoke out of my pocket and light it up, inhaling the nicotine into my lungs and letting it out slowly. I traded one vice for another, I suppose, and why the fuck not. A man's got to have an outlet. I won't touch drink anymore, and honestly rarely smoke, but tonight... tonight's a night I need fucking something.

Two years ago tonight my father was killed by a rival, a fucking Martin. We're at peace with them now. My brother Cormac married the tribute they offered. But they aren't friends of ours. We'll honor the truce between us, but the Martins are dead to us.

What would my father think of me now? Seamus McCarthy ruled with an iron fist. He worked tirelessly to establish the McCarthy Clan as the most powerful leaders in all of Ireland's underground. It matters to me to honor that.

I knew from a very young age, I never measured up to my father's expectations. He expected his boys to be strong and valiant, rulers of this land who feared nothing. And I let him down. Until recently, my older brothers felt the same. Keenan, the eldest, barely hid his contempt for me. But I can't blame him. I wasn't someone who earned respect.

But that was then. And this is now.

My brother sits on the throne as leader, Cormac heir to the throne, and I'm third in command. Keenan and Cormac are fathers now, their wee babies growing in number as the years pass. Keenan has two babes and Cormac one, but it's only the beginning of a new generation. Where do I fit in the grand scheme of the McCarthy clan?

My phone dings and I glance at the text from Boner.

Club tonight after the meeting, brother?

Boner would live at The Craic if he could, and hell, some days I don't blame him. We're well-known members there. Took me a while to get comfortable going without a drink, but now I welcome it.

I take another drag and draw it into my lungs.

Maybe Sheena will be there.

Sheena, the gorgeous, headstrong lass I've had my eye on for damn near as long as my father's been gone. The fucking investigative reporter that doesn't know what's good for her. The girl I love to hate.

Last year, there was an incident at the club that scared the hell out of her, and it took some time before she'd come back to the club. She keeps her distance from me, though. She knows I'm onto her. I caught her trespassing on our land once, and I thought I'd put a decided end to her snooping. But hell, if I'm honest, I hope I haven't.

I'd like an excuse to punish her again.

I frown out at the sea again. Now that I think of it, I haven't seen her recently.

Where's she been?

The better question is, why do I fucking care?

I kick another rock into the sea for good measure.

I swipe my phone on and my finger hovers over the keyboard. Do I want to go tonight? I shake my head. I want to see what the meeting brings, first.

I shove my phone back into my pocket, crush the cigarette beneath my heel, then pick it up to toss in the bin inside. The girls get all cranky if you leave a butt by the cliffs, and I know better than to get under their skin.

"Nolan." I look up to see Carson coming from the town centre, a steaming paper cup of tea in one hand and a paper bag in the other. His dark hair's cut short, and damp, as if he's just showered, his glasses perched on the end of his nose. Looks like he got his run in before the meeting tonight.

"What's the story, Carson? What's in the bag?"

Carson grins and looks down sheepishly. "Bit of pastry," he says.

I look at him in surprise. He's religious about his damn diet and working out.

"For Eve," he says, with a smile. "She's been cravin' it."

Carson's woman Eve is six months pregnant, and he's managed to keep it a secret this long. They've dated casually for years, but never made a commitment. I've no doubt the code of The Clan is to blame for this, since the men of The Clan typically marry for reasons that benefit us all: arranged marriages to form a truce, betrothal to solidify bonds, tributes as payment for sins.

"Did you tell Keenan yet?" I ask.

Carson shakes his head.

"Can't keep it quiet for that much longer, can you, Carson?" I shake my head.

He grimaces. "Aye. You're right."

"Tell him tonight."

He shakes his head. "Soon," he promises.

As the younger brother of The Clan, I'm the one they all approach first, to suss him out, I suppose. Keenan's an excellent leader, loyal and fearless, but tight as a drum. Stern. He followed in my father's footsteps. And though I consider Carson my brother, he isn't related by blood, so he's careful.

Carson's mum was an English woman by birth who worked for my family her whole life. Widowed when Carson was just a baby, she grew sick when he was only a child. She gave Carson over to my father to raise as his own. Said that she trusted him,

7

respected his code, and knew that her son would be taken care of for life.

He is. He lived in our home, then attended St. Albert's with the rest of us.

"You've got to tell him, Carson," I say. "For a logical braniac like you, I'm surprised you haven't made this conclusion already."

Carson's Clan bookkeeper, the smartest of the lot.

He runs a hand through his hair again, making it stand up on end, and for the first time, he looks scared.

"Well, no. Truth is, she doesn't want anyone to know."

I turn sharply to look at him, shocked at what he's saying. He was excited for this, eager, already the proud papa ready to light a cigar.

"Come again? Why not?"

"I mean, it isn't the first time she's gotten pregnant, Nolan. She's lost one before this. She's a bit... nervous, is all."

"Ahhh. Christ, brother, I'm sorry to hear that. And you don't want to tell Keenan until she's comfortable with that?"

"Aye."

I clap him on the shoulder. "Understood. So mum's the word for now, but don't let it get on too long. Reckon it's good not to wait too long, aye?"

Carson gives me a sideways grin. "Look at you, all responsible-like. I remember the days when you—"

The second clap on the shoulder isn't as friendly. He guffaws, trotting up the stairs ahead of me, but drops the conversation.

I can take crap from him, but the truth is, I remember it well, too. The days when I was carefree and drunk off my nut for most of the day. Seems those days weren't that long ago, and it'll take fucking years for my brothers to respect me again.

Boner's at the door, waiting for us. Tall and lanky, he bounces on the balls of his feet like he's ready to run a race. He takes a swig from a flask at his hip and puts it away when he sees me. My cousin by birth, he's as close as a brother to me, and he doesn't like to tempt me with drink. He knows it eats at me, though.

"Say yes, lad," he says, ruffling my hair. I duck, and give him a playful punch to the gut. "C'mon," he says, gasping. "It's Cinco de Mayo, brother. You know what that means."

"Fifth of May? Important if you're Mexican, but we're Irish, dumbass."

He opens the door and the three of us head into the main entrance. The house smells of freshly-baked bread and Irish stew. When we open the door to the study, a faint but pretty voice sings a lullaby in the distance.

"Aileen?"

9

"Aye," Boner says with a smile. "Newest babe doesn't sleep well, Aileen's got her in the library to give Caitlin a bit of rest."

I nod.

"Poor lass."

"Who's that?" Cormac's pouring himself a whiskey by the sideboard when we enter. My older brother, second in command, he's the biggest of all of us, burly and strong, with a thick dark beard and new ink on the back of his neck. Though he's the official Bonebreaker of the Clan, stern as hell and the first I'd want by my side in battle, he's got a gentler side to him as well. The only resemblance between us is the McCarthy family green eyes.

"Caitlin," I tell him. "I hear the babe's keeping her up at night?"

"Aye," Keenan says from the desk across the room. He's typing on his laptop and doesn't look over at us. His own eyes look bleary from lack of sleep. "Mam says it's colic or some such. I've been putting Seamus to bed and Caitlin's been taking the baby."

The eldest of all, Keenan resembles my father, his dark brown hair showing signs of gray at the temples and beard. He isn't as large as Cormac, but he still dwarfs the small desk. It's his wife Caitlin with the new colicky baby.

"Hire a nurse, brother," Cormac says.

Keenan shakes his head. "Caitlin won't hear of it.

Says it's her job and the time will pass." He smiles. "So I let it go."

Though Keenan's the stern, fearless leader of The Clan, he adores his wife Caitlin. He'll let her have this one thing.

"And anyway, you know mam's over the moon, helping with the grandbabies."

"Of course. Granny's in her glory." Cormac grins.

Carson takes a glass from the sideboard and pours himself a drink as well. Christ, I miss the drink, the social part of having a bevy together.

"Shouldn't you be celebrating your anniversary, Keenan?" They married the day my father died.

"Aye," he says. "We'll celebrate at the weekend, though."

I look around the room, Boner and Carson in one corner, having a drink, Cormac beside them and Keenan at the desk. Sometimes, Keenan only calls the inner circle, and sometimes he calls the larger group in as well.

"Is this it tonight?" I ask Keenan, kicking back in an overstuffed chair and propping my feet up on the ottoman.

"Lachlan's on his way in," Keenan says.

The door opens, and Lachlan enters as if summoned.

"Speak of the devil," Cormac says.

Lachlan grins. "What?"

He's large and strapping, but barely over the threshold of boyhood. With his dark brown hair cut short, he looks a bit more mature than when we first met. Back then, he had the look of a damp, freshly-birthed puppy with paws too big for his body. He's come into his own now, a real man of The Clan, though his bright hazel eyes are still full of mischief. I was the youngest member of the Clan until we recruited Lachlan from St. Albert's, our finishing school. As he's learned to curb his temper, he earned his way into our Clan with his sharp eye and quick wit.

"Alright, boys," Keenan says. He shuts off his laptop, leans back in his chair, and props his fingers together. It's a gesture so like my father's. I wonder if the others remember this is the anniversary of my father's death. "Got something to discuss."

We joke and kid like the brothers we are, but when Keenan speaks, the room falls silent.

"Father Finn's been to see me," Keenan begins. "Had a few things to say this morning. Seems the parishioners of Holy Family have some concerns."

Father Finn was my father's younger brother, the local parish priest, and our most valued informant.

Cormac sits up straighter.

"Concerns?" Cormac asks. "About us?"

"Aye," Keenan says. "At least, that's what it appears to be."

We keep our noses clean with the locals. We keep crime off their streets and amply fund their churches and charities. We've got half the police force in our pocket, and the other half doesn't care what we do as long as we keep the peace and the money flowing. It's unusual for any of the locals to question us.

Keenan frowns. "Seems there were some articles, and it seems there was a certain reporter who got their bees in a bonnet."

All eyes come to me. I know exactly who they're talking about.

"Why's everyone looking at me?" I ask. "I'm not her keeper."

"Maybe you should be," Lachlan says, and by the way the others nod, it seems they share the sentiment.

Jesus.

Sheena goddamn Hurston.

"Honest to Christ, haven't even seen her in a month or so."

"Maybe that's part of the problem," Keenan says.

For fuck's sake.

"How about you, Lachlan?" I say. There's something about the lass that spells danger for me. She tastes like the pull of liquor. I went there once, and it dragged me under. My gut says if I go there with her, I'll suffer the same demise. She's a drug, that woman, beautiful and dangerous, and her mission in life is to bring us down.

"Me?" Lachlan scoffs. "She doesn't look at me with doe-eyes, brother."

"Oh come off it. Doe-eyes? What is this, feckin' Disney?"

The men laugh, but they're still looking at me. I swing my gaze to Keenan.

"Keenan, what do you want from me?"

"Answers," Keenan says.

"Then I'm not the man for the job. She hates me. Doesn't trust me at all." And I don't blame her, not with how I've treated her. I don't regret it, but we hardly have a working relationship.

"Hate's just the start of a relationship," Cormac says with a smirk. "A very good start, and one you can work with."

He ought to know. His first encounter with his wife left her ready to kill him. One year later, she adores the very ground he walks on.

"Not all stories end in a fairy tale happy ever after, brother."

"Of course not," Keenan says. "But Cormac's right. Ask mam."

Keenan knows, too, having taken Caitlin as prisoner years back now. And my mother, she was wed to my father before they'd ever met, an arranged marriage between clans.

"Forget her for a minute," I argue. "Even if I could get her to pay attention, to fall for me as it were, I want nothing to do with the woman."

"Nolan," Boner says. "Who do you think you're talkin' to? This isn't the damn confessional, son. I've seen you around her enough times to know. The girl isn't hard on the eyes. And she's got a thing for you."

"Does not." I'm not letting this go. They won't cajole me into this.

"Does too," Lachlan says. "Tully and I noted it during the last party night at the club."

I glare at him. Who's side is he on?

"In any event, we've no choice, Nolan," Keenan says. Serious green eyes meet mine across the room. My oldest brother's always been the one in charge, our fearless leader, and he doesn't back down now. "Bottom line, we need answers. And she needs to know once and for all that she isn't to mess with us." He pauses. "You know I'm not above what the Clancys did decades ago."

I know what he's referring to. In the eighties, a reporter from American got in deep. She didn't know to leave well enough alone, but ran story after story about the Clancy Clan until they had enough. She was found dead in bed after running her stories, an example to the rest, and everyone knew who did it.

I don't respond at first. Keenan continues. "Only reason I haven't ordered a hit is because she could prove useful. An informant, as it were."

I don't understand why I clench my hand into a fist, why I want to slug my brother and make him bleed. A fucking hit for a naughty girl who doesn't know to leave well enough alone?

There's quiet in the room. Either they all agree with him, or they won't speak against him.

For fuck's sake.

I mull over his compromise.

Keenan continues. "So do it. This isn't a suggestion, Nolan." He's pulling rank, and goddamn it, he's given me no choice. "Find her. Interrogate her. Report back."

I stifle a groan. This is an order. I have no choice. Keenan might be my brother, and he's got enough respect for the rest of us to ask our counsel and tell us everything. But when he makes a decision, it's iron-clad. I'm bound by blood, honor, and vows to obey.

"Aye," I say. "I'll start at the club tonight."

Boner pumps his fist in the air and Lachlan gives me a grin. Carson looks at me thoughtfully, then goes back to his note-taking. When we disassemble, he comes to me.

"Nolan, a word," he says while we exit. The other men disperse, and I walk out with Carson. Those of us born McCarthy live here in this house, but the others live a little ways off.

"Aye?"

"Do you know where she lives?" he asks. "Do you know her family history?"

"No." I give him a curious look. "I've intentionally kept myself ignorant of anything more than the weight of her breasts and shape of her arse."

He snorts.

"You do?" I ask him.

"Aye," he says. "My girl was best mates with a neighbor of hers a few years back."

"Was she?"

He nods.

"Something I should know?"

"Piss fucking poor," Carson says. "Grew up in social housing just outside of Dublin. Still has three siblings and a mother at home she provides for."

Aw, feck. "Don't tell me anything that would make me sympathetic, now, Carson," I warn him. I don't know what I'm going to have to do with Sheena.

"Not why I'm telling you. But I know a few things, and I thought you should know, too."

"Anything else?"

"Aye. A scrapper like her, she uses her body to get what she wants. Long string of men she's slept with, all the way to O'Gregor's Chief."

I feel my eyebrows rise. "You don't say. Well, fuck."

Certainly doesn't warm me up to the girl.

"She stops at nothing, brother. Nothing. If she thinks there's a story, she's all in. Does what it takes to get her money."

"Maybe you should be the one to question her," I say, half teasing.

He shrugs. "I'll help you if you need me, but Keenan asked you."

I don't argue. I know he's right.

"I have the articles," Carson says. "I can send them to you."

"Yeah, do it," I say with a sigh. "You ever been to The Club?"

He grins. "No interest, brother. Got all I need at home."

I grin back. "Well done, you. Go, bring the pastry to your woman before she loses her mind."

"Aye," he says, giving me a salute before taking off.

I sit on a rough stone bench in the garden, watching the sun set over the water. I glance at my watch. Got about ten minutes before I'll have to get ready to go. Tonight, I'm heading to the club.

Chapter 2

Sheena

IT's hard to walk on heels with a mini skirt while carrying an armful of groceries, but I manage. I normally change before I come home—no, I can't call this place home any more. This is my mother's place. This isn't my home.

I didn't change tonight because I didn't have time. I have exactly one hour to drop these off, freshen up, and head into the club.

Someone catcalls behind me, and I grit my teeth. I've got twenty or so more paces to get to the door.

"Well, if it isn't miss high and mighty."

Jesus, no. The very sound of my ex-boyfriend's voice sends shivers down my spine, and not in a good way.

"Leave me alone, Cian," I say over my shoulder, not bothering to even turn to look at him.

"Lookin' mighty fine there, Sheena."

I try to mask the way I start when I hear him right behind me.

"Give those to me, now, lass. Pretty little thing like you ought not to be carryin' heavy things, eh?"

He's right next to me, reaching for the bags.

"I've got them, thanks."

His voice hardens.

"Give it here."

He's in my space, blocking me. I'd do anything never to see his shaved head and skinny, inked neck again. How I ever thought the man was attractive is a feckin' mystery. Now that I know him better, he resembles an underfed rat.

Though we stand eye-to-eye when I'm wearing heels, he's stockier than I am. More vicious. He reaches for the bags.

"Leave off," I say in my hardest voice. "I said I've got them."

"Course you have," he says, his black eyes narrowing. "You've got everything, don't you? Posh clothes. Fancy car. Fancy job. Aye, you've got this."

I try to walk around him, but he blocks my way.

"Need some help, there, Sheena?"

Relief floods through me at the sound of my brother's voice. I look to my left to see him approaching me at a good clip. Though Tiernan's only sixteen, and a tiny sixteen at that, he's fierce. He's determined to protect me, and just his presence brings a little comfort.

"Thank you, Tiernan. I need to bring these in and get back to work."

Tiernan takes the bags out of my hands.

"I told her I'd help her, boy," Cian says.

My brother's cheeks flame, matching his hair as he glares at Cian. "Aye, and she told you she didn't need it. So fuck off."

Cian takes a step toward Tiernan. "Or what, you fuckin' twat? You'll beat me up? You and what army?"

"Leave off, Cian," I tell him. "Go in the house, Tiernan."

He takes the bags, but before he leaves, he glares at Cian. I've got to hand it to him. He's brave. I wish he hadn't provoked Cian, though. The man will stop at nothing, and I fear some form of retaliation.

I walk behind Tiernan, ignoring Cian's curses and cruel taunts, until I get to the door.

"Tell yer mam you frequent The Craic, then, why don't you? Think she'd take yer filthy money then?"

I almost falter, almost give in to a smart retort, but he isn't worth my time.

I don't need him knowing I go there, dammit.

I open the door, cringing when it creaks on its hinges. One swift kick, and anyone could knock this down. They aren't safe here.

It's dark inside when I enter. The stale smell of whiskey and cigarettes lingers in the air. The sink overflows with dirty dishes, a soiled basket of laundry sits by the door, and the floor's in need of a thorough sweep. My stomach swoops with nausea. I hate that my siblings live in such squalor. Aine Hurston, my mother by birth but the woman I've done my best to disown, hardly deserves even this.

"Sheena!" Fiona hurls herself at me and gives me a huge hug. At thirteen years old, she's moving from childhood to adolescence, but she's still as exuberant as she was as a small child. I nearly topple over when I hug her back. I remember her as a five year old, when she still had the chubby cheeks of babyhood. She still has round cheeks, wide blue eyes, and my family's trademark red hair. I remember taking her onto my lap and brushing her long, gorgeous hair.

"Ah, hello there, Fiona." I hug her back. My throat tightens and my nose tingles. If I could, I'd pack the lot of them in the back of my car, leave, and never look back. But I can't. The courts would never allow it, and doing so could ruin my career. And if I lose my job, I wouldn't be able to provide for them any longer.

It's complicated.

Some day, though. Some day…

"Where's mum, sweetie?"

"Sleeping," Fiona says.

Passed out, then.

"Fucking sleeping," Tiernan mutters. He hates her as much as I do, though he won't admit it. He's old enough to know why she's sleeping.

"Language, Tiernan," I whisper.

Fiona twists a lock of hair between her fingers and bites it, looking down. I reach for her hand and gently extricate the hair from between her lips.

"Come and help me unpack the bags, and we'll get you a good meal, okay?" I brush her crazy, wavy hair out of her eyes.

"'Tis a mess, this hair of mine," she mutters.

"Would you like me to plait it before I go?"

She grins. "Please, Sheena?"

"Of course. Now go!"

She runs off to fetch the brush.

A loud, long wail comes from the other room. There's only two bedrooms, a tiny kitchen, and a bathroom here, so we know when the baby's up.

"I'll get him," Tiernan says, shoving his hands in his pockets and trudging off to where baby Sam's crib sits in the tiny, cramped living room. He comes in a few minutes later with the baby on his hip. One-year-old Sam's diaper droops, and he's still sniffling, but when he sees me, he reaches his chubby arms out for me. I won't lie, it breaks my heart a little.

I move quickly. My mother could get up at any minute, and I don't want to listen to her yammer on about me and my stuck-up ways. I change the baby's diaper, wipe his little face, brush and braid Fiona's hair, and feed them some soup I bought from the shops.

"Thanks, Sheena," Tiernan says.

I put the groceries away and quickly tidy the kitchen. "Wish I had time to clean up the dishes for you."

He shakes his head. "Leave it. I'd have done them myself but I just got back from work." I hate that he's working. Not only is he too young for a job, but the littlest ones are left unattended in his absence.

"What job do you have now?"

Since he was eight years old, Tiernan's found little jobs to do here and there. He brings in money and gives some to my mother. I hate that he has to. He should have years of childhood in front of him, but they've been stripped away. He stands on the cusp of manhood, and it isn't fair.

"Been making some deliveries," he says. "Here and there."

Fiona sits on the floor cross-legged, the baby between her legs drinking a bottle.

I could've slapped my mother when I found out she was pregnant.

A few years back, we lost my father, and my mother took to drink. He'd roll over in his grave to see the squalor they live in now. Though dirt poor, my father was a good man, a boxer who earned his living with his fists.

But I know who killed him. And they will pay for what they've done.

My mother went from one man to the next, spreading her legs for the next arsehole who'd pay the rent. The worst of the lot resurfaced last year, early release from jail. They had a one-night stand, and now the result of that night's sitting in front of me.

It isn't his fault, though. I can't deny he's adorable, the chubby little thing.

"Deliveries?" I ask Tiernan. "What sort?"

But before he can answer, I hear her. Her feet hit the floor and a second later, there's the strike of a lighter. Fiona looks at me with wide eyes, and Tiernan's jaw clenches. The baby gulps greedily at his bottle, unaware of what's about to happen.

"Go," Tiernan whispers. "I've got this."

"We both do," Fiona whispers.

I shake my head. I don't want her taking her anger out on them. And I don't run from anything.

The heavy sounds of her footsteps approach. Fiona

bites her lip. I continue cleaning up the kitchen as if it doesn't make me nauseous to hear her coming.

"Thought I heard you out here." My mother's behind me, and I keep my back deliberately to her.

"Aye," I say, wiping the counters down. "Brought some groceries, but I'll be leaving shortly."

"We don't need your handouts, you know. You can leave now."

It's how it always starts, every argument. The last time I came, she threw a teacup at my head and nearly hit me, because I had the nerve to bring Fiona new shoes.

It wasn't always like this. Before the baby, we were at least civil. But I was the one that saw to her boyfriend's recent arrest, and she knows it.

I may not be able to get the courts to grant me custody, but I'll be damned if I see the son of a bitch raise his hand to anyone. One black eye to Tiernan, and I pulled every fucking favor I had to get the son of a bitch's arse sent back to jail. I was successful, and she hasn't forgiven me.

"I know," I say, trying to keep the mood light. I don't want to fight with her. Not tonight. Not in front of my brothers and sister. "But I like to visit them, and I like to give them a little treat now and then."

She scoffs. "Bollox. You like to show off, is what you do."

My temper flares, and I keep it in check with difficulty. It's my downfall, every fucking time.

"Go," Tiernan repeats softly. "I've got this."

"Not until I know you're okay," I say in a whisper.

"She won't touch me," he says. "I can handle this. Don't worry."

But I do. I worry about all of them. I can't sleep at night knowing they're still under her roof. Wondering if they have food in their bellies.

Children shouldn't be raised in squalor. I ought to know.

I take a look at the time on my phone. I really should be going. I feel guilty, though, leaving them for what one could argue is a selfish reason.

But I can't save them. And I have a job to do.

I ignore mum's ranting and bend to kiss Fiona on her cheek.

"Thank you, Sheena," she says, giving me a smile. I pat the baby's head and stand.

My mother's rifling through the groceries I've brought. "Just what I thought," she mutters. "All high end, posh stuff. A reminder of how much better you are than us."

I want to tell her to go fuck herself, to shove those chocolate-dipped biscuits up her scrawny arse. Even a year or so ago, I would've. But not today. I have to

27

go, and I don't want her taking her rage out on the children.

"You're welcome," I say as pleasantly as I can, turning to leave, when I feel her grab me by the hair. I stifle a scream. I don't want to startle Fiona. I've learned a thing or two the past few years, though. I swivel with my arm bent and raised. She's weak. I easily smack her away.

"Don't touch me," I warn. "You really don't want to do that."

And she doesn't. She knows I won't take it.

Her eyes widen. It breaks my heart to see eyes that mirror my own, gray-flecked green. She was a pretty woman once, long before alcohol and misery aged her. She isn't even forty years old, having birthed me in her teens, but she's got the face and body of a much older woman.

The tattered gray top she wears sags on her, the black leggings filthy. She's barefoot, her feet smudged with dirt, and there are track marks on her arms. I still, noting the details. This is a new fucking conundrum.

I grab her wrist and spin her arm over, but she yanks it away. "Go," she spits. "Get your fancy arse out of here, and don't come back."

I step away and shake my head. "I'll be back," I say to Fiona, whose eyes have welled with tears at my mother's words. I give her a reassuring smile.

I wait until I turn the corner, half hoping Cian

comes out again. Even in heels and a skirt, I feel like I could take him right now. But he doesn't resurface.

I walk to my car and think. Maybe I could get custody. If my mother's shooting up and neglecting them, I might have a case against her. And I've made connections in my line of work. Connections that could help.

But if I were to take them, how would I finish the job I've set out to do? It requires flexibility and compromise. The very job I have to do tonight means if I'm successful, I won't return home. And I can't take men home if the children are there.

A part of me wants to call a friend to listen to me, to help me decide what to do. But I've hidden my past from the few friends I have. I don't let on who I was or where I came from. The squalor of my past remains in my past, and I'll do whatever I can to keep it that way.

Tonight, I'm going to The Craic. It's party night at the club. It'll draw all sorts, and I could get a lead on a story.

And I have a mission.

I avoided going there for a while, after one of the leads I followed blackmailed me. I was honestly scared. I knew my job as an investigative reporter was dangerous. I knew I treaded in shark-infested waters. But I'd managed to avoid getting caught and hurt so many times, I'd almost convinced myself I was invincible.

I was not.

I am not.

But after the incident at the club, I decided I wouldn't run with my tail between my legs. I'd do what I had to. I'd get my work done. I wouldn't let a bully and a run-in with danger push me away from doing my job.

So I went back, but I'm much more careful about who I interact with.

I tell myself I go back because I won't cower in fear. But I know there's another reason, one I don't like to admit.

Nolan McCarthy.

I hate him. I've been tracking his family for years, and he's onto me. He caught me on their property last year, he threatened and punished me, and I know I was lucky I got out alive. The McCarthy family is one of the most powerful mobs in all of Ireland. Spies don't live to see the light of day, and I know this.

They aren't the only ones, mind. The O'Gregors and Martins make up a good deal as well. But it's the McCarthys I'm after.

They're the ones I've set my eyes on. They're the ones who deserve my hatred and vengeance. And I won't rest until they've paid for what they've done.

I get to my car and slam the locks. I yank down the visor and flick the lighted mirror on. I fix my makeup and hair. I keep styling products and a makeup bag in my glove compartment, a change of clothes, and several wigs in the back. I've got everything I need, even a fake I.D. and passport. Tonight, I'll change when I get to the club.

Ever since I was attacked at The Craic, the owners and bouncers take good care of me. Probably helps they know who I am.

They all should know who I am.

I'm Sheena Hurston, and I take no prisoners.

Chapter 3

Nolan

WE SHOW up at the club at half past eight, and it's already teeming with people. Something about free food brings people out of the woodworks. Within two minutes of entering, Boner's got a plate of tacos, Tully's dipping chips in guac, and Lachlan's got a margarita in each hand.

Ah, to hell with it. I grab a sombrero from the bartender, fill a plate with mini tacos, and toss back a virgin margarita. Not bad.

"Filled your belly?" Lachlan asks. His eyes are already glossy, as if he hasn't eaten food all day and just made a meal out of margaritas.

"Aye. You ready?"

He nabs one more margarita, then jerks his head to the back.

"Brother, there's a girl up there who's had her eyes on you since you walked in."

"Yeah?"

"Ten o'clock."

I scan the room until I see her. Her jet black hair hangs down her back with waves that beg to be pulled, just grazing the top of a perfect, pert ass. She's got full red lips and exotic dark eyes done up with some sort of fucking magic. When she catches my eye, she grins at me, beckons one finger, then heads to the back.

I'm not here for a one-night stand. I've got a job to do. I'm supposed to find Sheena. I'm supposed to get answers. And I'm the one that does the beckoning.

"Should see what she wants," he says, grinning at me.

"Fuck off. I've got a job to do."

"But you have to fit in, don't you?" he asks. He sips his drink, then jerks his head to the back. "Got to have a woman on your arm, or you'll stand out."

"The boy has a point," Boner says, his arm already around the waist of a pretty blonde.

"Right atop his head," I say, right before I duck Lachlan's left hook.

We head to the back, the part of the club where the action is. The bar is almost a front, though not quite. At the back, we gain access to the hidden part of The Craic, where the real fun begins.

This is no tame club, but one of Ireland's most exclusive sex clubs, no vanilla allowed. Hell, I've missed this.

I miss the way it feels to have a woman under my control. To dominate and master. I miss inflicting pain mixed with pleasure. I miss the pleas and the screams when I grant an orgasm she begged for.

It's teeming with people here, but I don't have to look far to see the black-haired seductress from across the room. She's perched on a stool, her drink in hand. She takes a toothpick with a cherry on it out of the glass, captures it between her lips, and with her eyes locked on mine, licks it.

The low pull of seduction curls in my belly. It's been a while since I've had a woman at the club. I don't quite know why.

And this woman knows exactly what she's doing.

We had an incident last year involving Cormac's Aileen and fucking Sheena, the reporter. They were set up by rival mafia, attacked. We got to them just in time. Even though Sheena and I had a history, I was the one that wrapped her in a blanket, took her to the hospital wing of our estate, and made sure she was okay before we let her go. It was the right thing to do.

But I'm under no delusion. We aren't friends.

There's no love lost between us. I did what any goddamn guy would do in that situation. Hell, she probably hates me, and she'd have reason to.

"Any word on the reporter?" I ask the boys.

Boner's locking lips with the blonde, but he shakes his head no.

Lachlan snorts. "Did a thorough sweep. She isn't here tonight."

All the more reason to pursue the black-haired beauty. If Sheena isn't here, I'll have to move on to plan B to find her. And that means I've got the rest of the night ahead of me.

Just to be safe, I scan the place myself, looking from one person to the next. In the far right of the room I catch a glimpse of red, but when I make my way over, I see it isn't her at all, but a much older woman.

Sheena's on the young side. Fair skin dotted with freckles, delicately arched light brown eyebrows over beautiful light gray eyes.

Really a shame she's my nemesis.

The black-haired woman, on the other hand, promises a night of fun. I take in her vivid, dark brown eyes, clear porcelain skin. She's wearing a green and black snake-skin sheath dress that hugs every curve and leaves little to the imagination. I swallow hard.

"Evening," I say when I reach her. "Buy you a drink?"

She smiles and doesn't answer, but pushes herself off the stool and beckons her finger to me.

"Ah, no," I say. "I'm not about to blindly follow you. Not until we've at least made each other's acquaintance." I give her what I hope is my most charming smile. I'm interested. I'm totally fucking interested, but I'm not the type to follow a girl who beckons.

"It's too loud in here," she says in a French accent, her voice a soft purr. "Let's get some privacy? Then you can ask all the questions you'd like."

I'd follow her all night long to listen to that voice, that accent.

She turns and walks away, clearly confident I'll follow.

So maybe I am the type, because I find myself dodging between people, keeping my eye on her as she leads to the more private rooms.

She stills before we head down the hall, squares her shoulders, and swallows hard. Is she afraid? I wonder what scares her.

I watch her curiously. What's her game plan here? I've learned to translate body language, to learn how people give physical cues to how they feel. When we enter the hall, she's momentarily off her game, no longer the coy seductress. Finally, she takes a deep breath and moves on.

I look over my shoulder and catch Lachlan staring at me. He pumps his fist in the air, clearly eager to see me hook up.

Am I that uptight?

I give him the one-fingered salute and follow her down the darkened hallway. I need this.

A girl doesn't beckon a stranger at a sex club because she wants sweet, vanilla sex. The Craic welcomes all sorts, and even has a club safe word.

I've missed this. I've craved this. I need it.

She doesn't enter a room, though. She's waiting in the hall, leaning her hip against a doorframe.

"You came," she says in the same low, seductive whisper. Her accent is intoxicating. "Do you have plans this evening, sir?"

Fuck, she knows how to play the sub card well. I can already taste her.

I did, but my plans are shot to hell, so I'm thinking that's a no.

I shake my head. "No." I pause, folding my arms over my chest. "Do you?"

I don't miss the way she looks at me, her eyes roaming over me. She swallows hard, and for one brief moment, it seems as if her mask drops. Her nostrils flare with an intake of breath and her lips quirk up at the edges. It's an odd reaction.

Does she like what she sees? Or is it something else?

"You," she whispers. "I've seen you here before."

Has she? How come I've never seen her?

"Have you?"

"Yes, sir," she whispers. That sweet voice whispering that word I haven't heard in so long makes my need grow even stronger.

Sir.

I take a step toward her as if drawn by her spell, the faintest scent of her exotic perfume permeating the air between us. Her beautiful eyes widen as I approach, and she swallows visibly.

I reach for her and weave my fingers around the back of her neck. I close my eyes and kiss her cheek, a chaste kiss. Her skin is velvety soft, and when I kiss her, her breath comes in little gasps. One hand reaches for my wrist not to stop me but to steady herself, and her eyes flutter closed.

I pause. There's something about this that's so familiar, I stop for a moment.

I've met her before. I've touched her before. And it didn't end well.

But no, that isn't possibly. I'd remember a girl like her.

"Please?" she whispers. "The bedroom, sir?"

Yes. I want her alone. Maybe if I get her alone we can figure this out.

"Are you sure we haven't met?" I ask her, just to be safe.

She shakes her head. "No, sir. I'd remember a man like you." She's using all the classic lines, but hell, I like them.

I lead her down the hall to a room I'm granted permission to use. I may not have been here recently, but I'm part of The Clan. And they take good care of us here.

I reach for her hand, and again, I'm surprised that this feels familiar. I look back at her sharply, but she only gives me a wide-eyed look.

"Something wrong, sir?" she asks in that adorable French accent.

"Are you sure we haven't met?"

I don't miss the way her eyes quickly flit from mine before she answers. In my line of work, you learn to note signs of guilt.

"I don't know how," she says. "This is my first time here."

I'm either going mad or about to make a big fucking mistake.

"Are you sure?" I ask her.

"Of course, sir. I've just come from my home in

Paris. Visiting a friend. I'm told this club is one of the best in Ireland."

"Aye."

I open the door and lead her in. I'm dying to get her alone. We're both here for the same reason.

The room is small and immaculate, with a camel-colored leather loveseat, and an overstuffed chair.

We don't talk. Despite what she's said, we both know we aren't here for conversation.

I tug her onto the loveseat and she arranges herself easily on my lap, straddling me. My cock stiffens, pressing into her arse, and when she weaves her arms around my neck, I give into this. I need this.

She kisses my cheek and I wrap my arms around her waist.

"This is what I've wanted," she whispers. "A man like you, so big and strong. Mastering me. Dominating me. Will you do that, sir?"

"Christ, yeah." Hell, it's why I'm here.

"Thank you, sir. I will do my best to please you, sir."

She slides off my lap and onto her knees before me, her hands resting on my legs. She kneads my thighs, her dark eyes still holding mine.

"May I, sir?'

Christ, yes.

I swallow and nod.

"You may."

She squirms and bites her lip, her lowered eyes and panting breaths belying her arousal.

"Thank you, sir." She holds my gaze and unfastens my trousers, her eyes on mine, before she guides my swollen, stiff cock into her hand. She groans, bends, and licks the tip. I swear my eyes roll to the back of my head. God, I need this so bad my mouth is dry.

"Is that good?" she whispers.

I open my eyes and nod, just as she lowers her mouth to my cock.

She's good at this. She's fucking good, using her hands and lips, suckling and making me groan.

But as she continues, something's off.

I like to dominate a woman sucking my cock, and if she's a sub, she'll like that. I bend and fist her hair. She takes her mouth off me for a moment.

"No, sir. No hair, please."

No hair? When she's got gorgeous locks like these?

It's my first clue.

I move my fingers to the nape of her neck, and she continues to suckle. I look closer. The lighting's dim in here, but I think beneath her makeup I see the faintest dots of freckles.

Wait a minute.

I freeze when I notice a sliver of flaming red hair

where her forehead meets her scalp. She's wearing a wig. The disguise is excellent.

Bloody hell.

I try not to tense. Try not to let her know the fucking gig is up.

But I know why she's familiar.

She's the woman I rescued.

The one who trespassed on our property, who I punished soundly and warned never to come back.

I looked all around the club for Sheena Hurston, came here tonight to find her, and she's on her knees before me, sucking my cock.

I want to lift her up by the throat and instill the fucking fear of God in her. She doesn't know that I know who she is, but she's bright. If I let on that I'm angry at all, she'll catch on.

She didn't want a one night stand. She wants something far more insidious than that.

Two can play at this game.

I reach for the buckle of my belt beside me and yank it through the loops of my trousers. She watches me with a smile, her mouth still around my cock.

"You like to be spanked?" I ask her. I bloody well don't care if she does, she isn't leaving here until I whip her pretty ass red.

She grins. I wonder if it's part of the act, or if she really does like to be dominated. If she didn't, would she be here? In any event, she won't like the kind of spanking I'm about to give her.

I'm about to take control of this in a way she won't like at all.

"Touch yourself," I order.

With a moan, she sucks my cock and reaches her hand to her pussy. I fist the buckle and wrap my belt around my hand, leaving a little tail. I bend over, then slap the leather on her arse. Just a gentle stroke to excite her, even though I want to whip her to tears.

She flinches then moans, squirming, stroking herself. I intentionally give her light, sensual lashes with the belt, enough to stoke a kinky girl's arousal.

"Just like that," I tell her. "That's a girl."

She smiles around my cock, flinching a bit when I let the belt fall again.

The next stroke is harder. She jumps, and her eyes widen. She freezes, her mouth still on my cock.

"Too hard?" I don't fucking care if it's too hard. I've only just begun. Still, I don't want her to know that.

She pauses, then shakes her head.

She sucks me harder.

I hold her gaze, lift my belt, and slap the leather again. Harder. This is a vicious cut, one that will leave a lasting burn. She winces and her eyes water a little.

"Thought you liked a little pain?"

She release my cock. "I do. I do, sir."

But I've had enough.

Holding her gaze, I slide my cock back in my trousers and pull the zipper, even though it fucking kills me. I could take advantage of her right now, but I won't. Violating her is tempting as fuck, but I'll maintain my control. If there's anything I've learned in the brotherhood of The Clan, it's control.

Her brows furrow in confusion.

"Sir?"

"Thought you had me, didn't you?"

Her eyes widen with panic and she looks quickly to the door, when my phone rings. She takes it as an opportunity to try to escape. She pushes to her feet but I grab her arm and yank her back to me.

My phone rings again, and this time I realize it's in her fucking pocket.

She's over my lap in two seconds flat.

"Leave me alone!" she screams, all pretense of a French accent gone. "I'll call the cops."

"Ah, just like you did last time, mm? How did that work out for you?" I lift my belt and whip it hard on her upturned arse. She called our friend, Walsh at the station, who rang us directly. We've got plenty of local law enforcement on our side.

"Let me go!"

"Let you go?" I ask. She squirms, but I pin her in place. "You tried to con me, didn't you? Stole my phone? What else were you planning on stealing, hmm?"

"Fuck you!"

I lash her again, and again, deliberately laying the leather in hard, vicious strokes that make her scream and writhe. "You ought to know better by now, Sheena."

She howls and tries to get away, but she can't. I hold her down and whip her backside until I know she's good and sore. I don't overdo it. With folded leather I could welt and harm her, but I've left her fully clothed. Still, it'll hurt to sit for a fucking week. She'll remember this.

She's a sobbing mess over my lap when I'm done. I drop the belt and stand her up in front of me.

"Now that's for trying to con me," I tell her, panting from the exertion. I want to shake her, but again, I hold myself back. Still, she's due for a warning. "You ever fucking do something like that again, the next spanking you get over my knee, I'll bare you first."

"How dare you!"

I shake my head with mock regret. "You have no idea, doll."

"Don't call me that. Don't!"

As if she tells me what to do? Telling me she

doesn't like it means she just guaranteed that's exactly what I'll call her.

She's glaring at me and swiping at her tears. I reach for her and yank the wig right off. Vibrant red hair cascades down her shoulder. She growls at me.

"How'd you change the color of your eyes?" I ask her. "Your eyes were gray."

"Are you that dense?" she asks.

"No, but maybe you are, talking to the man who just whipped your little arse like that."

"You can't do this," she says. She wriggles and squirms in my arms.

I tuck her easily against one arm, take my phone from her pocket, and dial Boner. "Situation in a private room."

I tell him where I am, and half a minute later, Lachlan, Tully, and Boner stand in the room, staring at Sheena's disheveled appearance, the black wig on the floor, tracks of black mascara streaming down her cheeks.

"Guess you found the reporter," Lachlan mutters. "Bloody hell."

"Clearly."

"Need help, boss?"

"Aye. She isn't going home tonight."

She screams so loudly, Lachlan jumps, but Boner's prepared. With a grin, he steps over to her and shoves a ball gag in her mouth and fastens it behind her head.

"Anything else, boss?"

"Call Keenan," I tell him. "Tell him I'm bringing home a visitor."

She mumbles and squirms against the gag but can't speak.

Lachlan grins. "On it."

Chapter 4

Sheena

I PUT up quite a fuss when they take me out, but it's only so they think I don't want them to take me. This didn't go exactly as planned. I didn't think he'd strap me, but if I'm honest, I've taken worse. Frequenting The Craic isn't just for business, mind.

Still, Nolan McCarthy can deliver a thorough belting, and I'd be smart to remember that. He lashed me over my clothes this time and promised the next would be bare.

I'm experienced with deviant sex. I've been whipped and caned, paddled and belted before. But I know if he bared me to punish me, he wouldn't take it easy on me.

He didn't the last time he caught me, the last time I ended up at his mercy. He caught me trespassing on their property, captured me, and dragged me to a windowless room in the basement of their massive mansion that overlooks the cliffs of Ballyhock.

I remember it well. I know I'm fucked up, but I've replayed that night. I was angry at the time. Helpless and infuriated. But I could tell he held himself back when he punished me then, and I've remembered how he did. How it felt to be restrained in the cuffs he had. The way his stern voice lectured me as he inflicted measured pain with a stout-handled whip.

I let him think I caved. I cried and wept for mercy. He didn't know I'd frequented The Craic to learn tolerance, and found a bit of myself in the process.

And he will never know.

I can't scream with the gag, which is just as well, because being taken to their property is exactly what I want. Still, I have to protest some. So I wriggle and squirm and yell against the gag, my pleas coming out in muffled protests. Nolan's still angry, I can tell by the way his green eyes flash, and his jaw goes all hard.

I've watched him for over a year. I know so much about him, I could write his biography. Former alcoholic, he went to rehab and quit the drink. He's been stone sober ever since, no small feat for an Irishman. The youngest of the three McCarthy brothers, he defers to Keenan and Cormac's leadership. My research says he's Lieutenant, but as McCarthy blood, he's high ranking in command.

Though he likes to joke and tease his brothers, he's got a darker side. Perhaps it's why I find him at the pinnacle of my focus when I think of the McCarthys. The others come here to dabble and play, but for Nolan, the need to dominate is in his blood.

I've watched him brooding over the cliffs. I've seen him scene with woman after woman at the club. But I also know he has a soft spot in his heart for his mother, the matriarch of The Clan who lives in the mansion and fancies herself mother for the lot.

They will all pay, every last one of them. Maeve McCarthy is just as guilty as the lot of them.

I suppose they fancy themselves some sort of fucked up altruists, and the truth is, they don't dabble in the harder games the other mobs of Ireland do. There's no human trade, no hard drugs, and as far as I can tell, they haven't fulfilled a contracted hit since Keenan took to office. They bring arms from the coast and sell them at home and abroad. I suppose they think their generous contributions to the church and town buy them clemency.

Fuck them and the horse they rode in on. There is no pardoning the evils of the mob.

They're Irish mafia through and through. The list of casualties in their wake grows by the day. They live by a ruthless code of loyalty and vengeance, and illicit funds pad the pockets of the lot. They may fancy themselves the Robin Hoods of Ireland, kind-hearted criminals. But I know better.

I will bring them down, from the very top of leadership to the very base of soldiers. All of them. Every last fucking one of them.

Naturally, they steal me away with ease, since the McCarthy brothers walk on fucking water. No guards come running to my aid, and when one looks our way, the tallest of the bunch has a word, and he leaves. I don't care. My cell phone's strapped to my inner thigh and I've secured my car with a club friend. I'll get back onto the McCarthy's property, find what I need. Then I'll escape.

They leave the club with me as effortlessly as if they were heading out for a smoke. Balancing me between them, Nolan's got a tight grip on one arm and one of the burly guys has me on the right. He's being none too gentle on me either. At first I don't recognize him, but when I remember, I cringe.

Tully. I used him last year to onto the property. A friend of mine slept with him, got his keys, and we were able to get onto their estate. That's what started this ball rolling.

I have no friends at the McCarthys. I'll have to play this just right.

I don't fight them when they put me in the back of a car. I feel the reassuring coolness of my phone where I've hidden it. This car, not surprisingly, is large, with a driver up front and room in the back for several people. They don't all pile in, though.

"Leave us alone," Nolan tells them. "Take the other cars home."

My pulse spikes at his words. He wants me alone for a reason.

It's part of my job, though. If I do this… if I do what I've set out to do, vengeance will not only be mine, I'll be paid amply for the information I send back to my boss. If we can do a full-on exposé of the McCarthy Clan, we can bring them down. I'll be paid richly, and maybe I'll even have enough to go to court and fight for my siblings.

I wonder if he'll interrogate me. Perhaps there's an even meaner side to him than I've yet seen. I know that although his record's clean, he was accused of murder several years back, but he was acquitted. Naturally. Ballyhock thinks the McCarthys wear tilted halos.

I know better.

He unfastens the gag they put on me while he asks me a question.

"So tell me, doll. Why'd you try that?"

Doll. I hate it when he calls me that because a part of me likes it. A tender term that would make a girl feel wanted, I think, but since there's no tenderness between us, it grates.

Nolan leans back in the seat and laces his fingers behind his head. Sandy blond hair falls on his forehead, his green eyes glint at me. When he leans back, his muscles bulge. He might be a bastard, but those arms, those hands. Strong arms like that could hold a woman close and make her feel safe.

But I'm not that woman.

He waits for an answer, his gaze so nonchalant he could be watching a rugby match.

"Do what?" I ask.

"Try to distract me by sucking me off."

I swallow hard. The way he says it makes something like arousal stir low in my belly.

I had him. I had him, right there, on my knees.

I shake my head. I need to throw him off kilter as easily as he does me.

"If only you were patient. I'd have swallowed, you know."

His nostrils flare and his eyes heat for one split second before he schools his features and gives me a slow, sadistic grin.

"Not so fast, doll. Don't make assumptions."

"Assumptions?"

He smiles, and it's a chilling sort of smile. I shiver.

"Assumptions," he repeats.

"What am I assuming?"

"That it'll be the only time you'll get on your knees for me. That your opportunity to swallow's gone."

I shiver, suddenly nervous. I prepared myself for many things, but somehow rape wasn't one of them.

Would he? Have I managed to convince myself there is good in this man after all?

Am I wrong?

I grit my teeth and don't respond at first. He wants to scare me. He wants to intimidate and threaten me. I won't let him.

I give him a grin. "Is that right, sir? I'm eager for another chance."

I have to admit, I feel a little smug. I hope it doesn't show. But if I won't cower with a spanking and I look forward to being used sexually, what else is there he can do to me?

His eyes darken as he stares at me.

"Why are you on our arses?"

Maybe playing stupid will help. It's worth a shot. So I shake my head at him and roll my eyes. "Are you that dense? Do you really not know?"

But it was the wrong thing to say. He unclasps his hands, leans forward on his seat, and reaches for my hair. I gasp when he tightens his fingers and yanks my head back. Pain shoots along my scalp, even as a shiver slides down my body.

I love to be dominated. Mastered. Manipulated, and used. I don't come to The Craic for the drinks.

"Mmm," I say. "I did peg you as a hair-puller."

A lesser man would cave, maybe lose his temper and hurt me. But he doesn't even register surprise.

He leans his mouth to my ear and whispers, his hot breath tickling the sensitive skin. "I've wanted to tangle my fingers through your hair and pull it since the day I first saw you."

Oh, Christ, his hand's traveling down my body, slides under the top of my dress, and cups my bare breast.

"Oh, have you then?" I ask, trying to mask my arousal and give him a grin. "You fancy the red?"

He gives me a wicked grin. "Oh, I fancy the red, all over. Your hair, my bite marks on your neck, your freshly-spanked bottom. Now, lass. Answer my question."

I want him to think he doesn't affect me, because hell, I like his hands in my hair and on my body. "Or what? You'll make me come to threaten me?"

He shakes his head. "You shouldn't do that, doll."

I swallow again when his green eyes narrow on me.

"Do what?"

"Lie. Manipulate. You've underestimated us."

I don't reply, because for one brief moment, I'm afraid he might be right. Have I gotten in over my head?

But no. Cast me to the furthest depths of the ocean. I always swim.

Always.

"Hard for you to say, isn't it?" I ask. My voice comes

out in a pant, because he's tugging my hair so perfectly I might come undone, right here, right now, with the streets of Ballyhock zooming out the window and his rough, strong hand cupping my breast.

"That you've underestimated us?"

"Aye. You don't even know what I think of you, so how can you make such a judgment?"

He thumbs my nipple in reply, and frissons of arousal and awareness skate down my skin. My core aches, my pussy throbs, and my breasts swell.

He shakes his head. "'Tis a pity you've done wrong against The Clan, Sheena."

I look at him curiously. I wonder where he's going with this.

I don't reply. He leans in closer to me, so close I can see light flecks of gold in his gorgeous eyes, a line between his brows, and a tiny scar to the left of his nose. I wonder where he got that.

"I'd have liked to give you a chance," he whispers, just one second before he lowers his mouth to mine. For one brief moment, I'm not Sheena Hurston the reporter, thirsty for vengeance and ready to destroy. He isn't my prey. When his mouth brushes mine, he could be mine.

I've been with many men, but most were for a purpose. They didn't kiss, and I didn't want them to. No one's ever kissed me like this.

I sink lower into his arms, losing my ability to remain aloof. He yanks my hair and teases my nipple as he slides his tongue into my mouth. My pussy clenches and my body throbs. Aching. Hungry. So needy for more.

I can't do this, I tell myself. I can't let him seduce me with such ease. I can't enjoy this. I'm lecturing myself with one part of my brain while the other is helpless to protest. I've fantasized about just this, being held in Nolan's powerful, unrelenting hands, and touched.

Hell, can he kiss. It's perfection, the softness of his lips, the harsh contrast of his beard, the way his hands roam purposefully over my body.

He releases me too soon. Takes his hands away from me. His eyes are cold and hard when he drops me on the seat. It's ice water dashed on my face.

"I can't do that, though," he says. "Can't give you a chance. You've done wrong against my brothers, and we have a code we adhere to."

I pretend like he doesn't affect me, but it's the hardest thing I've had to do tonight.

"Ah, right," I tell him. "If I'd left well enough alone you'd have asked me on a date, hmm? Dinner and a movie? Something vanilla, perhaps."

His lips quirk up and he shrugs a shoulder. "Dinner and a movie, maybe. Vanilla?" He laughs mirthlessly. "No fucking way."

A glimmer of excitement coils in my belly. I knew he was a kinky bastard.

The car comes to a halt, and all humor vanishes from his face.

"We're at my home. You'll come with me. You'll keep a civil tongue in your head when you address my family, or face punishment. Is that clear?"

"Sure. Sounds terrifying."

His narrowed gaze tells me he doesn't buy my quick response.

Hell, I don't either. I wonder again if I've bitten off more than I can chew.

I take in every detail when he opens the door.

There are two more cars that park when we do, but the others let him go ahead. Some of the men stand around us, watching. One has his hand on the butt of his gun, as if he's prepared to draw and shoot if I do anything rash. I give him a wide grin, then Nolan tugs me along by taking my hand.

"You typically bring your prisoners up to the house by the hand?"

He doesn't reply.

I'm familiar with the layout of this house. It's fucking gorgeous, and I have to admit a part of me, a very teeny, tiny part, is a little jealous. After what I'm familiar with, such opulence and wealth stings like nettles.

The massive house overlooks the eastern coast of Ireland, the blue green sea churning below. The docks and ports of Ballyhock are below us. They have men that work those ports. It's where they do their arms trade. Of course they don't do it in the open, but it isn't hard to note the work they do when you're trained to observe.

Before you reach their house, there's a beautiful garden, with a stone bench and a trellis. Maeve McCarthy tends some of the garden. A well-manicured lawn and flowering bushes and plants line the walks, and one walkway goes away from the house and toward the back, where they've placed a woodshed and greenhouse.

The garden's an excellent place to hide if need be. I should know. I've done it before.

I know the inside of the house as well, though "officially" I've only spent time in their windowless room on the basement level. Last year, when he captured me and punished me.

I shake my head to clear my thoughts. It isn't time for a trip down memory lane.

We walk up the stairs to his house, thirty-five stone steps to be precise. I've counted every one of them. I've wondered if the location of this house, with so many large steps to get to the top, was intentional to deter visitors. There are no neighbors, and no one drops by unannounced.

The McCarthy brothers, who've taken over leadership roles since their father's death two years ago, all live here. I know every detail. Keenan and his wife Caitlin, with two small children. Cormac and his wife Aileen, a woman with former connection to their rivals, the Martins. Their mother Maeve resides in the house as well since she's been widowed. There are servants aplenty, and the rest of the men of the Clan, from the lowliest soldier, lives within walking distance of the McCarthy mansion.

We enter the front door, and his grip on my arm tightens. He stops when he sees Maeve by the entrance. She's got a large bouquet of flowers in her arms, and she freezes when she sees us enter.

"Nolan."

He nods to her. "Mam."

She eyes me coldly, looking me over from head to toe. "And you must be Sheena Hurston, the reporter that's been up our arses."

I give her a broad smile. "Nice to meet you, too, Mrs. McCarthy."

She inclines her head in greeting and doesn't reply.

"Where's Keenan?" Nolan asks his mother.

"Just helped Cait put the babies down for a nap. Want me to ring him for you?"

"Aye," he says. "Tell him to give me a call when he has a minute. I'll be in my room."

She looks to me again and back to him. "Will you be needing the interrogation room, then?"

I wonder why she asks him this in front of me. Does she want me to know she's complicit in what they do? I know this already. Or does she want me to know she hopes he hurts me? It's an odd thing for her to say.

"All set, thanks," he says. Then under his breath as we head to the stairs, he says, "I've got plenty of methods of interrogation in my own room."

"I bet you do."

He smiles wryly. Maeve turns away from us as we reach the large staircase. I've never been here before, though I know the entire layout of this house. The bottom floor houses their windowless "interrogation room," as Maeve called it, as well as the library. This floor holds the dining room and meeting rooms and offices, and the rest of the floors are the residences. Nolan takes me to the second floor, still gripping my arm tightly as we march down the hall.

"Nice place you've got here," I say, pretending to be friendly and even maybe a little nonchalant.

When he doesn't reply I carry on.

"Have you lived here your whole life?"

I know he has. I want to pretend I'm not afraid of him. That I don't fear what he'll do to me when he has me alone. And it's probably best he isn't aware of how much I know about him.

A muscle ticks in his jaw, and he still doesn't respond.

"Perhaps later you can show me around," I try again.

His eyes narrow on me.

"Just trying to make small talk," I mutter. "You don't have to be so aloof."

Still, no response. We reach the very end of the hall on the second floor. He opens the door, pushes it in, and drags me inside. My heart beats faster. This was a mistake, I know, and no matter how brave I pretend to be, I'm scared. My pulse races, and my palms are sweaty, slipping in his firm grip.

He slams the door behind him once we're inside. It's a small room, with a few bar stools propped up to a bar, an electric kettle and bags of tea besides cups nestled on a wooden tray, and behind that, a living room with huge windows that overlook the sea.

For what this room lacks in size, it makes up for with the view. From here, we can see the waves crashing on the shore, the beautiful cliff beneath wispy white clouds. But I can't look for long, as he's tugging me to his room.

I don't know what I was expecting Nolan McCarthy's room to look like. But it certainly wasn't this.

I've seen the layout, I know some of what their mansion looks like, but the bedrooms are a mystery to me.

His bedroom's three times the size of the anteroom. A huge bed dominates the center of the room, with large, sturdy rings anchored on posts. I shiver in fear when he tugs me along. The door to the bathroom's to the right, and from here I can see a massive circular tub. It's decorated in creams and browns, not the traditional bachelor pad. But neither the bed nor the bathroom are the focal point here. Along one wall is a large, sliding glass door with the shades pulled wide open. A balcony that overlooks the beautiful, tumultuous sea below. People would pay millions for a view like that. Hell, maybe he has.

"On the bed," he says, his voice sharp. "Strip. I want you belly down, arse in the air."

I look at him in shock. I can't strip. For fuck's sake, if I strip he'll see my phone, and that's the least of my worries.

"Excuse me?"

"On the bed," he repeats, louder. "Strip. I want you belly down, arse in the air."

Still holding my hand, he slaps my arse, hard, then points to the bed. "Now."

"Ah, well, then. Seems someone didn't get his fix at the club," I mutter, marching off to the bed.

I won't let him intimidate me.

I won't.

I'm not prepared for the clink of metal, or the hiss

of leather being pulled through loops. His hand on my lower back, pushing me belly-down on the bed.

I reach a hand back on instinct to stop him, but he easily takes my wrist and pins it to my lower back.

I cringe, knowing what's coming even while I crave it.

"Do you think this is a joke, doll?" he asks, so placidly you wouldn't think he was ready to hurt me.

"A joke, well, no," I begin, when the first line of fire lights up my ass. I hiss and draw in breath when he gives me another sharp lash, then another. My hands on the bed scramble for purchase and I fist the thick navy duvet to brace myself before he strikes me again.

"Then stop playing these games," he says. "You're on our property now. You're prisoner here. You have no way to get out. You can call the police, but they won't help you here. You can call your friends, but they can't help you either." He strikes me again, and I'm starting to feel like maybe I should take him seriously. His belt fucking hurts, and it seems he likes to wield it.

He punctuates his words with a hard, searing slap of leather.

"No. More. Games."

And then I'm on my back and he's pinning me down, and I'm dazzled by his scent and power. My wrists are in one of his hands, anchored to the bed above my head, and his mouth is on mine. He yanks the top of my dress down. I'm moaning into his mouth as he tweaks my nipples, and I'm stunned when I feel the hard length of his erection pressed up to my belly. Something should flash warning in my mind, but I live for this, I crave it, and all I feel is the seductive pull of domination.

He kneads my breast and kisses me with such primal possession, I can't stop him. I feared rape, or something like it, but this is far worse. If he took me against my will, I could fight him. I could tell myself he was wrong, that I hated him. I could do what I've grown excellent at doing: wall myself off from all emotions that surround sex. I could fight him.

But this... *oh, God*. This is something else altogether. It's like he's read my fantasies and played them out with perfection, controlling me and forcing my body to respond of its own accord. I'm losing control, and that can't happen.

My body throbs from the lashes, my pussy aches for pressure, my breasts tingle in his grasp. He stops kissing me and stares at me, panting from the exertion of belting and dominating me.

"Need a breather, then?" I ask.

He shakes his head. "I'll enjoy every minute of breaking you, doll."

Chapter 5

Nolan

SHE THINKS I don't see right through her. That I don't know she's spied on everything we do, from our work to our home to our personal lives.

She thinks I don't know that she feigns nonchalance when she's really not only afraid, but aroused. I've got a masochist on my hands, and that spells fucking danger.

Thanks to Carson, I know a little bit about her background. I know she frequents The Craic, and she knows every damn one of us.

The only thing I don't know about her is why the fuck she's determined to fuck with us. And that's exactly what I mean to find out.

In time. I'm going to go enjoy myself in the process.

I slide my hands up her thighs and shove her panties aside. I'm not surprised to find her wet and throbbing. She loves being dominated, maybe even craves it. I'm not sure why, and I'm not sure that matters.

But one thing I do know for sure. If I bring her to climax and pleasure her, she may be more malleable to me than she is now. The more I strip her down and pleasure her, the more she'll draw closer to me. Rely on me. It's the only way to control her.

I stroke her pussy until her hips rise to meet me and she's panting on the cusp of release.

She's attracted to me, to this.

Fucking dynamite.

"That's a girl," I say in her ear. "Move your hips and take it."

I bend my mouth to her nipple and draw it between my lips, suckling until her mouth parts, and she gasps, while I stroke and fondle her.

"Oh, God," she pants. I grin, working her faster, until she's right on the edge. Her eyes roll back in her head and she's right on the cusp of release when I take my hand away.

She mewls and pants, pushing her torso up for pressure, but I shake my head.

"Do you really think I'd reward you so easily?" I say to her, shaking my head. "After what you did? You're a naughty little kitten, aren't you?"

She pushes her wrists against my hands and glares at me, but I shake my head like a stern professor giving a lecture.

"Now, then, Sheena. Behave yourself and give me answers, and I might grant you pleasure. But you see, doll, I don't take too kindly to being manipulated or used, so no reward until you've been suitably punished, see?"

"Fuck you," she says, glaring at me.

"Ah, now, we'll have none of that." I roll her to her side and give her arse a good, hard slap. "Now, you'll do as you're told or suffer the consequences."

"Fuck you," she repeats.

Twice now I've spanked her with my belt, and it hasn't made an ounce of goddamn difference. But I have many tools at my disposal, and giving her a spanking is only one of them.

"I've told you to watch that smart mouth of yours, or I'll punish you. But maybe that's exactly what you want, isn't it?"

I don't think she's really angry. I think she's playing a part, rehearsing a script of hers she prepared. It's how she always behaves, her automatic response. She thinks I expect her to behave this way, so she's giving me what she feels she should.

But I won't get the answers I need playing games. Not her game, anyway.

She gives me a coy smile. "Oh, no," she says with

mock surprise. "A spanking? No, sir. I hate the thought of going over daddy's lap."

Heat flares in my belly at her words, her tone, the seductive cut of her eyes. I hold her gaze, bring my hand back, and slap it against her arse again. Her mouth drops open and her eyes grow heated with arousal.

"You think I'm playing, Sheena?" I ask, holding her gaze.

She grins at me and doesn't answer.

I hold her gaze, bring my hand back, and give her another firm, unyielding slap that makes her hiss in breath.

She's the one playing, and this is a game she's going to lose.

"I told you to strip," I say, shaking my head with mock regret. I'm not at all upset about having to take her clothes off. Hell, I've been dying to do just this. "And you disobeyed me."

I grasp the edge of her dress and lift it up. She wriggles and squirms to stop me, but her efforts are laughably futile. I'm above her, twice her size and weight, and she's pinned belly-down on the bed.

But when I lift her dress as far as her lower back, I see why she protested.

Cold, hard metal hits my palm. Her mobile's so small and well-secured, and I'm not sure how I missed it when I touched her before. She's got it taped securely against her inner thigh.

I shake my head. This can only mean one thing.

She planned on being taken tonight.

She hid this as a precaution, not something a girl heading to the club would normally do.

"Very clever, lass," I tell her. "And yet, so stupid."

She flinches at my words, and this time I'm not sure she's playing.

I could take this and destroy it, but something tells me that would be a mistake. She could have contacts on this phone, evidence we could use. And if I give her a little slack and find out who she's in touch with, I could piece information together.

This could come in very useful.

"Give that to me!" Her words are strangled and laced with panic. Now this is a side of Sheena I haven't seen yet. She isn't play-acting.

"Not a chance, doll," I say, sliding it in my pocket and easily arranging her limbs again as I continue to strip her.

Now she's fighting me in earnest, wriggling like an over-excited puppy, as I tear her dress off. It nearly shreds in my hands, thread and fabric giving way to her perfect naked skin. I ignore her protests and pull it over her head, through her arms, undressing her until she's totally naked.

I've seen Sheena naked once before, but the circumstances were wildly different. At the time, she was every bit a victim, stripped by the men who wanted to hurt her, tied up, her most private parts exposed for all to see.

I rescued her that night. Against my better judgment, I rescued her, but it wasn't even a conscious choice. We came in the room to fight for Aileen, Cormac's wife who was abducted and abused. But Sheena was taken, too. When I saw her, I acted on instinct. I grabbed the nearest blanket, threw it over her naked body, and unfastened the bonds that held her.

It was the only thing to do.

And hell, how I've thought about that since then. Fantasized, even?

Why?

It's stupid as fuck to fancy myself Sheena Hurston's savior.

But for one brief moment in time, when she looked at me, I felt like I could be. The men of The Clan are old-fashioned, high-handed. We were raised to be unequivocal heads of our households. When we find the woman we're meant to cherish, we're all in. My father was that way for mam, Keenan is for Caitlin, and Cormac for Aileen. Deeply embedded in who I am as a McCarthy man is the need to protect and cherish a woman who needs me.

But Sheena is dangerous, deadly, out to destroy my

family, and anything that even smacks of romance between us is as flimsy as a sandcastle. One gust of wind, one wave, and it collapses.

She's the most beautiful, dangerous enemy we have.

I have to break this woman. Tear her defenses down and find what she's after. Make it clear that her threats against my family will not go unpunished.

But hell, if I do, won't I be saving her, even a little? The rules of the Clan state that spies are to be killed. Everything she's done puts my entire brotherhood at risk and her penalty is certain death.

I can't save this woman, but I can save her from execution.

A fucking conundrum.

Once her clothes are removed, I restrain her wrists with one hand and drag her to the edge of the bed. I can tell she likes this, though, being dragged around and manhandled. Christ, she likes being used. This knowledge is as dangerous to me as a goddamn drink.

I have handcuffs in my pocket I've readied for this, and my room's the perfect place to restrain her.

"You're a kinky little doll, aren't you?" I ask her, flipping her onto her back and taking one wrist to the ring fastened to my bed.

"I'm the kinky one? You have fucking O-rings mounted on your bed. Suppose you've got nipple clamps and anal plugs in the little drawer in the jacks where others store toothpaste and dental floss, hmm?"

My cock stirs to life. She knows what O-rings are. Naturally. And the mention of the other tools of the trade brings a sudden, beautiful vision.

"Ah, you have me all figured out, don't you?"

She doesn't respond. For some reason, this question sobers her a little. She watches curiously without a trace of fear or surprise when I fasten her right wrist to one ring, then her left to the other. I have them spaced apart enough so that her arms are stretched but not that uncomfortably.

Her eyes do widen a bit when I take out the spreader bar.

A moment later, she's on display for me, a gorgeous little kitten with full breasts, dusty pink nipples that taste like ripe berries, her pussy shaved bare and her little toes painted a sheer shade of peach. Her gorgeous red hair's all tumbled on the bed like a swath of ribbons. I stand beside her, admiring my handiwork. I can see the faintest lines of red across her thigh from where I've spanked her. Gorgeous.

I pace beside her, fully clothed, and observe her unhindered. Her long fingers taper like pianists', delicate and slender, her fingernail polish matching her toes. No ink, but she's got a birthmark right beside her bellybutton, and something else on one of her shoulders. I lean in to take a closer look.

I brush my thumb across the silver scar that runs alone one side.

"You have a scar, here. The location and size... it's a knife wound, isn't it?"

She pinches her lips together and doesn't respond. I shake my head.

"Ah, right. You still haven't gotten the message. Good that I'm ready for that, hmm?"

I open the drawer beside the bed and remove a long, slender riding crop, then turn back to her. Once more, her eyes grow heated. She tries to school her features, but she can't. I brought this woman to my room as prisoner, and I've given her exactly what she fucking wanted.

But I want to test that theory.

I take the little leather squared-tip of the crop and touch her cheek with it, first the left, then the right.

"Kiss it," I whisper, dragging it across her lips.

She obeys, her full lips placing a kiss on the leather, her eyes on my mine.

"Good girl," I say approvingly. I drag it down her cheek to her neck, trace the outline of her jaw, then retrace down the column of her neck until I reach her breasts. I caress first the left, then the right, gently dragging the little strip of leather over her hardened nipples. Her hips jerk when I touch the tender buds.

"Fuck, woman, you're sensitive, aren't you?"

74

When she doesn't respond, I lift the crop and slap her naked breast. She yelps, and the faintest light pink blooms on her naked skin.

"You'll answer me when I ask you a question."

"Thought that was rhetorical," she pants. "And yes, I'm sensitive. I thought that was obvious."

"You'd think that, wouldn't you?" I ask, dragging the crop between the valley of her breasts. My cock aches, she's so fucking beautiful. "But no, doll. Nothing's obvious in this game."

I drag the crop to her pussy, and she begins to tremble.

"Have you ever had your pussy punished, Sheena?"

She nods, and it looks as if she's trying to toss her shoulder with nonchalance, but restrained and vulnerable like this makes the action difficult. Instead, her movements are jerky and nervous.

"Of course," she says. "Loads of times."

I lift the crop and tap her pussy. She hisses and gasps, but can't get away.

"Loads of times? Is that the truth, doll?"

"Okay, well," she begins. She bites her lips. "At least once."

I shake my head. "Lying again, then? I won't put up with that."

I lift the crop and snap it on her inner thigh once,

twice, three times. She hisses and yelps, but she can't get away, not now.

She's here to be questioned, it's the very purpose of her being held prisoner. No one said I couldn't have a little fun with it.

"You'll tell the truth when I ask you a question. Do you understand me?"

She nods and squirms, still aroused, but now it looks like there's a touch of fear in her eyes.

My phone rings. I keep the crop propped on her belly and leave it there while I step away to answer the phone.

Keenan.

"Yeah, brother?"

"You have any answers yet? I heard you found her and you've taken her."

"Found her, yes. Taken her, also yes, she's in my room."

"Ah, you've got her in the love shack?"

My brothers love to give me crap about my room.

"Aye," I say, leaning against the wall and eying her perfect, naked body on display. "You could say she's good and well secured."

I give her a wink. If her wrists weren't restrained right now, she'd probably flip me off.

"Any answers yet?"

"Of course not, brother. Interrogation's a fine art, you see. I've only just begun preparing the canvas."

Her eyes widen slightly and it might be my imagination, but I swear she finally looks a little nervous.

He grunts. "Fine art, my arse. You brought her here for questions, and I expect—"

"Calm your titties," I tell him. Christ, I need a smoke.

"Nolan," he says warningly. As my older brother and Clan Chief, I do owe him respect, but for Christ's sake, does he think me a magician?

Still, I want to prove myself to him. For years, I know he thought me worthless and spoiled, and fuck, maybe I was. But not now. I've shown my loyalty to The Clan time and time again, he just has to give me time.

"I will, brother. Trust me, Keenan. I'll get answers in time."

Right about now would be a good time to smoke a cigar and sit on the balcony that overlooks the sea. Let the salt breeze unwind my nerves and calm me. But not when I have a job to do.

There's a pause on the other end of the line, then I can almost hear him nodding when he says, "Absolutely. Of course I trust you. Do what you think's best, and let me know when you have something for us to go on. If you need answers, call Carson. He's ready and willing to investigate."

"On it."

We disconnect the call. She's watching me with those wide, beautiful eyes of hers. She notices everything. It's her job to note every detail. I slide my phone back into my pocket and go back to her.

"Your brother," she says. "Keenan?"

I nod. "You know who my brothers are," I say. "Don't pretend you don't."

"I'm not," she says. "But I'm trying to get them straight in my head. He wants you to get answers from me. Why?"

"Why? You're a smart girl. Of course you know."

Her look grows cold and detached, her jaw clenched and her eyes icy.

"I just wondered if there was any new reason for you to get all up in arms about my investigation is all. I don't know everything. Suppose you think you do."

I lift the crop and hold it, crossing my arms on my chest. Warning. She swallows again and gives me a placating smile.

"New article that came out recently," I tell her. "The locals are angry at the McCarthy Clan. We've been on amiable terms with the locals for decades, and you're ruining that. You're the informant, you're the one causing trouble. What do you have to say for yourself?"

She holds my gaze. "Isn't it obvious?"

"Much is obvious, Sheena. But I asked you a question."

For some reason, she looks away when she answers me.

Why?

"You're mafia," she says. "You might fancy yourselves some sort of benevolent do-gooders with their own code of ethics or whatever, but you're still organized crime. You flaunt the law. You don't bring security to Ballyhock but misery and devastation, and it's time the villagers knew the truth."

She's lying. There's more to it than that.

"Ahhh," I say, circling the bed. I tap the crop on my hand and she flinches when it makes a snap sound. "So you're the one in charge of policing us, then. Did you sign on with the police force, then? Did I miss your badge somewhere?"

"Oh fuck off," she snaps, clearly forgetting she's bound and at my mercy. She cringes when I raise the crop and snap it on her thigh.

"Watch that smart mouth, doll," I warn. "I'll not have you speaking to me that way."

She grits her teeth and doesn't answer.

"So who put you in charge, then?" I ask. "The villagers here, the local church and police, all know what we do. We've gotten along just fine until you came along."

Her lips thin, and she looks away. I take the crop

and place it on her cheek, guiding her eyes back to mine. She grits her teeth but looks my way.

"So answer me, Sheena. Why us? Why now? There are other mobs in Ireland you could just as easily trail."

She looks away from me again, and her lack of response is telling. I've hit something here. Her vendetta against us is personal, as we've suspected.

She doesn't answer me. This isn't something she'll joke about. There's no smart retort, no wise crack. I've struck a nerve then. If this is something personal, I'll have to dig deep to find out what the truth is. I pretend like I don't know, that she hasn't given anything away.

"So let me ask you a question, then," I say. Standing in front of her again, I'm reminded why she's here. I may have enjoyed dominating this woman, wielding my crop and belt and tasting those full, beautiful lips. I may enjoy the sight before me even now, while she's restrained and at my mercy, bearing the marks I've inflicted on her.

But this isn't about a quick, hard lay or a night of fucking.

This isn't about picking up a girl at The Craic, or even about normal interrogation.

This woman has betrayed us. She's dragged us through the mud and by Clan code, deserves death. My mission to extract the truth from her both vindicates The Clan and saves her from certain execution.

My phone rings again, and I go to answer it without taking my eyes off her. But when I lift my phone, no one's calling. It rings again. Takes me a minute to realize it's her phone that's ringing, not mine.

She's not getting this phone from me.

"Huh," I mutter. "Same ringtone. That's odd, isn't it?"

Every mask that she wears falls when she realizes it's her phone that's ringing.

"Give it to me. Please, Nolan. Please let me answer my phone."

Nolan? She's supplicating with as much as she can muster, and it throws me off a bit. Why is she so desperate to answer the phone? Doesn't she know anything she wants that badly is the very thing I won't give her?

I look at the name on the caller I.D.

Tiernan.

Heated jealousy rips through me.

Her fucking boyfriend? She thinks I'll let her talk to her fucking boyfriend?

I'm half tempted to whip her phone across the room and smash it. I go so far as to wind up to throw it, but she screams.

"No! Don't. Please don't!"

What kind of a woman with a boyfriend seduces a man with a blow job? I shut it off, shove it in my pocket, and stalk out of the room. I kick the door open, march to the large framed print above the sofa, and tear it aside. I flick open my safe, slide her phone in, then relock it. I place the painting back, toss the crop to the couch, and go to leave.

She can think about who she is, what she's done, and what she's yet to do for a good long while. I'm having my smoke and letting her fester.

Chapter 6

Sheena

OH, God. *Oh God.*

Panic causes my breaths to come in ragged, shallow gasps. I'm drowning, unable to catch a breath. I made my way through the club, tried to seduce one of the most dangerous criminals in all of Ireland, got kidnapped and brought to their house, fucking punished and restrained and interrogated and nothing has made me panic until now.

Tiernan never calls me, but that ringtone's specifically his. I have my phone set on silent unless he calls me, and he only ever rings in an emergency.

Oh God.

If he's calling me, something terrible's happened. I have to answer. It's only been a matter of hours since I've seen him, and he wouldn't call unless this was an emergency, I know he wouldn't.

"Nolan!" I yell. If he hears me, he doesn't answer.

"Nolan!"

Christ, even if I did get his attention, what would I say? Oh, hey, I know I'm your prisoner, but do me a favor and let me answer my phone?

I try to take another breath, but my chest feels as if someone's sitting on it. With my wrists restrained and my legs spread apart like this, I can't do a damn thing to move from this position, to draw a deeper breath, to quell the rising panic.

A sob rises in my chest and I scream a second time. "Nolan!"

I close my eyes when panic darkens my vision.

I can't breathe. I can't draw in breath. My lungs are constricted, my need to breathe instant and terrifying.

I'm a little girl again, trapped in a closet while my mother fucks her boyfriend. She's punishing me for being stupid, in this dark and dank room. I can hear the baby crying in the other room, a sick cacophony that clashes with the grunts and moans on the other side of this door.

I can't open the door. I can't get the baby. She's kept me in here to silence me, but I will not be silent. One day I will escape from here and I will never be silent again.

I'm sobbing, tears falling freely down my cheeks, so caught in my misery and panic that I don't even hear him entering the room until I feel strong arms on my wrists.

"Easy, lass," he says. "For Christ's sake, you've worked yourself into a feckin' frenzy. Take a deep breath and relax."

I try but the air's too thick or my mouth won't open, I don't know, but I can't. He removes my restraints, and for one brief moment, I remember. Back at The Craic, the night I was abducted and he and the others saved me. How he wrapped me in a blanket and took me to safety. It was the one and only time I've ever seen tenderness from Nolan McCarthy, and I've not forgotten it.

"I—I can't," I gasp, trying to catch a breath.

After my wrists are free, he goes to my ankles next and unfastens those. When I'm finally free, I don't flee. I curl up in a ball, gasping for breath. He climbs up in bed beside me.

"Shh, now." He's holding me, naked and trembling, to his chest.

"Sheena. Easy, doll. What the hell happened? I was only out of the room for a minute."

But I still can't breathe.

He spins me over to look at him, his strong hand cupping my face to hold my gaze.

"Are you having an asthma attack?"

I shake my head.

"Do I need to call the doctor?"

I shake my head harder. "No," I gasp. "No doctor. Panic."

Understanding dawns quickly, and he nods.

"Okay, Sheena. Look at my eyes." His voice grows stern and commanding, and I instinctively obey. "Now. Do what I do."

He draws in a deep, steadying breath, then lets it out. I can't breathe on my own, but when he does this, I can imitate him. I hold his gaze and draw in a deep breath. Cool air fills my lungs and the haze of panic begins to ebb away.

"Good girl," he says softly. "Just like that. Again, now." He draws in a huge breath again, his shoulders rising, and again, I imitate him.

I do it again and again, until I'm breathing freely.

"There, now," he says. "Better."

My hair's plastered to my forehead, my whole body dotted in a fine sheen of perspiration.

I try to put my wall up, to defend myself against the rush of emotion and relief. I don't need to see the tender side of Nolan McCarthy again, goddammit.

If I do, I might lose control.

All this work, all this effort to get here, to follow my script and find my answers, vanishes when I devolve into a sobbing fucking mess. I'm so angry with myself I could scream.

Once I'm breathing freely, he holds me at arm's length and gives me a serious look, his eyes probing and sober.

"Y'alright?"

I look away. I don't want him to see the devastation I can't hide, how stupid and foolish I am for showing weakness.

I take in one breath, let it out, then take in another, steadying my nerves.

I nod. "Yeah, I'm fine."

He's still guarded, on edge, as if he's waiting to see if I'm fooling him. Hell, I don't blame him. I've feigned panic attacks before to get something I needed, and I'd do it again. Big, strong men like him enjoy being the protector, and I know how to play that.

I'm not playing now, though, and a part of me wonders if I'm the girl who cried wolf. If I keep manipulating him, will he ever really trust me?

Do I want him to?

He sits up in bed and releases me, watching how I react. I reach for the duvet, grab the corner, and pull it over myself. I feel so wildly exposed, and I don't like it. Minutes ago I was restrained and naked and it didn't bother me like being bared to him does now.

He didn't just see my body. My body's a vessel. I've learned to detach as a matter of survival.

But just now, he saw so much more than that, and I hate that he did. He's seen my fears. He saw me lose my mind, and I want to take cover.

I can't, though. Too little, too late.

"Why'd you panic so?" he says, and the sharpened tone of his voice makes me look at him. That quickly, the kindness he showed me evaporates. He's on edge again, the hunter watching the moves of his prey. His voice hardens to granite. "Your boyfriend calling you?"

I hold the blanket tighter. I'm no fucking wilting violet, and I won't let him intimidate me, but still, I can't help but cringe a little.

What the hell is he talking about?

"My boyfriend?"

He rolls his eyes and swings his legs over the side of the bed.

"Your fucking boyfriend," he says. "I saw the phone. I saw the name come up. Tiernan wants a word, does he? Afraid he'll dump your pretty arse when he finds out who you really are?"

I can't stop the sudden fury he inspires in me. It isn't fair how easily the fucker can make me snap. I won't tell him I don't have a boyfriend. He doesn't deserve to know it's my brother that calls me, that they depend on me. It's too close to the vest, and he doesn't deserve to know anything that personal.

"Fuck off."

A muscle ticks in his jaw and he crosses his arms on his chest, shaking his head.

"You really haven't learned, have you?"

I blink, unable to respond. My fucking gob. Gets me in fucking trouble, every time.

"Probably not," I say, still seething. "But I suppose you're willing and able to teach me."

He holds my gaze, his eyes narrowed and his jaw tight. I wonder if he regrets holding me just now, soothing me. "Ah, lass," he says so softly I can hardly hear him. "You have no fucking idea. Now tell me, or we'll have another session of ask and tell. Was it your boyfriend calling you?"

My plan not to tell him something's crap. If Tiernan called, there's an emergency. And if he called, I need to find out why.

"No," I tell him. If I give him enough truth, maybe he'll buy it. "Not my boyfriend. Tiernan's a friend of mine, and he only ever calls if there's a very serious emergency."

He blinks, absorbing this, then nods slowly. "Right," he says. "So if I call Tiernan back, then, I won't find a pissy boyfriend on the other line?"

Is he testing me? I swallow and hold his gaze. I can't let him intimidate me, not this time.

"You will not."

A knock comes at the door, and he curses under his breath. "I'll be right back. You stay right fucking there, or that spanking you got earlier will look like a joke."

He waits until I respond. All I manage is a curt nod. I won't move. Not yet.

He goes to the door, and I hear him talking to someone. Their voices rise and fall, and then the door slams shut. I wait for him to come back to the room, but he doesn't at first. I get out of the bed and stand, half tempted to go in the other room to see what he's doing, but I'm not sure it's worth provoking him again. I don't hear his footsteps because of the carpeting. A moment later, he's darkening the doorway to the bedroom and my phone rests in his hand.

"Password protected," he says wryly, crossing the room to me. "And when I say stay right there, I fucking mean it." He places the phone in his pocket, grabs the duvet, and yanks me back over to the bed, forcing me into a sitting position.

"Who was at the door?"

I've learned to be the pain in the arse. You get a lot more answers that way, even if it pisses people off. I've grown used to that part.

But he's good at this. He doesn't even bother to respond, and hands me my phone. "Unlock it, then hand it back to me."

I don't want him to know my secrets, but my need to find out if they're okay trumps my need for this tiny bit of privacy. I take the phone he hands me and punch in my passcode.

"Good. Now disable the privacy settings."

I pause when he gives that instruction. If I disable my passcode, he'll have total access to my phone, and I don't like that at all. I've hidden most of the important files, though, and he's not giving me a choice. So I do what he says and disable the passcode. I'll get it later. I'll wipe it. Right now, I need to call Tiernan.

"Good," he repeats. "Now call Tiernan back on speakerphone. Find out why he called."

"I don't want to call him in front of you," I protest, but a narrowing of his eyes warns me. I'm not sure what choice I have. I have to find out why he called. I grit my teeth and do what he says.

I swipe the speaker on and dial.

The phone rings, and Tiernan answers on the second ring. His voice is descending, but he still sounds like a child. Nolan will know this is no man.

"Sheena?"

Relief floods through me at hearing his voice. He's okay.

I bow my head and look away from Nolan so he doesn't see my face.

"Is everything okay?"

I hate that we're having this conversation in front of him.

"No," Tiernan says. There's a fist around my belly, squeezing. I take in a deep breath and let it out again.

"What's wrong?"

"She left tonight with some man. Came back drunk off her arse, forgot her key and wanted in. The baby was crying, Fiona came out dazed, was half asleep, and told them to leave. The man lost his mind, broke the door down. They started throwing things. Hit Fiona's wrist, damn near hurt the baby. Came at me."

I'm on my feet. "Oh, God, are you okay?"

"I made them leave, kicked them out. Gave her all the cash I had as bribery. I thought of calling someone, but I—I'm afraid they'll separate us. Not sure who else to call."

Christ.

Nolan snaps his fingers. My eyes fly open. I almost forgot he was there.

"Mute it," he mouths.

"Tiernan, just a minute." I hit the mute button and look at Nolan. He looks even angrier than before. What the hell is that about?

"You have children?"

"Of course not," I snap. I sigh. "That's my brother."

I want to get to Tiernan. I want to rescue them, but how?

"Then who's that on the phone?"

I swallow. I hate giving him any truth. "My younger brother."

His eyes widen slightly. "And you've got siblings left unattended?"

"Aye," I say angrily. "Their mother's an alcoholic, likely passed out on some arsehole's couch."

He holds my gaze for a moment, working his jaw.

"I'll tell you right now, woman, if I find out you're lyin' to me I will flay you alive."

My heart thumps. I glare. "I'm not lying," I tell him. Everything else I've told him is a lie, so I'm not sure why it bothers me so much that he questions the only truth I've given him.

"Son of a bitch," he curses. "And he's got no one to watch them?"

I shake my head.

"I see," he says, stroking his chin. "Alright, then. Get dressed. Let's go."

"Let's go?"

He points back to the phone. "Tell Tiernan you're on your way."

Chapter 7

Nolan

THIS WOMAN IS way more complicated than she appears.

So fucking complicated.

When I came into the room just now and saw her in a full panic attack, it took me by surprise. I've never seen her lose herself like that, lose such self-control. She's mastered every emotion. It's part of her armor.

I couldn't help but comfort her, to help her calm down. But I don't trust her, not one bit.

But now I feel a little like a douchebag. I assumed Tiernan was her boyfriend. What the fuck am I, a jealous fucking lover? What the hell?

I don't trust her, and I need answers, but hell, I'm

not a monster. If she's got children she's responsible for…

Still, it's crap like this that pisses Keenan off. I was given a job to do and I have to do it, damn it. He'll kill me, maybe even step in and do the job himself.

"Suppose you can't wear that damn dress to go see your brothers or sisters?" I ask, frowning at her. She looks at the dress with chagrin, and shakes her head.

"You got someone you can call that will go to them until we get there?"

She thinks for a moment, then bites her lip. "Aye."

"Call them."

Her fingers hesitate over the phone. Does she have to think that hard about it? If I needed help, I'd have an army of support at my fingers. Does she have no one?

Why does this surprise me? Of course she doesn't. She's disingenuous and conniving.

She finally dials someone, but it only goes to voicemail.

"I can call Walsh," I tell her. He's one of the officers on our payroll.

"Christ, no," she says. Her eyes flash at me. "Are you out of your fucking mind? He'll have them in child protection before the day's out."

"Then call someone," I repeat, my voice hardening. I've no patience for this.

She calls a second person, then a third. No one answers. No one's going to help her. She can't hide the way her face falls.

"Fine, then," I say, when my phone rings. It's Keenan. I shove my phone in my pocket. I'm not going to answer.

"Let me go alone," she begins. "I swear to God you can send a guard with me, I'll—"

I'm chuckling before she finishes her sentence.

"Ah, no."

She's still pleading her case when I dial my cousin Megan.

"Hello?"

"Need a favor, Megan."

We were born the same year, me and Megan. She's as close to me as a sister.

"Of course," she says. "What do you need?"

"Some clothes. Girl clothes."

"Girl's?"

I clear my throat. "Ah, woman's."

Megan laughs out loud. "You're a hot ticket, Nolan. You bring a girl home so fast she lost her knickers on the way?"

"Ah, no, she's got the knickers."

Sheena watches me with wide eyes. She can likely hear Megan's laugh all the way over there.

"Right, then. About what size is she?"

I mute the call, get the details from Sheena, and tell Megan.

"Okay, I'm at Aileen's right now. Sounds like some of her clothing would fit her, no?"

"Maybe," I say, frowning. "Bring me a variety, will you?"

"Aye."

"Who's Megan?" she asks when I hang up my phone.

"None of your damn business," I tell her. Doesn't she know enough about us?

But I recognize that jealous look she's giving me. Does she think what I did about Tiernan?

Are we that fucked up?

She's my prisoner, my enemy. I've punished her and haven't even begun extracting the truth. Why the hell do I care who's connected to her? Why does she?

"Cousin," I tell her.

"Right."

She looks away and bites her lip. "Look, Nolan. It

matters to me that my brother doesn't know who you are. If he does, it'll scare him."

I snort. "Am I that terrifying?"

She looks back at me. "Yes. You are."

I shrug. "I won't go in with a gun drawn or anything, if that's what you're afraid of. But you'll do well to remember I shouldn't even be bringing you there. That you're captive here, and what happens outside this room doesn't matter."

I wonder if I'm making a mistake.

Maybe going to her siblings will tell me something about her I need to know. Suppose this is what I tell myself to justify what I'm doing.

A knock sounds at the door.

"That'll be Megan. Stay here."

She rolls her eyes heavenward. "Like there's any fucking place for me to go?"

Megan can wait. I step over to Sheena, tangle my fingers in her hair, and hold her gaze. "That's ten, doll. Care to up the count?"

She swallows when I place my hand on her neck. Warning. I can feel her pulse quickening under my palm.

"The count?" she repeats.

"How many smacks you'll get over my knee tonight when we return to why you're here."

"Is that all you like to do?" she asks. She's trying to unsettle me or distract me, I'm not sure which, but I won't have it. We weren't planning on leaving, and I won't tell my brother I haven't gotten answers.

"You'll see about that," I say with a rueful smile. I flex my hand on her neck. "Now sit on the bed and behave yourself."

"Fine," she whispers with a nod. I push her to sitting and hold her eyes as I walk to the door. I need a good, long night with her before I find out anything at all, I know it, and even then I'll have to employ a variety of methods. But I won't get far if she's distracted with thoughts of home.

I open the door to find not only Megan, but Caitlin and Aileen. Megan is grinning, Aileen eying me cautiously, and Caitlin looks a bit sheepish. I shut the door behind me and step into the hall.

"What the fuck is this?" I hiss. "I don't need a goddamn posse." I glare at Megan. She's responsible for this. The brown-haired, jolly cousin of ours doesn't know enough to leave well enough alone.

Aileen, her long blonde hair woven into a braid, is shorter than Megan, but just as bold. She places her hands on her hips and faces me.

"Nolan, if you've brought a woman here, we ought to meet her."

I turn my glare to her, but it doesn't intimidate her. She's married to Cormac, the biggest and most fierce of all, and he's wrapped around her little finger.

"Is that right?" I ask her. "Every time I bring home a lass for a quick fuck we should put the kettle on? Hmm?"

She rolls her eyes and Caitlin speaks up. Taller than Aileen and thinner, she's willowy and fairy-like, Keenan's wife and the first that married into our clan in our generation.

"Now, Nolan. We know she isn't here for a quick f—" she blushes furiously. I've never heard her utter a curse word. Even slang is usually beneath her. "For that," she amends. "She's here for a greater purpose, and you know it."

Megan tugs a lock of Caitlin's black hair. "You're adorable, you know that?"

"And at what point in time did your husbands tell you our greater purpose was any of your goddamn business?"

Aileen rolls her eyes heavenward, but Megan grins at me. "Husbands? Did you forget who I am, cousin?" I haven't. Megan and I have sworn off marriage, and it's one thing that draws us together as friends.

She scoffs. "The day I put a band on my finger's the day pigs fly over the Irish Sea. Now, are you leaving the poor lass stark naked and waiting, or are you going to let us in?"

"You're not coming in," I say, reaching for the pile of clothes.

"She might need a friend, though," Megan says.

"She needs a firm hand is what she needs," I say, shaking my head. I turn away from them. "For all the nerve."

I open the door and they're smart enough not to follow.

"Keep me posted, cousin!" Megan says. The other girls giggle. I almost regret even asking for her help.

I shake my head and slam the door behind me. "Thank you," I say to the closed door. I don't want to be a total arse.

It doesn't take long for Sheena to find something to wear. I marvel at how different she looks with her red hair, sporting a pair of leggings and top, instead of the black wig and fancy dress.

She's stunning, even in these simple clothes.

When she looks at me, she isn't playing anymore, but dead serious. "You should bring a weapon," she says softly. "It's dangerous where we're going."

"Lass, I never go anywhere without a weapon. Where exactly are we going?"

She swallows and looks in the distance when she answers, "Stone City... just outside of Dublin," she says. "Probably never heard of it."

But she's wrong. "I know Stone City." Reminds me

of Limerick City a few hours away. The area where we're going is drug-infested and riddled with crime, and she's right that I should bring a weapon. What I also need is back-up.

I call Lachlan.

"Nolan?"

"You free, brother?"

"Aye. Something the matter?"

"Need to get to Stone City. Need back up."

"Christ, Nolan. Stone City? Keenan know?"

"No."

He's silent for a minute. He knows my job tonight and can assume why I need to go.

"Right then," he says. "Where do I meet you?"

I give him instructions to meet him by the car.

"I'll see you there. I'll keep an eye out for Keenan."

It feels weirdly like I'm a teenager sneaking out past curfew. Keenan's a good leader, the very best. Loyal and just, and he holds himself to even higher standards than he holds us. But he's uncompromising. And I've no doubt he'd think leaving here with our prisoner I'm supposed to question to go to a dangerous, crime-infested city where I'm certain to be noticed, is a fucking mistake.

But after this, she'll owe me a favor, and hell,

though I don't want to be that bastard, she's left me no choice but to play hardball.

We don't go down the main stairs but the back stairway that leads down to the kitchen and garden. I march her along, my hand on her arm, to remind her she's my prisoner and not to pull anything fast.

She'll try, though. I fucking know she will.

When I get to the garage I find not only Lachlan but Carson as well.

"Fancy a party?" I ask. "What the hell, Lach?"

"We were having a drink when you called. Thought it'd be better to have three of us than two."

"More conspicuous that way," I mutter.

Carson flips me off. "I can leave if you want."

"Come off it, Carson, it's nothing personal."

"Eh, I know," he says with a shrug. "But I got into a fight with Eve, and she locked me out."

Sheena watches us, her eyes flitting from one to the next without a word. She says nothing. Notes everything.

"What'd you do?" I ask, going over to the passenger's side and opening the door. I point to Sheena. "You. Here." She rolls her eyes and I slap her arse before I even think about what I'm doing. I place her in the car as if she's a small child, grab the belt and buckle her in. I lean in close and whisper in her ear. "Care to add to your number?"

She flushes, purses her lips, and doesn't respond.

I go to the driver's side. Lachlan and Carson go to the back.

"Address," I say.

She gives it to me and I punch it into the GPS.

Carson whistles in the back. "No foolin', Nolan? You fancy gettin' knifed tonight, brother?"

Sheena whips her head around and glares at him. "I'll thank you to keep your fucking opinions to yourself."

I grip her thigh and squeeze. "Watch it, woman. You're captive here, and not allowed to speak freely."

"Is that right?" she snaps. "Or what? Twenty?"

I pull out onto the street and follow the directions. She notes everything as the gates open to let us out.

I grit my teeth. "Don't tempt me, Sheena."

Lachlan chuckles in the back. "Figures you'd end up with a mouthy one, brother."

"End up with? What do you think this is, a fucking reward?"

"Aye," he says cheerfully. "You're second in line to the throne. Of course it is."

"Oh come off it," I mutter.

"Is he?" Sheena asks over her shoulder.

"Aye," Lachlan continues.

"That's enough. We don't need to give her any more information than necessary, for Christ's sake."

We drive in silence, and as the time passes, the view out our window goes from the glittering rocks that line the coast of Ballyhock to dilapidated streets of Stone City.

Lachlan whistles. "Never been here," he mutters to himself.

"Well good for you," Sheena says.

"Sheena," I begin. I've had it with her mouth, but I don't get very far when someone runs straight out in front of the car so quickly I come to a screeching halt.

"Mother of God," I mutter, as two teens dressed in all black laugh and jeer, running away from us.

"Pull the car over," Lachlan fumes in the back. "I'll teach them to be so feckin' stupid."

"No time, brother." He's got a temper he keeps in check with effort, which sometimes proves useful. Other times, not so much.

"Careful, Nolan," Carson says. "Pull 'round the shops here, and to the left. To the right's where the dealers are. Likely to be more crowded this time of night."

Sheena looks over her shoulder at him, frowning. "How do you know anything about this city?"

"Don't answer her," I tell him. He's silent, and she huffs out a breath, but before I can respond, she points a finger.

"There," she says. I glance quickly at her. Her face has paled, and she bites her lip. When she speaks, her tone of voice carries more than anger, though. Hurt? "I'd thank you to keep your nasty comments to yourself."

"Nasty comments?"

"Aye," she says, reaching for the handle of the door. "Not all of us were raised in a mansion, Nolan."

Touchy, seems like. I didn't say a word to her about where she came from. I have to admit, it surprises me, though. There are few places more run down than Stone City, and I didn't peg her coming from a place like this.

She opens the door and leaves. The rest of us follow.

"Christ, brother, good luck with that one," Lachlan mutters.

I give him a wry smile. "It isn't luck I need."

Carson smacks me on the back. "Aye, Nolan's up for this job."

I go round the car and beckon for Sheena. She walks to me without giving me trouble, and takes the hand I hold out. It feels strangely intimate.

"Didn't know you'd be introducing me to mum and dad already, did you?"

She lifts her head high and doesn't respond at first. Her nostrils flare and her cheeks redden, before she tosses her hair and shrugs. But she's acting again. I needled her. It's easy to do.

"Right then. Be sure to make a good impression, will you?"

I snort. "Aye, lass, I always make a good impression."

"Really?" she asks. "Don't know about that. First night I met you, you tied me up and punished the hell out of me. Did you forget?"

I squeeze her hand a little tighter. "Of course not. But it seems, doll, that I'm not the only one who hasn't forgotten, eh?"

She looks away, abashed, when someone crosses our path. He's tall thin, with a shaved head and beady, angry eyes. My body instantly tightens when he takes the stance of a guard dog ready to defend its territory.

"Back again so soon, Sheena? But you brought a few of your quick lays with you?"

My fingers roll into a fist. For fuck's sake, I didn't come here to knock someone's teeth out, but he may leave me no choice.

"Fuck off," she says.

Jesus, she doesn't know how to handle bullies. You don't mouth off to them or needle them. That only feeds them. You either ignore them or take control, and if they attack, you knock them out or slice their throat, whichever the situation calls for.

But I've no patience for a dumbass prick barring our way, so it's my turn.

"Move aside," I tell him. "We're here for a reason and you're in our fucking way."

The dumb bastard's looking for a fight, because he yanks his hand out of his pocket and a blade snaps open in his hand. Sheena gasps, but within seconds, Lachlan, Carson, and I all have our weapons drawn.

I take a step toward him, my gun trained on him.

"One more word, motherfucker."

Moonlight glints in the man's eyes, and he widens them almost comically when he sees the ink on my neck. "Feckin' mafia, Sheena? Are you out of yer fucking mind, you—"

I cock my gun. "Finish that sentence, it'll be your last," I tell him, and I mean it. I'd just as soon splatter his brains on the sidewalk as I would look at him. I'd have a clean-up crew here before his body hit the ground.

He lowers his hands as if in surrender, but the next thing I know, he lunges at me. I duck the blade just in time. Shots ring out but we're on the ground, fists flying. He catches me in the gut and I can't breathe, but I roll over and get the higher ground. I've been trained in this, how to incapacitate and kick someone's arse without letting myself get hurt. Again, and again, my fists fly. He's beneath me, bearing my weight and the vicious strikes I deliver, one fucking blow at a time. Bone snaps, and his face is a bloody mess. Lachlan and Carson stand by, prepared to help, but I don't need them. The prick's easily beaten and damn near crying. I give him one last vicious blow before I stop.

He holds his hands up in surrender, damn near sobbing.

"Okay, alright," he says, turning his head to the side and spitting blood onto the ground. One eye swollen, his lip split and pouring blood, but he's fucking lucky he's alive.

Lachlan leans over, plucks the blade out of his hand, folds it, and pockets it.

"Thanks for the souvenir," he says.

"Now run along, lad," Carson says, his voice dripping with condescension, icy with a hardness we rarely see. He seems placid and calm until you try to hurt one of his brothers, or worse, someone defenseless.

"And if you ever threaten her again, I won't hesitate next time," I say. "I'll put a bullet in your head without a backward glance, you hear?" I fucking hate bullies.

He gets to his feet. His eyes are swollen, blood dripping down from his broken nose. Still holding his hands up in surrender, he backs up until he trips, and when he gets to his feet, he runs.

"Well, if that wasn't a sight for sore eyes," Sheena

says. I look at her in surprise, but she only shrugs. Most women can't bear to witness the violence, but she seems almost happy. "Never saw anyone put the fear of God in Cian."

"Who was he?" I ask her.

"Ex-boyfriend."

"Bloody hell, lass, if I knew that, I'd have pulled the fucking trigger."

Chapter 8

Sheena

HE'S MY ENEMY, for God's sake. I should hate him.

I do.

Well, I don't.

I do.

When he does things like that, when he protects me and steps in as my savior, I can't help but wonder if I've been too hasty.

I can't think of this now. I won't. I'm here for a reason, and they need me right now.

I hate that he's here, that he's witness to the misery and squalor that ties me to my past. He already hates me and it shouldn't matter now what he thinks, but honest to God, I want to curl up in a ball and cry that I've had to bring him here.

What will he think of me?

Why do I care?

But I have no choice. They need me. They aren't safe, and I'll have to swallow my pride and do what I've come here for. Why must I always be forced to swallow my pride around Nolan?

I open the door and head straight in.

"Tiernan!" I yell. "Where are you?"

"In here, Sheena."

I almost cry when I walk into the living room. Tiernan sits on the dilapidated sofa. He's got a black eye, and Fiona's curled up beside him with her knees tucked up to her chest. She's wearing faded pajamas that are too small for her, and her hand's wrapped in a messy bandage that's falling off. Tiernan's eyes widen in surprise when he looks at the company I've brought.

"Thought you were coming alone," he say reproachfully. He stares with distrust toward Nolan, his gaze dropping to Nolan's blood-covered hands. Nolan wipes his hand on his trousers and clears his throat, then holds Tiernan's gaze for a long moment, takes in our surroundings. He speaks in a hushed voice to Lachlan and Carson. They leave.

Did he command them? Or was that a word between brothers?

"Sheena," Tiernan says, getting to his feet. "Who are they?"

"Well, about that," I begin, when Nolan interrupts.

"Thought it would be safer she not come alone," Nolan says.

And even though I know I'm here because I'm their prisoner, a part of me wonders if he speaks any truth at all. Would he prefer I not go alone? And why does a part of me hopes that's true?

Tiernan glares at Nolan, arranging the baby on his hip.

"And who the fuck are you?" he asks.

"Tiernan," I say reproachfully. "Language." I don't like him talking that way, he's better than that, and for goodness sakes, I don't want him provoking Nolan.

Nolan takes another step toward him.

My breath freezes, and I don't move. If Tiernan had any idea who Nolan was, who any of them were, he would watch his tongue. Fiona's eyes go from me to Nolan in wide-eyed silence.

Nolan doesn't respond at first, as if he's mulling his words over before he speaks. Finally, still holding Tiernan's gaze, he says in a voice much softer than I expect, "I'm guessing you're Tiernan."

"Aye."

Nolan extends his hand. "Nolan. Pleased to meet you."

Tiernan stares at Nolan's lacerated hand.

"You get into a fight?" he asks.

"I mean you no harm, Tiernan," Nolan continues, ignoring the question. "I came here because your sister and I were... together when you called. I didn't want her coming here alone."

Tiernan works his jaw, then nods.

"Now, no more questions," I say with the firmness of an older sister. Lying is a way of life for me, but I don't lie to Tiernan if I can help it. I'm concerned that if I give him any more space to ask questions, one of us will have to do just that.

"Aye," Nolan says. Tiernan hasn't shaken his hand, so Nolan withdraws it, but he doesn't look angry. He pockets both hands, a gesture of surrender, I think, and jerks his chin toward Tiernan. "Where'd they enter?"

Fiona watches us with wide eyes. The plaits in her hair from earlier have loosened. Little wisps of hair frame her face, giving the appearance of a reddish halo and makes her look younger than her thirteen years.

She walks to me and stands beside me in silence. Tiernan shows us the broken door in the kitchen, the splintered wood and broken lock. Nolan curses under his breath.

"Need a proper locksmith to come in to fix that," he mutters. "And who the f—who knows if they'll be back tonight. Often the way, you know."

Fiona hasn't spoken before now, but she's watched Nolan the entire time.

"What's that on your arm?" she asks, waving a finger at the ink that shows just beneath his shirt sleeve. The dim overhead lighting doesn't reveal much, but it does illuminate his trademark ink.

Tiernan draws in a sharp breath, and takes a step back.

Dammit.

"Mother of God," Tiernan mutters. "Sheena, what have you done? Who've you brought here?"

Nolan looks to me. I don't know what to say.

When neither of us responds, Tiernan continues. "You're mafia, aren't you?" he asks Nolan.

Nolan's busy with the locks and doesn't answer. He straightens, and still not answering Tiernan's question, he turns to me.

"They'll come with us, then," he says. "Can't all fit in the one car."

What?

He opens the door and calls out to Lachlan.

While he steps out, Tiernan hisses to me, "Sheena."

"What?" I hiss back.

"Is he mafia?"

I grit my teeth. "Is it that obvious?"

Tiernan curses, and Nolan steps back inside. "Right, then," he says. "We'll take the children with us, Lachlan and Carson will wait for a ride to come get them."

I shake my head. "No. Absolutely not. They can't go with you. I'll stay here, and—"

Nolan's gaze darkens, and he shakes his head. "Can't do that, Sheena," he says, his voice tight and laced with meaning. "It isn't safe for any of you here. And anyway. You have promises to keep."

Tiernan takes a step toward him but I raise my palm up to stop him. "He's right, Tiernan. Staying here isn't safe." I think about this opportunity.

If my siblings are at the McCarthy house, how will we possibly keep my status with them a secret? How will I find what I need to, spy on them and bring them down? Will this put a complete wrench into everything? Or... will it buy me even more time at the McCarthy's?

"A word, Nolan?" I ask as pleasantly as I can.

"Go on," he says.

I blow out an exasperated breath. "Privately."

He takes my hand, too firmly I might add, and with a tight nod, says, "Aye. One minute. Tiernan, pack what you need but don't take much."

Tiernan doesn't move.

Nolan drags me into my mother's room and shuts the door. I curse when I see a mirrored plate of pills beside a used needle and spoon, the rumpled sheets, and piles of dirty, rancid clothing. I push it away, pretending I'm not here, that he isn't seeing this. I put up a wall between my logic and my pride, and swallow the lump in my throat. I open my mouth to speak, but I can't. The lump prevents me. I swallow and try again, but when I try to talk, nothing comes out.

Nolan reaches for me, wraps his fingers around the back of my neck, and pulls my forehead to his. But the way his green eyes flash and his voice is laced with tension bely any tenderness.

"No fucking around, Sheena," he says. "I came here tonight because I'm not as big a prick as you'd believe. I might be mafia, but I won't abide children being abused, do you hear me?"

He squeezes my neck. My nose tingles, and something strange is happening still because I can't speak.

"You'll still be my prisoner. You'll still answer for what you've done. But Jesus fucking Christ, the least we can do is get those kids out of this hellhole first."

I blink, and the worst thing possible happens. Fat, hot tears roll down my cheeks. I go to swipe them away, but I can't because he stops me. His mouth is on mine before I know what's happening. I taste salty tears and the strength of this man as he kisses me, his grip tight, his lips soft, the prickle of his beard scraping my tender skin. Too soon, he pulls away.

"Impossible fucking woman," he growls. One hand grabs my arse and he pulls me even closer to him. "You ruined everything."

"Go to hell," I hiss.

To my surprise, he grins at me, and his green eyes look wicked. "Aye, lass. No question that's exactly where I'm going. Question is, are you coming for the ride?"

"Jesus, Mary, and Joseph," I mutter. "Jesus Christ."

"You've got the mouth of a fucking sailor."

"How funny, so do you," I say. "Who knew?"

He shakes his head. Through the flimsy door I hear Carson and Lachlan enter, talking with Tiernan and Fiona.

"What are we going to do?" I ask him. "This is the worst possible situation. How will we keep what's… how will they not know that… how will you…" I don't even know how to ask the questions I need to know.

"Sheena," he says, his voice a hoarse whisper. "It's the dead of night, lass. Those children haven't slept. They need a proper night's sleep, a clean place to lay their heads, and safety and protection. We'll deal with the rest in the morning."

Goddamn him, he's got logic on his side. At least partly. He can't explain away the rest of our conundrum so easily.

My throat's tight again. I can't help it. I reach my hand to his cheek.

"Damn you, Nolan McCarthy," I whisper.

He looks at me quizzically.

I shake my head. "Sometimes you make it hard to hate you. But don't worry, I'm sure you'll give me reason again before the sun rises."

"Will do my best," he says, then he shoots me a grin I feel straight between my damn legs. He releases my neck, and grabs my hand. He opens the door and leads me out.

Something like hope blooms in my chest when I see the McCarthy men in the little kitchen. It's so incongruous, the big, massive lot of them all alpha male and dangerous, in this little hellhole of a kitchen, but they're big, they're strong, they're fearless.

And oddly... it seems like a contradiction, somehow... I feel safe with them.

I immediately dismiss that line of thinking. I didn't get to where I am by being foolish and helpless, and I'm not going to start now.

"Alright, then," I say briskly, and I swear to God I stop myself just seconds before I clap my hands like a teacher trying to get her classroom's attention.

"What do we need to bring? Nappies, bottles, tooth-brushes."

"Just about all we'll need is the baby things," Carson says. "Everything else, we'll get back at the house."

"Aye, I agree," Lachlan says. Fiona looks up at him with such wide eyes, it breaks my heart a little. She hasn't said a word. He notices her staring up at him and smiles.

"Hey," he says. "Name is Lachlan. What's yours?"

She looks to me for permission to speak her name. I nod at her. "Go on," I say. "It's okay."

"Fiona," she whispers.

"'Tis a beautiful name," he says, and for that one brief moment in time, my heart softens toward him.

Tiernan isn't having any of it, though. He scowls at the lot of them.

"Just for tonight," he says. "We won't need their help for any longer than that."

I nod. It's not time for me to argue with him. Not now, when we need to leave so quickly.

We hear voices right outside our door, and we all stand still and listen. Lachlan's hand at his holster.

"Don't you dare," Tiernan warns, but Lachlan gives him a warning look and ignores him. I admire Tiernan's bravery, but I have to have a talk with my brother. He has to watch it with these men.

The voices go away, and Lachlan removes his hand. But a few seconds later, a loud crash sounds just outside.

We have to get out of here. They were in danger before, then Nolan had to come in here with fists flying. It'll be trouble, I know it.

"Right, then," I say. "I'll go get the baby."

I turn toward the doorway and freeze mid-step when Nolan comes through the doorway with the baby in his arms.

Mother of God.

Bloody hell.

Nolan's a fucking natural with baby Sam, curled up in those powerful, muscular arms of his like he's done this before. I wonder if he has, but then I remember, he's an uncle now to several babies. I try not to go all hormonal, but I can't help it. I honestly think my ovaries twitch.

"Let's go," Nolan says. I go to reach for the baby, and he hands him to me. His arms brush mine, warm and strong, and for one brief moment he isn't my captor, my enemy, the very man I've set out to destroy, but something… else.

I take the baby, draw him to my chest, and kiss his wee head. He stirs and rolls closer to my chest. I imagine for a moment that Nolan's eyes grow wistful, but the next blink of an eye he's all hard and determined again.

"I don't want to be here if there's blowback," he says. "Would defeat the feck—" he stops mid-sentence "Would defeat the purpose," he finishes.

I nod with the others, and we leave the dank hovel. My imagination goes wild, pretending for one brief moment that once I take them out of here I don't have to bring them back. That they can have a safe place to stay, regular food in their bellies, security, and the comforts of home.

But it's a dream, something I can't bring them now. Not until I complete my mission. Until I establish myself and seek justice for what the McCarthys have done.

Two cars are waiting out front. I'm no fool. I'm aware of the fact that every person in this small, cramped neighborhood is either aware of my coming here tonight with the McCarthys or will be soon. Rumors will circulate, and there's no telling what will come of this. There are too many questions right now and too few answers, but I can't deal with any of those quite yet.

Fiona walks beside Lachlan as we go outside. Tiernan glares at the lot, his fists shoved into his pockets, but he can't hide the look of relief when we open the car door.

"Don't know about this, Sheena," Tiernan mutters to me, in a low voice so only I hear him. "How do we know we're not jumping from the frying pan into the fire?"

I swallow hard. Damn him for saying exactly what I fear myself.

"I know it, Tiernan. But you have to trust me. Can you trust me?"

He nods immediately, as if there's no question, and it tugs at my conscience. If he only knew what I've done, what I'm planning still... he wouldn't find me as trustworthy as he does now. Hell, he may be the only person in the world now who does.

"Let's just get to safety tonight."

"But that's just it," he says. "Are we safe?"

I clear my throat. "For tonight."

Tiernan slides into the back seat and he gestures for Fiona to go with him. She looks to me, then Lachlan. My heart aches for her, for the girl who hasn't had the safety and protection she so deserves. "Come, sweetheart," I tell her. "Into the car and we'll get you to a nice, warm bed, okay?"

She nods and walks with me. Lachlan watches her go, and a shadow crosses over his face. I wonder what his story is. I know he was recruited young by the McCarthys, that he went to their finishing school, but that's all I know.

The drive back to their house is silent. Tiernan broods and stares out the window, I hold the baby in the back of the car, and Fiona sits next to me, resting her head on my shoulder. Nolan drives in silence. I try to silence my brain, but I can't seem to. Fiona's asleep when we get to the house, and

Nolan's phone rings just before he parks the car in the garage.

"Yeah?" He sighs at the voice on the other end of the phone. "Doesn't matter which entrance," he says. "He'll know soon enough, and I'll answer to him in the morning."

I wonder who they're worried about. Keenan, most like.

He parks the car and we exit. A shadow lurks in the doorway between the garage and entrance to the house. I'm surprised to see long red hair tucked into a messy bun. He's alerted Maeve? Or was she roaming about and noticed our arrival?

"They'll go with mam," he says, reaching for the baby. I turn from him and won't let him take him.

I shake my head. "No. I'll help them get—"

"They'll go with my mother," Nolan repeats, more forceful this time. "Care to be reminded of our agreement?" His voice is tight, laced with meaning, and I know he's trying to keep Tiernan from knowing too much.

Maeve approaches. She's wearing a dressing gown, her brows furrowed as she draws near. I almost forgot for a moment that it was the dead of night.

"Why, hello there," she says to Fiona, but Fiona pulls into my side and turns her face away from her. Unperturbed, Maeve turns to Tiernan. "Pleased to meet you," she says, but doesn't wait for a response. It's a good thing, as he only glares right back at her.

Nolan's jaw clenches. "They've been through an ordeal," he says to his mam, then gives Tiernan a stern look. "We'll work on manners in the morning."

I glare at him. If he thinks he's going to bully my brother into behaving a certain way, it'll be over my dead body.

"Give mam the baby, Sheena, and you'll come with me," he says firmly. "We'll go over all of this after we've had a good night's sleep."

"I'll take the baby," Fiona says, the first time she's spoken since we've left the house. She reaches for Sam, who curls up into her arms and rests his head on her shoulder.

Carson and Lachlan join us, and we all go inside.

Maeve leads them through the kitchen to the main living area, then up a flight of stairs. "They won't be far from you, Sheena," she says gently. "And they'll have everything they need, you have my word."

"Why isn't she coming with us?" Tiernan asks, his brows furrowed together.

Nolan squeezes my elbow in a silent warning. I clear my throat. "Get some rest tonight, Tiernan, and I'll see you in the morning."

His eyes narrow on Nolan, but Nolan doesn't pay him any heed. He takes my elbow and leads me away. When we're several paces away from my siblings, my heart is in my throat.

"Have you forgotten why you're here?" he scolds.

"How could I forget?" I snap. "You've reminded me ten times."

"Perhaps I need to remind you more clearly back in my room?"

Reluctantly, I clam up. Exhaustion suffuses me and I don't want to spar with him again, not tonight.

"That won't be necessary," I say through clenched teeth.

We get back to his room but my heart is down the hall. The only people I love in the entire world are alone with strangers, and I'm here as a prisoner.

I wonder if he'll interrogate me tonight, what he has planned for me still.

He shuts the door harder than necessary. It's dark in here, but a faint glimmer of moonlight illuminates his face. A shock of blond hair falls over his forehead, and his jaw's clenched.

"Keenan will kick my arse for this," he mutters. "You know that, don't you? Probably hope he does."

He fastens a series of locks before he stalks over to me. I don't respond to him. I don't even think he's looking for an answer, and I'm so tired, so confused and scared for my brothers and sister that I don't even know what to say. I can only assume they're safe for tonight, but they're apart from me. I can't reach them and have to trust the very people I despise with their safety.

"I couldn't care less if Keenan kicks your arse for this," I mutter, but it's a lie. I don't want him to get in trouble for helping out my family. He could've left them. Then what?

He walks to me and my heartbeat quickens. Have I pushed him too far? When he reaches me, he runs his fingers through my hair, his grip at once tight, primal, erotic. My head falls back, baring my neck. If he were a vampire, I'd be his prey, my lifeblood pulsing beneath him in the light of the full moon outside his window. He'd bite me, and I'd be his for eternity.

"You don't care, do you?" he whispers.

"What happens to you? No."

He smirks at me. "Might be the first fucking honest thing you've said to me all night."

I swallow and don't respond. It isn't.

"Back in the room," he says. "We'll get some sleep and pick this up again in the morning."

I'm not so sure what "this" is, but I know what I plan in the morning.

He half-drags me back to his room, tugging me along. If he has any tenderness in him, he's exhausted it. We reach the bed, and he tosses me onto it.

"Clothes off."

I don't fight it. I'm exhausted and fearful, and I need to reserve my energy for the next battle I'll face. I don't care that he wants to remind me of who I am, what my place is, or that I'm his prisoner. It's as if he needs to force this knowledge on me because he's shown weakness with tonight's rescue.

Is it even a rescue? I've no idea. If he plans to use tonight as leverage, it isn't. It's merely a bargaining chip.

So I strip my clothes off and toss them to the floor like this doesn't demoralize me, like my body and mind are two separate entities that don't entwine.

Are they safe? The baby, Fiona, and Tiernan? Are they scared? Will anyone hurt them again?

I don't know if I want to hit him or cry, but of course I'm not given a choice. When I'm stripped, he brings me back to the bed, removes a pair of cuffs from the drawer, and fastens them around my wrists. He tosses a blanket over my naked body and turns away from me as if I disgust him.

"Sleep," he orders. "We've got a big day ahead of us tomorrow."

Chapter 9

Nolan

I SLEEP in my boxers on my sofa reluctantly. I could've slept next to her, but I needed some space to think.

The next morning I rise early after only a few hours of sleep. There's a crick in my neck and my back aches. Toss pillows aren't made for fucking comfort. I look out the window, at the sun rising over the ocean, and for one moment I let it bring me peace. I wish I was in my own room. I like to sit on the balcony of a morning and drink tea with the sunrise.

I reach for my phone and power it on, grateful there are no messages from Keenan. I've got video feed to my bedroom on it. I zoom in on Sheena.

It took her a while to fall asleep. I watched her until she did. It isn't easy to fall asleep with your wrists cuffed. I've been there before. But she finally did, and after I could tell she was out, I rolled over and got some rest myself.

It's dark in the room, with only a faint glimmer of light, but I can tell she's still sleeping. Her red hair's all tumbled about her, and the blanket's fallen off her shoulder. Gorgeous and peaceful in sleep.

I wonder what makes her tick. Up until last night, I'd allowed myself to only demonize her in my mind. A bitch on a mission to destroy my family. But after seeing those children in that disaster of a house, after seeing how she came apart and dropped her defenses when she was near them, I know there's more to her than meets the eye.

If I'm honest, I've known that for a while. Hell, it may be the very thing that draws me to her.

Today, I'll dig deeper. First, I've got to cover my arse and act proactively.

I shoot Cormac a message.

You up?

A reply comes back almost at once.

Cormac: Aye.

Need to talk.

Cormac: Right now?

Yeah.

Cormac: Phone, house, privacy?

Privacy.

Cormac. Meet me by the cliffs in ten. Bring tea. Bonus points for food.

I smile to myself. He eats all damn day.

I toss off the covers, and pull on the trousers and t-shirt I left on the floor. I lock the door behind me and head to the kitchen downstairs, grab two cups of hot tea, and nick a plateful of scones. When I reach the cliffs, Cormac's already staring out at the sea, waiting.

I hand him the tea and scones, and we sit in silence. He doesn't like to talk unless he's got at least one cup of tea in him.

Like Keenan, Cormac didn't have much faith in me when I was younger, when I'd taken to drink and fucked up everything. But he's got a softer heart than Keenan. He's the peacemaker in our family. He was the first to come to me when I needed him, and I know he's got my back faster and more reliably than any other brother in The Clan.

I stare out at the sea. It's cool this morning, a brisk, salty breeze coming off the water. I inhale deeply. It's fucking mesmerizing, a balm to my soul.

"Right, then," he says, after he's polished off his tea and three scones. "This have anything to do with you boys rolling in last night after you'd taken the girl?"

I nod. "Aye."

I fill him in. When I get to the part of entering Stone City and the beating I gave the arsehole, he groans. When I tell him about taking the children back home, he smacks his head. By the time I'm finished, he's cursing under his breath.

"Haven't talked to Keenan, then, yet, have you?"

I groan. "No."

"Have any answers from the lass?"

"Also no."

He curses. "So all you've done, then, is manage to bring trouble here."

"Don't forget, I also did a right good job of dirtying up Stone city."

"Oh, right," he says with a groan. "Well that makes things better."

"Tell me about it."

"So you know what you have to do today, then, don't you?"

"Aye. I do."

He lifts his brows questioningly.

"Get the answers I need."

"Aye. You've a plan for that?"

I tell him what I did the night before, how I plan on getting answers from her, and he nods. "Seems about right." He takes another scone. "You let me handle Keenan, alright?"

I appreciate the gesture, but shake my head. "No, I'll handle him myself."

Cormac grins and smacks my shoulder. "Good lad. Aye, you can. Now best get up to her and see what you can get before breakfast."

"I'll use this to my advantage," I tell him. "She's indebted to me with her family here."

Cormac stands and brushes crumbs off him, looking out at the sea. "Aye," he says. "If Keenan lets them stay."

Christ, I didn't think about that.

Seems I've got two jobs today.

I glance at the feed on my phone and see she's still fast asleep. Cormac looks over.

"*Jesus*, she's a sight, eh?" he mutters.

"Aye," I say, not quite sure why there's a note of pride in my voice. "Fucking gorgeous."

"I mean she isn't as pretty as Aileen, but she's passable," he says. I punch his arm, and he laughs, rubbing out the sting. We walk together back up to the house.

"For what it's worth, Nolan, I think you did the right thing."

I look at him sharply. "Do you?"

"Aye." His voice thickens a little. "Maybe even what dad would've done. I mean, he was ruthless. I saw things at a young age I'll take with me to my death.

He had a heavy hand, but he didn't have a heart of stone."

"Aye." My throat is clogged myself. I didn't realize until he said this how much I needed to hear it.

My father never knew me as an adult sober.

Maybe it isn't Keenan I need to prove myself to.

When we reach the garden, I'm surprised to see mam out front, bent over, holding the hand of the littlest one. He's toddling around the garden and speaking in gibberish, pointing to one thing and then the next. Jesus, he's cute.

"Christ," Cormac says. "I don't blame you, Nolan, I really don't. The hardest of hearts couldn't have left a babe like that endangered."

I nod, glad he's on my side. Mam hears us coming and beams at us. "Morning, boys."

I'll be seventy years old and she'll be hobbling around with a cane and still, she'll call us "boys."

"Morning," I say to her. "Didn't sleep?"

Her face softens and she smiles benevolently down at the wee one. "Ah, well, you know it's hard to sleep when you have a whole world out there to explore, isn't it?"

She's lapping this up. She comes alive when she's with the little ones.

"You reckon his mother will come looking for them?" she asks, not meeting my eyes as she shows

Sam how he can sit on the stone bench. He swings his little legs and raises a chubby fist to wave at me. It's a marvel to me that such a little one remains innocent when he's been handed the life he has.

"Don't know, but we'll have to prepare."

She nods.

"Bring him to breakfast, then?" I ask her.

She nods. "I'll see to it they all get what they need."

Cormac leaves to take a run on the beach. I thank her, trot up the stairs to the house, and crash straight into Keenan.

Christ.

"Morning, Nolan," he says. I can tell by the tone of his voice and posture he knows some of what happened last night. Hell, maybe all of it.

"Morning," I respond. He looks out the large windows out to the garden, his hands in his pockets, the early morning light reflected in his green eyes.

"I'm assuming you've got something to tell me?"

He might be my older brother, but as Clan Chief, he's the father figure of our group. I owe him the truth.

"Aye." I take in a deep breath, then I fill him in.

I sugarcoat nothing.

"Jesus, Mary, and Joseph," he curses. He stands with

his arms folded on his chest, so like my father it's uncanny. The hints of gray at his temples were just like dad's, the sharp green eyes boring into me the very same. "Christ, Nolan, what the hell were you *thinking*?"

Also words my father could've uttered.

"I was thinking it was the right thing to do," I tell him.

"We're not in the goddamn business of saving families," he says. "We're not philanthropists, for Christ's sake."

"Aye," I tell him. "But think on it, Keenan. She threw us under the bus with the locals, didn't she? It's the very reason you wanted her brought here. Maybe we catch more flies with honey than vinegar. She wanted to be brought here. It's time we took control, and having her family at our mercy could do just that."

He curses and looks out the window. "You have a point, brother," he says. I'm actually surprised he's agreeing. "But I'm not as concerned about the children being here as I am about you causing trouble in Stone City. Did you know the O'Gregors do their biggest drug sales there?"

Motherfucker.

I groan. "Didn't know that, no."

He nods and looks out the window again. "That'll come back to bite us," he says, but at least he says *us*. We're still in this together. He continues, mulling it over while he strokes his chin. "I get why you brought them here, but they can't stay. I think a call to Father Finn could help. Let's find out what's going on."

He goes back to pacing, his hands shoved in his pockets. "But fuck, Nolan, we'll have to have a meeting to prepare for blowback from the O'Gregors."

I nod, stifling a groan. "Aye."

He still stares out the window. "Go to her. Find out what you need. I'll call a meeting."

Today, I need answers. I need to do my job, and do it fucking right.

I check my phone again and can tell she's waking by the way she stirs. When I get to the room, I shut and lock the door behind me and hear her calling me.

"Nolan? You there?"

"Aye." I come into the room, and take a moment to observe her unhindered. Light streams in from the window. She tosses her head to the side, her vibrant red hair cascading onto the bed. Bright gray eyes meet mine, beautiful and uncompromising.

She changes with the wind. Which Sheena will I meet today?

I cross over to the window and pull back the blinds all the way to reveal the sea before us. "Morning, lass. Did you sleep well?"

"Aye," she says behind me. "Better than I thought I would with these damn cuffs."

We're dancing in time to the music. I lead and she steps along with me. But I'm tired of playing this game, of waltzing around what needs to be said. I want truth.

I stare, looking out at the sea from the balcony window. The sky's a bit overcast today, but the sun peeks through. It's high tide, waves reaching high on the cliffs. A herring gull flies overhead. I open the balcony door, inhaling the scent of salty air, before I turn to her.

"I imagine you'd like to see your brothers and sister this morning."

She eyes me warily and doesn't speak for a moment. She swallows, then nods. "Aye."

I walk to her, my hands in my pockets. She follows me with her gaze, apprehension written on her features.

"Then let's play a little game, shall we?"

Her lips quirk up. and she nods. "Sure. Why not? I'm naked and cuffed in your bed. What could possibly go wrong?"

I can't help but chuckle. She drives me fucking crazy, but hell, I love that mouth of hers.

"The better question, doll, is what could go *right?*"

She licks her lips, and this time, I don't think she's

playing. Her chest heaves when I draw near. I'd do well to remember how she ticks.

She responds well to being dominated. I sit on the side of the bed and reach for her hair. I can hardly stop myself from weaving my fingers through the soft, fragrant mass of it.

She closes her eyes for a moment, tipping her head back. "I know I'm fucked up," she whispers. "I know it, and I won't pretend otherwise. But I do love when you touch my hair."

I drag the tips of my fingers along her scalp and tug so that I've got her in my grip. Her mouth parts. I lean in and kiss her, and hell she tastes good. She kisses me back.

"You like that, do you?" I whisper in her ear.

"Mmm."

"Remember how you address me, lass, will you?"

"Aye," she breaths. "Yes, sir."

I reward her with another hair pull. I watch her body's response, the way her breasts swell and the tips of her nipples harden with just the hair pull. I lie beside her and hold her hair in one hand, tightening the grip while I drag my palm down her body.

"Let's start at the very beginning." I need many answers from her, but it'll go better if I start with the easier questions. "Did you know the O'Gregors run Stone City?"

Her half-lidded eyes fly open and she stares at me.

She blinks before she responds. "I know my ex was involved with them," she says. "I know I've seen them in the city before. But no, I don't know the intricacies of their involvement there. Damn."

I nod, reaching my thumb to her nipple. I pinch and squeeze. "Is that the total truth?"

She gasps. "Yes," she pants. "They peddle drugs there. My ex-boyfriend's in with them."

I release her nipple, bend down, and lap at it lazily. She moans and moves closer to me.

"Is he, now?" I ask. "Does he work for them as well, then?"

She nods. "Aye."

"Would've been helpful to know that before I busted his arse, no?"

I bite her nipple. She gasps and writhes but can't go very far with her restraints.

"Aye," she says. "Probably would have, but honest to God, you didn't ask, and I didn't know if you'd care or that he'd even be there."

I look in her eyes, still holding her nipple between my teeth. It seems as if she's telling me the truth.

"Not care?" I ask around the tender bud in my mouth. "Not care that I ventured into rival mafia territory to save your family and now I'll have to deal with that aftermath?"

I lap lazily, and she bites her lip.

My phone rings. I leave her restrained on the bed and go to answer it. She follows my every move.

It's mam. "Yes?"

"Nolan, will you be coming to breakfast?" she asks. "The children are asking for her, and I don't know what to tell them."

I glance over at Sheena. I want to test my theory. "Aye," I tell her. "Tell them we'll be down in ten minutes."

I hang up the phone and look at her for a moment before I fill her in. "Imagine you'd like to see the children."

She swallows hard, and her voice wobbles a little. "I do. Please, Nolan. Please, sir," she says. "I'll give you what you want if you only let me see them."

I fold my arms on my chest and hold her gaze. "And what will you give me if I make sure they're cared for? If they're safe and protected, well-fed?"

Her eyes brim with unshed tears. Either she's a very good liar, or I've struck a nerve.

"Anything you fucking want."

"I'll remember that."

I unfasten her cuffs and send her to the bathroom to get ready. We dress, but before we leave, I pull her over to me and lift her skirt. Cupping her arse, I whisper in her ear. "Today, you give me answers. Down there, you'll stay by my side. You'll speak when spoken to, and keep things normal with the children. You don't leave my side."

"Aye," she says, nodding.

I continue with my instructions. "You speak respectfully to my family. You earned a spanking last night I'll deliver today, and how that goes depends directly on your behavior at breakfast. Am I clear?"

Her eyes heat but she nods. "Aye. Yes, sir. Of course, sir."

Her compliance spurs me on. I never know if she's telling me the truth, but right now, I've got a compliant little kitten on my hands. I'll use that to my advantage.

"Let's go."

Chapter 10

Sheena

I CAME HERE FOR ANSWERS. I came here to spy, to find what the McCarthy clan has done so I could bring them down. But now... oh, God. I'd convinced myself that I hated them. But right now, they hold the safety and wellbeing of the only people in the world who matter to me in their hands.

And Nolan... the way he talks to me, touches me, commands me... I'm losing my grip on my self-control. It isn't just because I enjoy it, the response is far more instinctual. My body's alive with the masterful way he touches me, my mind consumed with thoughts of what he'll do next. It's hard to remain detached when someone orchestrates things the way he does.

I woke confused but determined. I would do my best to take care of my siblings, to do my job and stay strong. But one pull of his fingers through my hair, and I melt.

I wear the borrowed clothing and take a quick look at myself in a mirror by his bedroom dresser before we go. My cheeks are flushed, my eyes bright, my bright red hair is a mass of tangles I tamed with a quick bun at the nape of my neck. Damn, there's no help for it.

I gave him the truth just now. I knew that Cian was involved with drugs, and I suspected the O'Gregors were behind it. I know they're involved in Stone City, but I wouldn't have gone so far as to say they "own it." I have as little to do with the city as I can.

Rumor has it I slept with the O'Gregor's chief, but it's only partially correct. I slept with the captain, next in command to the chief, and it's because of him I know the McCarthys are responsible for my father's death and my family's ruin.

"You're lovely," he says, with sincerity, as we get ready to go downstairs.

I'm a bit taken aback. Does he really think so?

"Oh, I'll do," I say, and I'm not fishing for compliments. "I'm wearing borrowed clothing, I have no makeup, and my hair's got a mind of its own."

He laces his fingers through mine and smiles at me, his handsome face breaking into a grin and those mesmerizing green eyes of his making my belly swoop. "You'll *do*?" he says incredulously. "You drive me crazy, lass, and I haven't forgotten our purpose here. But I mean it when I say you're stunning, Sheena." He laughs. "Sometimes I wish you weren't. Would make my job easier."

"Your job of tying me up and punishing me? Ack, seems you do *that* job just fine."

"With pleasure," he says.

I'll give him this. He might be my enemy, but he knows how to compliment a girl. I'm a good judge of truth and lies; it's the nature of the beast in my job. And for some reason I can't quite fathom, when Nolan tells me I'm beautiful I know deep down he's not just telling me to placate me.

I don't know how to take it. I can't quite process his compliment, so I drop the subject.

As we head downstairs, he asks me about my family, and I tell him the basics. Nothing that'll give too much away. How my mother was a teen when she had me, how she fell in love with my father and gave birth to us three oldest. I say little about my father except to mention he's deceased, and how his death contributed to my mother's downward spiral.

It isn't until we're halfway down the landing on the way to the dining room that I realize with surprise that I haven't been doing what I set out here to do. I've observed nothing, my head's so in the clouds with his touch, his compliment, the sound of his voice as he talks to me. I'm supposed to be noting every detail.

When we reach the landing, Cormac stands waiting

for us, his large, hulking frame dwarfing the picture windows in their entryway. He doesn't trust me, and hell, I don't blame him. I'm here as their captive. He knows my purpose is to bring them ruin.

I know he notes my hand in Nolan's by the way his gaze locks on our entwined fingers. Cormac might even be trying to scare me, standing all badass and intimidating as he stares up at us. And hell, it's working a little. He's massively huge and muscular, like the Irish version of the Hulk or something.

"Good morning," I say to him as pleasantly as I can. I won't let these men intimidate me. I *won't*.

Cormac gives me a curt nod. "Morning. Nolan, get her clothes of her own today," he says. "I don't enjoy seeing her wear clothes that belong to my wife."

Ouch.

"Aye," Nolan says. "I'm on it, brother. Where are the others?"

I'm assuming "the others" refer to Tiernan, Fiona, and Sam.

"Dining room," Cormac says. "You first."

Nolan leads me toward the dining room, and Cormac follows behind us. For goodness sakes, it's like they think I'm a bomb about to go off, and they're ready to shout the warning to head for cover.

"Are they that scared of a girl like me?" I ask Nolan.

He quirks a brow at me before responding. "Scared? Hell no. But we do assemble together for a reason. They're not afraid of you, lass. But they won't let you forget you're my prisoner."

I shrug, feigning nonchalance. *Right.*

I'm not prepared for what I see when we enter the dining room.

There's a massively long dining room table and several smaller circular ones. The room's well-appointed and immaculate. Along one wall lies a table laden with food, buffet style, certainly more food than my brothers and sister have ever seen in once place.

I swallow hard. I'm starving. But that isn't what surprises me.

Maeve sits at the table, her gray-tinged red hair tucked into a bun. She wears a simple white top, and looks the part of *granny* quite well. Little Sam sits on Maeve's lap, happily drinking a bottle, his head on her chest. She holds him to her, her arms loosely about him, content as can be. Gently, almost imperceptibly, she rocks him back and forth.

Beside her sits Caitlin, her long, long black hair hanging down behind her on the chair. She's got the appearance of one of the sprites in Irish mythology, fairy-like and ethereal. I don't know how she does it. Her clothing's simple, and if she wears any makeup it's minimal. Maybe it's her eyes. When they meet mine, there's kindness in them.

It makes me self-conscious. I don't deserve her kindness.

Beside Caitlin sits Aileen, Cormac's wife. She doesn't look up when we enter, nodding her head while Fiona talks a mile a minute. She stands out as the only blonde. Her bright, round eyes dance as she smiles and nods, bouncing a little child on her knee. She's entertained by Fiona, it seems. Cormac approaches her and puts his hand on her shoulder. She reaches up and squeezes his hand, a gesture both intimate and private.

Tiernan sits nearby, taking it all in, nursing a steaming mug of tea.

I try to pull my hand out of Nolan's, to get to them quicker, but he holds me fast. "Easy, lass," he says in a side whisper so the others don't hear. "You'll not cause a scene. They're fine."

I both love and hate that they're safe here. I don't want them to grow comfortable.

Tiernan's eyes meet mine, and he's questioning, probing, his gaze traveling to my hand in Nolan's, then back to my face. He clenches his jaw and waits for us to approach. Light streams in from the window, illuminating his features, and for that one brief moment in time, I see the boy he is now on the cusp of being the man he'll become.

"Sheena!" Fiona spots me first. She waves to me.

"Do you know them? This is Maeve, Caitlin, and Aileen, and can you *believe* this place?"

I blink. She seems taken with their home, but she's ignorant. If she only knew… it grates on me that she doesn't, though I'm loathe to dash her dreams.

Reality sits in my belly like a rock. Fiona has no clue that it's Maeve's husband that's left her fatherless.

When we reach the table, Fiona stands, reaches me and hugs me. Nolan lets me go long enough for me to embrace her back. "I don't care," she whispers in my ear.

I lean down and look into her eyes. "Don't care about what, Fiona?"

"What mum thinks of any of this," she says, before she turns from me and goes back to the table.

I blink in surprise. I haven't cared what mum thinks about anything for so long, it didn't even occur to me.

Nolan pulls out a chair for me, and I sit with Tiernan on my right and Nolan on my left.

"You all slept well, then?" I ask.

"Aye," Tiernan says. He looks begrudgingly at Cormac, then Nolan. "Thank you." He doesn't trust them, and for good reason, but he's not above thanks when it's due. He'll be a good man one day.

Nolan reaches for a basket in the middle of the table and hands it to me. I take a scone for myself. Caitlin hands me the butter dish, but Aileen watches me distrustfully. I don't blame her. Last year, I was blackmailed by the O'Gregors to trick her into coming to the club. We were both assaulted by them, though rescued by the McCarthys. I'm sitting in her dining room, wearing her clothing, a stark reminder of what I've done to the people she calls family.

Aileen turns away from me as if I don't exist and smiles at Caitlin. "Seems the baby slept well for you last night?"

"Aye," Caitlin says. "Nothing like a good night's sleep to make you feel better about things."

"Of course," Aileen says. "But you let me know if you need any help, will you? You've done so much for me, it'd be my pleasure to help you when you need me."

They chatter on about their babies and sleep, soothers and bottles. It's hard for me to piece what I know about these two with the women in front of me. Until now, I've known them only as the wives of criminals. But here are two women who love each other like sisters.

And right then, in that moment... I hate all of this.

The lies. The betrayal. How far I've let myself sink for the sake of vengeance. I wish for all of this to end, and for one brief moment in time, I wish that I didn't have to keep playing this game. That I could have good, lasting, solid relationships with people I trust. I wish I didn't have to be the only one holding everything together.

"This place is beautiful," Fiona says, chattering on about everything from the paintings that hang on the walls to the lovely cut of the juice glasses on the table. "Never seen fabric napkins, can you imagine, Sheena? This place is grand, no lie."

"Fiona, stop it," Tiernan mutters, but she doesn't pay him any heed. For all his sulking and being guarded, she makes up for with bubbly enthusiasm.

"I've never seen such a nice place," Fiona repeats. "And my goodness, Maeve, your cooks must be the most talented in all of Ireland. Sheena, have you ever *tasted* such scones?" She butters one and eats it greedily. Seems she's gotten over her shyness.

"Never," I say, and catch Nolan's eye. He winks at me, and my tummy does a little belly-flip.

Carson and Lachlan enter, and it's the first time Fiona stops jabbering on. She clams up when she sees Lachlan enter, her fork raised halfway to her mouth.

My God, does she have a schoolgirl crush on one of the men?

I look sharply from him to her, but he only smiles and gives them a little wave.

"Morning," he says to Tiernan, who doesn't return the greeting. Fiona finally waves shyly at him.

"Morning," she says.

"Y'alright?" he asks, filling a plate full of food. Fiona

151

only nods. Her eyes are wide and her cheeks are faintly flushed.

My goodness, my sister's crushing on mafia. What have I done? Have I led the lambs to slaughter? I remember Tiernan's question the night before, how he wondered if we were going straight into the fire.

The baby reaches for something on the table and knocks a glass of juice over. The girls scramble to clean it up, and I try helplessly to mop at it with napkins, but Maeve brushes me off.

"Leave it, Sheena," she says. "We'll have the girls in the kitchen clean it, no worries."

Fiona watches her with wide, curious eyes but doesn't say anything.

Nolan turns to me, leans down, and whispers, "Your sister's entertaining us."

I narrow my eyes on him. "She's a *child.*"

His eyes widen back at me. "Of course she is," he mutters, "which is the only reason why we brought her here to begin with."

I don't know why I'm so defensive, why I feel the need to make sure he knows she's innocent. I know what these men can do, what they have done and will yet. I hate that I've brought my family anywhere near them, though the thought of leaving them alone in my mother's house makes me nauseous.

I eat a scone, and though it's tasty, it feels dry and crumbly in my mouth. I've worked hard to keep my worlds separate, so my work and my personal life don't collide. And now... now that's exactly what's happening.

Lachlan and Carson sit together at one end of the table. I don't miss the way Tiernan and Fiona watch them. Tiernan knows who they are from the night before, and Fiona is a smart girl. She'll catch on soon herself.

"How's that wrist of yours?" Lachlan asks Fiona. She stops her yammering and looks down at her arm, as if just remembering she had one.

"Ah, well. Pretty sore," she says, flushing pink.

Nolan pushes out of his chair and walks to her. "Let's see it," he says. She stands and lifts her arm up. Frowning, he takes her arm in his hand and gently inspects.

No, my mind protests. I can't bear to see him tender with her. It picks at my resolve.

"Very sore?" he asks.

She winces when he touches her with his index finger. "Aye."

"I'll call Sebastian," he says, then looks to me. "Clan doctor."

I swallow hard, then nod. "Thanks very much."

I don't trust that they're being so kind, that they're taking care of them.

"Baby Sam has quite a rash," Maeve says. "We'll ask

Sebastian about that as well."

"Hasn't been changed often enough," Fiona says, blushing deeper when all eyes come to her. "We did our best, but…" her voice trails off. My heart squeezes, but when she looks at me I only smile at her.

"I know you did, Fiona. No one blames you."

Footsteps sound in the doorway and I look up to see Keenan coming in. The men fall silent, and my stomach plummets. The record I have on him would fill a diary. Nolan takes his seat beside me and draws in a deep breath.

"Morning, Keenan," Maeve says, unperturbed. She breaks off a piece of toast and hands it to Sam, who waves it in his little fist.

"Morning," he says. He pours himself a cup of tea, looking over all of us. "Mornin' Sheena," he says to me. The tone of his voice sends a chill straight down my spine. I'm not one to cower, but he's harder than the rest. He doesn't trust me.

"Morning."

"And who are the rest?" he asks. I introduce them all.

"Well, then," he says. He pulls a seat out next to Caitlin and sits. "I'm guessing you're here because you aren't safe at home?"

Tiernan nods, and facing Keenan, tells the truth succinctly. How they were endangered the night before, how they called me, how Nolan and the rest came and brought them here.

"We don't mean to intrude," he says. "We know we don't belong here, and we'll be going just as soon as we know it's safe."

Keenan eyes him thoughtfully as he states his story.

"Doesn't sound like it's safe for you to return home," he says. He turns to me, his gaze sharp as granite. Nolan grips my thigh, a reminder to watch my tone and behavior with the Clan Chief. "And Sheena has some business with us here, don't you?"

Business with them. My God. He's right, though. I do.

"Aye," I say.

"They'll be Nolan's responsibility," Keenan says, buttering a scone. "Nolan, you can call Father Finn and he can help you sort things out. Get them taken care of."

He says it as casually as if he were ordering cream for his tea instead of issuing an order that could tear my family apart. My body stills, and before I can respond, Nolan does.

"The hell I will," Nolan says. Keenan's eyebrows shoot heavenward and he pauses, the scone halfway to his mouth. The room falls silent, even baby Sam watching everyone with wide, curious eyes.

"You know how that will go," Nolan says, glaring at Keenan.

Keenan takes a bite, swallows, then follows it with a pull at his teacup. "Careful, brother," he says quietly.

"You will not call Father Finn," I say. My mind's made up. I'm prone to making dumbass decisions on the spur of the moment. I should keep my mouth shut, goddamn it, but I can't seem to stop.

"Who's Father Finn?" Tiernan demands.

"Parish priest," I tell him. I don't even bother to hide the fact that I know who every single person connected to the McCarthys is. "If we call him, you'll all be sent to social protection before breakfast is over. And I can't let that happen."

Keenan purses his lips, working his jaw. Caitlin leans in, placing her hand on his arm, and speaks in a soft, gentle voice. "Keenan, you can't call him. Fiona told us what happened, what it was like. It breaks my heart to think of sending them back there, where they aren't safe, or sending them to social protection, where they'll likely be separated."

I make up my mind and clear my throat. "I'll finish my business here with you," I tell him. "And once we're done, I'll take them back home with me."

Keenan's eyes don't leave mine. He stares at me, unblinking. "Will you, then?" he asks. "Are you that sure your business with us won't take very long?"

My throat tightens. Does he mean to keep me here prisoner forever?

God, I'm so stupid. *So stupid.* I thought I could waltz

right in here, spy without being noticed, then waltz right back out again. That they wouldn't know who I am, what I've done, and maybe even what I plan to do yet.

Keenan folds his arms on his chest. His voice is quiet but dangerous when he asks, "Does the Clancy Clan mean anything to you, Sheena?"

My *God*. Of course I know of them. Every reporter in Ireland knew that story, how the American reporter tracked the mob and harassed them, doing an exposé and story that brought them to ruin.

How she was found dead in her bed not one day later.

"Are you threatening me, Keenan?" I ask, holding his gaze.

He turns to Nolan. "Perhaps we need a private meeting, brother."

Nolan's jaw clenches. "Aye. After breakfast, inner circle."

"That's fine, boys," Maeve says. She runs her fingers through Sam's hair, unperturbed. "You have your meeting, you make your decision. But you know we've a spare room right here in the house beside mine. You know it isn't safe for them to go home. And you further know that a call to Father Finn could separate them. We may not be in the business of charity, but I think our decision here is clear."

Keenan mutters something, shaking his head, but

Fiona looks hopeful. My body feels both warm and cold, my belly tight.

Nolan gets to his feet, and Keenan watches him. "Meeting in thirty," he says. Turning to his mother, he gives her a nod. "Get them situated in the spare room for now, no call to Finn. Call Sebastian and have Fiona's wrist looked at."

"Looks like you could use a visit with Sebastian yourself," Maeve says, gesturing to his lacerated hands from the night before.

"I'll be the judge of that," he says. "Don't you worry about me."

Nolan reaches for my hand. "Sheena."

Tiernan's on his feet while Fiona watches everything. She knows something's awry, but it's Tiernan I need to worry about.

"I'll see you in a bit," I tell him. "Nolan and I will talk to the others is all. We'll be sure you're safe here."

I want to scream against Nolan, beat my hands on his chest and rail for what he's doing to me, what he's putting me through. And I want to weep with relief. I'm so confused, not sure how I should even react.

Nolan's on his phone, his grip on me firm.

"Meeting," he snaps into the phone.

My heart does a little somersault when he commands these men. He was born for this.

Keenan nods. "I'll prepare the office."

"No Finn."

Keenan nods. "I won't call him. You have my word."

When the men have dispersed, Nolan turns to me. "Before the meeting? You and I will have a talk."

There's something ominous in the way he says it. *We'll have a talk.*

I wonder what precisely he has in mind.

He reaches for the handle of a door right behind him. I don't know where I am, what he's doing, or what's happening. He pulls me into the darkened room, shuts the door, then pulls the latch behind us.

Chapter 11

Nolan

I SAW how close Keenan came to ruining everything. I won't allow it to happen. I can't.

She angers me like no one else, but there's more to this fierce, brave woman than meets the eye. Anyone would want to see to the safety of her young siblings. Well, nearly anyone. But Keenan's right. We aren't in the business of charity.

But I just put my neck on the line for her. I'm on the cusp of defying my brother, and the responsibility of how this all goes fall squarely on my shoulders.

I yank her into one of our meeting rooms, lock the door behind us, and shove her up against the wall.

"This again?" she says with a coy, breathy whisper.

"Not now, Sheena." My body shakes with the need

to dominate her, to convey to her how important it is she not fuck this up. I keep myself in check with effort. "Now is the time for you to drop the game. We're playing life and death here, doll, and you're outnumbered."

The teasing glint in her eye fades, and her voice wavers a little.

"Don't let him call the Father, Nolan," she says. "I can't… I won't… Goddamn it, Nolan, I'll give you what you want, but you have to make sure they're safe."

"Of course," I tell her. "What do you think I am, a monster?"

She closes her eyes briefly before answering. "Sometimes? Yes."

I don't blame her. I've done wicked, cruel things in my life, some things I regret and some I don't. I'm not sure what she knows of me and what she only surmises, but I do know one thing. The pull between us, this thing, whatever it is, is undeniable, and I'll be a damn fool to ignore it.

"I'm taking you into a meeting with my brothers," I tell her. "You'll be expected to answer. And how you answer will determine how we treat you. Understood?"

She nods. "Of course. Yes."

I weave my fingers through her mass of red hair. The knot at her neck comes loose when I tug her head back.

"Try again, doll."

Her lust-filled eyes meet mine, and she lets out the breath she was holding. "Yes, sir."

"Good girl."

She's too eager to be used, too turned on by being mastered. I can't threaten and hurt her to get answers, nor do I want to.

I'll have to try other methods.

We're in a small room used for bookkeeping, and brief, private meetings. There's a small desk with a computer, a cup filled with pens, some papers and notebooks, and in one corner, a large, overstuffed chair.

I take her by the hand and lead her over to it, sit heavily, and draw her over my lap. There's a fire that builds between us I need to stoke, and roles I need to clarify.

If I leave her wanting, she's less likely to fight me in front of a roomful of my brothers.

"Nolan!" she protests, but I'm certain she only fights me because she feels she ought to.

"Counted out your punishment last night, didn't I?"

"Oooh." Her recognition is part moan, part assent. "You did."

"I can't neglect your discipline now, can I?"

She shakes her head. "No, sir. Certainly not."

I lift the edge of her skirt, baring her ass.

"Good girl," I approvingly, run my hand along her inner thigh. "You're already wet, aren't you?"

"Y-yes," she pants, wriggling as if to seek pressure from my fingers. I raise my hand and give her bottom a sharp, quick swat.

"Good. Now it's time for a little game of ask and tell. I ask a question. If you answer well, I touch right there." I bring my fingers higher, and give one stroke across the silky strip of fabric between her legs. "If you don't, I'll spank you. Cooperation will end up with you climaxing, right here, over my knee."

She tries to respond, but it comes out in a strangled moan. She nods, her mass of hair bobbing all over the place.

I promised I'd interrogate her. I have my methods.

I pat her bottom. "Ready?"

She tenses. "Yes, sir. Ready."

Good.

"Was your plan to come here last night?"

She grips my pants leg, takes a deep breath, then nods. "Yes. Yes, sir."

I part her legs and stroke my fingers purposefully upward, grazing the edge of knickers between her thighs.

"Was your plan to get your family to come here for safety?"

"No."

I stroke her again, feathery light brushes of my fingertips. Her panties are damp. I'm aware of the seductive scent of her arousal.

"Were *you* planning on lying to us?"

She pushes out a resigned sigh. "Yes."

I crack her ass so hard she bucks. "Hey! You said no punishment if I told the truth!"

"I did not. I promised a reward if you did. I said nothing about not giving you the punishment you earned."

I give her another searing swat, the palm of my hand landing straight across the fullness of her arse. "That's for planning to manipulate me," I tell her. I raise my hand and give her another hard smack. "And that's for putting yourself in danger. For God's sake, you could've been killed." Another swat, then another lands. I'm spanking her in earnest now and it feels fucking perfect. "What do you have to say for yourself?"

"I'm sorry," she says. "I wanted to—I needed to—I had to investigate." She's panting, writhing, trying to get out of my grip but unable to.

"Why?" I ask, my hand poised. When she doesn't answer, I slam my palm against her ass again.

"I wanted answers!"

Now we're getting somewhere. I part her legs and stroke her pussy, no light teasing this time but firm, deliberate strokes of my fingers aimed at working her toward climax.

"That's a good girl answering my questions," I say approvingly. I'm fucking pleased she's giving me answers now before I meet with the rest of the Clan. If I go in proving she's answered me some, it'll go better for the both of us.

I've got her in my power, her family at my mercy and her body bending to my will. I took Sheena Hurston prepared to break her, to interrogate her, to demand answers only she could give. And now… now that I've got her, it seems there are more effective methods of finding the truth.

I move her panties aside and groan when I find her sopping wet and swollen. I love how responsive she is, how eager. I stroke her pussy, work her clit, glide my fingers effortlessly over the bundle of nerves that will bring her to climax.

"What answers do you want? What are you trying to do?" I ask.

I pause, my finger poised just where she wants me. She tries to wriggle and get closer to me, but I taunt her with my touch just out of reach. I pinch her inner thigh. "Answer me."

"Isn't it obvious?" she pants. "I'm trying to find the truth. Who you are, what you do, and why."

I reward her with another stroke. "Good girl," I tell

her. She's panting, her breath hitched and guarded. I know she's on the cusp of release. "Are you a good girl, Sheena? Should I let you come?"

"I—I'm… yes, well, of course you should let me come."

Goddamn her for being so adorable. I slap her arse again, a good, hard slap that makes a red print like a tulip bloom on her cheek.

"Answer the question."

She moans and wriggles but doesn't respond. My body tightens, my resolve firm. If she won't cave, if she won't tell me the truth, she earns nothing but punishment. I spank her again, until she cries out in pain, then stroke her pussy until I can tell she's ready to fly. Then I lift her off my lap and stand her in front of me.

Her hair's a mess, her eyes watery, and her lower lip wavers. "I'll tell you the truth, but you won't like it. And I'll only tell you the truth if you promise not to hurt them, to keep them safe."

She's crying, and hell, her tears seem so real I don't know what to make of it. This isn't a game anymore.

"I can't—I won't—" her shoulders rack with sobs. "They're the only people I care about in the world, and I won't stand by and let them get hurt. Don't let them get hurt, Nolan. Please. Don't. I'll drop this. I won't pursue you. I'll—I'll—"

She's telling the truth, and she's so beautiful when

she does, I feel like a ray of sunshine's illuminated her features, even as she's breaking right before me. She's been walled up, closed off. I hate seeing her fall apart like this, but I know that it's necessary. For me to get to the real woman inside, we need to get past this.

"Let's hear it."

"I did come here to spy on you. I knew if I provoked you at the club after what I did with Aileen, that you'd probably take me. I decided if I could get apprehended by you, I'd be able to find out more about you, if I could actually get into the place where you live."

I don't realize I'm gripping her harder until she flinches. I don't like hearing this, but hell, I do think she's actually telling me the goddamn truth. To her credit, she's unperturbed by my anger.

"My plan was to do an exposé. A big story, as it were, bring the truth of what you do to light. It would be a breakthrough for me, you see. And if it worked… if I did it… I would have the funds and stability to fight the courts for custody of my siblings."

I believe she's telling me the truth, but there's more to it than this. Her grudge against us goes deeper. It's personal. But for now, this is a good start.

"You did well, lass," I tell her, granting her a small smile. "So well. And I'll remember that you told me the truth." I'm proud of her. She drives me crazy, this woman, but it would be a lie to say I'm not damn proud of her.

My phone rings. I ignore it, but on and on it rings. She watches me, then swipes her hand across her eyes when I curse and finally take the phone from my pocket. Keenan.

"We're ready. Seems the O'Gregors have found out what happened last night," Keenan says. "Come to the meeting room now. Bring the girl."

"Aye. On my way."

Fucking O'Gregors.

I shove my phone in my pocket and drag her over to me. I grab her jaw and hold her gaze with mine, my fingers splayed on her perfect skin. "That was Keenan. Says the O'Gregors know what happened. No doubt they've got their eyes on us after last night."

She grimaces, nods, and doesn't look away. "I've done terrible things and you know I have. But lass, so have you."

She flinches as if I struck her, but still holds my gaze.

"Doesn't mean either of us are past redemption. Doesn't mean either of us don't have a fucking *heart*."

She nods, blinks, and another tear rolls down her cheek. I continue. I have something to say and it's important. "What it does mean is that we have to find where our loyalties lie. And that means right now, we go in front of my brothers and we tell them what you just told me. Do you understand me?"

She grimaces, but nods again. "Yes."

I stand, tug her to my chest, and wipe my thumbs across her cheekbones, wiping her tears away. "Don't cry, doll," I tell her, unable to help comforting her. "We'll find a way. But I won't let you harm my family, and I'll have a *very* tight leash on you. Understood?"

Her eyes are bright when she looks at me, both smiling and sad at the same time. "Aye, I understand. Thank you, Nolan." She gives me a watery smile. "Tight leash sounds fun."

I groan. "Don't thank me yet. You've never been to a meeting with my brothers."

I've no idea how we'll handle this, how I'll remain loyal to The Clan and keep my word to her as well, but I feel as if I've no choice in this.

I have to.

We walk in silence to the meeting room. We hear a baby's laugh, and both of us look out the large windows to just outside the lawn where Maeve and Fiona walk with Sam between them.

"They trust you," she whispers. "Wish I could, too."

Once she says it, she bites her lip and looks as if she wishes she could take it back. She shakes her head. I don't respond. Truth is, I wish I could trust her, too.

When we arrive in the meeting room, the men of our inner circle are there: Carson, Lachlan, Tully, Boner, Keenan, and Cormac.

Sheena freezes next to me when we step inside the room.

Bloody hell.

Father Finn sits beside Keenan. When Sheena sees his priestly garb, her eyes flash at Keenan.

"You told me you wouldn't!" she shouts, pointing an irate finger at him. I yank her back to me. I'm angry as well, but I can't let her speak to him that way. I've broken the bones of men for less than that.

"Sheena." She flinches at the sharp sound of my voice. I wrap my fingers around her accusatory hand and bring it down.

"That's enough. You won't speak to the Chief that way. You watch that smart mouth or I'll punish you right here, right now, with all of them watching."

And I will. I'm fully prepared. She needs to know she can't do this, and they need to know I won't let her. *Goddamn* this woman. I've got to get her under control, and now, before this spirals out. I can already see her splayed across Keenan's desk, while I give her a proper belting.

The other men are watching, all their eyes on the two of us. Even though I don't blame her and want to deck Keenan myself, I take her jaw in my hand and force her eyes back to mine.

"Sit. Do not speak unless spoken to." I tug her hand and make her sit beside me. She still seethes but at least she obeys.

Keenan's still as she watches the two of us with narrowed eyes.

"Are you done?" he asks Sheena. "Ready to listen, now?"

She barely contains her contempt while she nods, and thankfully keeps her mouth shut.

Keenan takes in a deep breath, and his gaze comes to mine. "I didn't call Father Finn," he begins. "This has nothing to do with what we talked about earlier. He came to us, and she better listen to what he has to say. He's here to bring us news."

Sheena sits silently beside me, but I can still feel her fuming.

I trust Keenan. She doesn't. He told me he wouldn't call Father Finn, and Keenan's a man of his word. I look over at Finn.

Father Finn looks older than the last time I saw him. His hair's nearly white, though he's only a decade or so older than Keenan, and his eyes look tired. I wonder at times if he wars with his vows of allegiance to the church and to us. Still, his placid voice and calm demeanor haven't changed.

"You must be Sheena," he says placidly, his voice as calm and soothing as if he's prepared to pray the morning office instead of witnessing an irate woman about to tear the mob boss' head off with her bare hands.

She nods. "Aye."

He nods. "Pleased to meet you. Name's Father Finn, uncle to the boys here and pastor of Holy Family."

"I know who you are."

He carries on as if she hasn't spoken. "I've come to speak to Keenan about something that affects your family," he says. "When I came today, I didn't know you were here. But now that I do, there's something you ought to know. Several things, actually." He pauses, as if waiting for her attention. When she nods, he continues. "For one, it may come as news to you that I knew your mum when she was a child."

Sheena blinks in surprise. "Didn't know that."

"We went to school together," he says. "I was friends with your father."

Her cheeks flush pink. I don't miss the way her body grows rigid and she clenches her jaw. She's barely masking fury, and I'm not sure why.

Does her purpose here have something to do with her father?

He leans back in his chair. Though he speaks quietly, he holds the attention of the room. "Something else you may not know, Sheena. I presided at your mum and dad's wedding."

She blinks, then shakes her head again. "Didn't know that either."

He sighs, closes his eyes, and pinches the bridge of his nose.

"I've given many of the Sacraments to your family, lass," he says. "Including last rites the night your father died."

It's too much for her. She can't hold her temper in check any longer. Before I can stop her, she's on her feet, her eyes flashing, pointing an angry finger at Father Finn.

"Don't you *dare,*" she says. "Your family, this *family,* was to blame for my father's death. And you have the nerve to pretend as if you were friends! How dare you—"

Keenan's on his feet, but not before I am. I yank her back toward me.

"*Enough,* Sheena." I sit and yank her onto my lap and wrap my arms around her body. She heaves with anger, but closes her mouth when my grip tightens. I lean in and whisper in her ear, "*Stop.*"

Father Finn watches us with one brow casually raised. He doesn't speak until she's subdued. Her whole body trembles with rage, but she knows I mean what I say. She's one breath away from being taken across my knee and strapped in front of the lot of them.

"Is that what you think, lass?" Finn says quietly. He

shakes his head. "I'm disappointed in you. A brilliant girl like you ought not jump to conclusions."

She stills. I grip her thigh and give her a firm squeeze. She needs to stay silent, to hear what he has to say.

"As I said, your father was a friend of mine," Father Finn continues. "When money got tight after the birth of their third child, your father got involved with the O'Gregors. Stayed on the outskirts, or tried to." He swallows, his Adam's apple bobbing, before he continues, as if it pains him to remember. "But you don't dabble with the O'Gregors. Your father tried to pull out, but it was too late. One of them wanted your mum, you see," he says. "And for the O'Gregors, all's fair in love and war."

"Are you trying to tell me it's the O'Gregors who're responsible for the death of my father, not the McCarthys?" I can tell she doesn't believe it by the way she shakes her head and snorts. "Wouldn't that be convenient?"

Father Finn's placid gaze doesn't waver. "Not at all convenient. Not when you've brought the wrath of the O'Gregors on our doorstep."

Her jaw drops in shock and she looks like she's about ready to lose her mind again, when I intervene. I squeeze her thigh and address Father Finn.

"Tell us how you know this," I say. "Do you have proof the O'Gregors are responsible for Hurston's death?"

"Witnessed it myself, Nolan," he says. "He knew they were coming, knew his death was imminent. He came to me for the final Sacraments. They took him when he was still on church property. They don't have the same scruples as you. And yes, I have proof. Security footage from the church, to be exact."

We don't do any type of business on church grounds, hallowed as they are.

Video footage is as clear as it gets. In any other place and time, security footage of a murder would go to the police and the O'Gregors would pay. But not here, not in Ballyhock. Law enforcement's on our payroll and theirs. Executions at our hands are left between the clans.

Sheena's trembling, but I can't tell if it's from anger or something else.

No one else has spoken since Father Finn began, but now Carson chimes in.

"I knew it, too," he says. "The O'Gregors are responsible for the drug trafficking in Stone City and every other surrounding town."

"I'll... show you the footage if you'd like," Father Finn offers.

Sheena doesn't respond.

"I'll see it, please," I tell him. "Later. For now, I trust you've told us the truth." I've known him my entire life, and he's never told a lie to me.

Sheena shakes her head. Keenan addresses her, his voice laced with warning, and for some reason it makes me want to deck him. I don't often want to hurt my brothers, but Keenan's stepping on my last nerve.

"Did you have a different story, Sheena? Another take on things, as it were?"

She lifts her head and meets his eyes, squaring her shoulders and drawing in breath. "Aye, do you think I've been on your arses for sport, then?"

I feel the corner of my lips tip upward. Christ, I love that smart mouth of hers. Still, I grip her firmly.

Keenan shrugs. "Wasn't quite sure why you've been on us. All I know is that you are and that it's time to put an end to it."

"An end to it?" she says, her temper flashing again.

Keenan leans on the desk, his body rigid with authority. *"Aye.* An *end* to it. You think we'd be bothered to bring *you* here for sport? Got better things to do with our time than fuck with the likes of you."

She flinches as if someone slapped her.

I've had it.

"Fuck off, Keenan," I say quietly. The entire room goes silent, the only sound the ticking of a clock on a shelf behind Keenan. Boner squirms beside me, and even Lachlan's eyes widen in surprise. Christ, I can't even believe I said it myself.

Keenan doesn't look angry, though, but surprised. I

shouldn't have said it. Even privately is unacceptable, but in front of the others... He's Clan Chief, my older brother, my superior. Insubordination can incur not only his wrath, but severe punishment, and I know it. Hell, I'll take it. I should've kept my mouth shut.

"Nolan," Cormac warns. He sits beside me, shaking his head. He's likely trying to prevent a pissing match I won't win. "You don't speak to him that way, brother."

But Christ, the way Sheena's eyes look at me, whatever happens now is worth it.

Father Finn clears his throat. "Boys," he says. "Tempers are high. I won't have you warring among yourselves." Aye, but there won't be a war. Keenan will have my arse kicked and I'll fucking take it, but I won't apologize. I won't allow him to talk to Sheena that way.

Finn continues. "The strength of the McCarthy Clan has always been the loyalty and brotherhood we've fostered since its founding. And we won't let *anyone* —" he pauses, his eyes coming to Sheena. "Destroy that."

Keenan sits up straighter, picks up a stack of papers on his desk, and straightens them, tapping them like a judge banging a gavel.

"Aye," he says. "I agree. So it's time we clarified a few things, then." He doesn't speak to me of what I said, but continues discussing business. "First, the O'Gregors are responsible for the death of Sheena's father. They also own Stone City, where several of you went last night to rescue Sheena's family. Any word on her mum?"

Carson shakes his head. "No, but I'll see what I can find out."

Keenan nods. "Do that." He turns to Father Finn. "I gave Nolan my word we wouldn't involve social protection. We'll keep them here in the meantime, and you're not to interfere." He turns to Sheena. "Under *one* condition."

She holds his gaze for a long moment, before finally nodding.

"By your own admission, you were on our tails under the assumption we were responsible for the death of your father. Aye?"

She nods in silence.

"Assuming you were trying to bring us to ruin with the locals as retribution. Also true?"

It's clear to me now, it all makes sense. She's been terrible to us, but damn if I don't blame her. She doesn't have the power we do to set things to right, and sought justice it in her own way. I need to know why she thought us responsible. I'll find out.

Keenan continues. "Now that you know we had nothing to do with the death of your father, you'll clear our names. We've spent decades establishing a reputation here, and I won't allow you to destroy that. You'll do whatever it fucking takes to undo the damage you've done. Understood?"

He's being gentler with her than he could be. He knows she means something to me, I'd guess. And anyone with a heart would take pity on the littler ones.

She looks to me and I give her another reassuring squeeze of her thigh. "Won't be easy," she says. "Got to make sure they don't think I'm being bribed, and with my family here..." her voice trails off.

"You're a smart girl," Keenan says sharply. "You'll figure it out."

She breathes in deeply, squares her shoulders, then nods. "Aye. I'll do it."

"Good," he says. "And you'll remain under our custody until it's evident you've cleared our names and we're back in good standing with the locals. Understood?"

She huffs out a breath. "Yes."

"I'll have you know, lass, we've granted leniency to you only because of him." He jerks his chin at me. "If not for Nolan, you'd have already paid the ultimate price by Clan code. Is that clear?"

She swallows and nods again. "Aye."

He turns his gaze to me. "Nolan. You'll head the battle against the O'Gregors. You brought it on us, and we weren't exactly friends with the O'Gregors before all this began. They will not disturb our family. You'll be sure to prevent fallout in whatever way you have to."

"Of course."

There's warning in his gaze. "And you'll keep this woman of yours under control in the meantime."

I squeeze her thigh again. "On that you have my word, brother."

Lachlan snorts but covers it up with a cough.

Keenan continues. "Find out what you can about what they're planning. Find her mother and make sure she doesn't pose a threat. For today, we find out who our enemies are. We won't act defensively, brothers, but proactively."

All around us there are murmurs of agreement, nods and promises. We could be on the cusp of battle, and we have to prepare. We talk about the possibilities, how we'll approach this, and I delegate jobs to various men until we have a plan in place.

Keenan closes the meeting with one final admonition. "The lives of the Clan depend on you, Nolan. I know you won't let us down. Sheena's the best goddamn reporter in Ireland and I'm sure those skills of hers can be put to good use. She'll help, won't you?"

Sheena nods.

"Keep your eyes open. Be prepared, boys. This has only just begun."

I take in a deep breath. He's right.

"Before we go, Keenan, I've something to tell the

group." We look over at Carson, who meets Keenan's gaze bravely.

"Aye?"

He smiles. "Eve's expecting."

Lachlan pumps his fist in the air and hoots. Tully slaps Carson on the back, and Cormac bumps his fist. Keenan smiles. "Congratulations, Carson. Mam and the girls will be thrilled."

"Aye," Carson says. "Thanks very much. Not sure how well she'll fare, but… well, I didn't want you lads finding out any other way."

"Much appreciated, Carson," Keenan says, then he looks to me. "And all the more reason we re-establish the safety and well-being of The Clan."

Sheena looks wistfully at Carson, then the others, but she says nothing. Her face is drawn and pained, for some reason. I wish I knew why. I wish I knew how to make it better.

.

Chapter 12

Sheena

I DON'T KNOW what to do, what to think. It's as if my entire purpose has been swept out from under me. Until now, I've been on a vengeance mission to bring the McCarthys down, and now... if I'm to believe what the priest said... I've been misinformed.

I'm deep in my head when Keenan dismisses the meeting, filled with so many thoughts I don't even know how to begin to sort them.

They can prove they didn't kill my father.

I've been chasing the wrong people.

The O'Gregors are the ones responsible.

It's up to me to bring vindication to the McCarthys.

This has only just begun.

Just now, Carson told the lot of them his girlfriend's expecting, and their congrats brought a pang to my chest. I don't have a support system like this. I have no one.

Nolan rises and takes my hand, a decided firmness to his gaze and tightness to his grip on my hand that gives me pause. I don't know if he's angry or just determined, but something tells me I'm about to find out. I try to shove all my thoughts and fears away, but it's hard.

I can't believe how stupid I've been, how arrogant.

I was set up. I was lied to. And I've built my hopes and dreams on a sand castle premise. The tide's washed everything away.

As we're leaving the meeting room, Father Finn calls my name. "Sheena."

I turn to look at him. I knew who he was before I met him, having done my homework. The younger brother of the late Seamus McCarthy, he looks much older than he is. I imagine his dual role as McCarthy clan chaplain and pastor to Holy Family isn't an easy job.

"Father Finn."

He sweeps a hand across his brow and runs his fingers through his gray hair.

"Your father was a good man, lass."

My throat is tight, and my nose tingles. "Aye," I agree. My voice is husky. "The very best."

"He didn't deserve to die the way he did. And it broke my heart to see your mother's undoing."

I nod. "Me, too."

Nolan watches us thoughtfully but doesn't speak.

"Between your connections and mine, we'll see to it that social protection leaves them be. I've a contact in the main office in Stone City. I imagine you do as well?"

"I know a few people, yes."

Even though I feel like I need a good, hard cry, another, inexplicable feeling comes over me as well. My heart feels lighter than it has in years. Our meeting today's shed light on the truth. And now instead of a mission to bring down one family, my job is to vindicate. And I like that. I'll do my damned best.

"Good," he says with a sad smile. He pats Nolan's shoulder. "Nolan's a good man. Follow his lead, and he won't steer you wrong."

I don't expect this, and it seems Nolan doesn't either, for we both stare at him as he leaves the room. The others leave until it's just me, Nolan, and Keenan left.

"Nolan, stay in touch," Keenan says. "I want a blow by blow."

Nolan nods. "Aye. I'm sorry, Keenan. Shouldn't have said what I did."

Keenan looks to me then Nolan, before he nods his head. "I defied dad once on behalf of Caitlin. And because of that, I'll forgive what happened." His eyes meet mine, though he's addressing Nolan. "See to it she doesn't interfere, that you do what I've asked, and we'll move past this."

I now know that Nolan telling Keenan off probably broke some kind of Clan code.

Nolan nods. "Aye. You have my word."

I've heard them say this before. It's like a McCarthy brother thing.

We leave the room and head for the stairs. I can still hear Fiona, Tiernan, and Sam in the garden. It seems almost surreal, as if I'm existing simultaneously in two separate worlds.

I look out the window. They're happy as can be, Maeve sitting on the lawn weaving a wreath of flowers from her garden. Fiona's blowing bubbles with Sam, and Tiernan's hands are in his pockets as he stares out at the sea in the distance.

To my surprise, Nolan brings us outside to join them. He talks to Maeve, while I chat with Tiernan and Fiona. They don't know my vendetta against the McCarthys, so there's nothing to tell them. But I have to put their minds at ease.

"I've a job to do," I tell Tiernan and Fiona. I watch

as Sam toddles after a large, iridescent bubble. He squeals when he reaches it and pops it.

"What kind of a job?" Tiernan asks. "And how long will we be here?"

"Just an investigative job, Tiernan," I tell him. "I've promised to vindicate their family in exchange for protection."

He looks at me sharply. He knows there's more to the story than what I'm telling him.

"Why does their family need to be vindicated?" Fiona asks. She drops her voice to a whisper. "Sheena, are they bad men? Do they do evil things? They seem so nice."

I honestly don't even know how to answer that. Yes, of course they're no innocents, but at the same time... have I been telling myself lies about the McCarthy clan all these years? Have I allowed anger and hatred to fester for naught?

"Well," I say to Fiona. "They've brought you here, haven't they? And you're safe. That's something that matters."

"Right," Tiernan says.

Nolan approaches us, bends to one knee, and picks up a bubble wand that lays forgotten on the grass. He dips it into the bottle, lifts it to his lips, and blows. A large bubble floats in the air. Sam squeals, chasing after it. Nolan grins, and my heart squeezes.

He defended me in there. He told Keenan off, at his own personal risk. He's made sure that my family is protected.

Why?

I make it my mission in life to find out the "why" behind things, to know the reasons why people behave the way they do. And I can't figure Nolan out.

"Sheena," he says. "You and I need a private talk." He gets to his feet. After what he's done, after what his family's done, I feel I owe him my compliance.

I nod. "Right, then. You lot behave yourselves and we'll see you…" My voice trails off. When *will* we see them?

"Dinner," Nolan says with a smile.

I look to the large, wrought-iron gate that surrounds the estate. I remember what went on at the meeting, and I'm grateful for this protection. Will my mother try to come here? Will the O'Gregors?

Nolan takes my hand and leads me back to the house.

"Are they safe out there?" I ask him.

"Aye, lass. Probably safest place in all of Ireland for them right now."

"Are you sure?"

"Positive."

"Then why can't we stay with them? Why must you—"

"Because we've much to discuss, Sheena." His voice drops. "And it's time I got you alone again. You heard what Keenan said. There's not much that's changed between us."

But he's lying. There's so much that's changed between us it's unsettling.

Nolan promised with near glee to keep me under control. I haven't forgotten what he did just before this meeting. I can still feel the punishing smack of his palm, his fingers stroking through my most sensitive parts. Just the memory has blood pumping through my veins again.

He holds my hand and leads me upstairs. "Come along, now, Sheena."

"You talk to me like you're coaxing a puppy," I mutter.

He grins. "I could collar you and lead you with a chain if you wish. What's your kink, lass?"

"Nolan, you can't talk like that when my brothers and sister are *right outside that window,* and your own brothers are probably milling all about the place."

"Is that right?" he asks. "Or what?"

"Or I'll—" I don't finish the sentence, because he's got me pressed up against the railing, his fingers woven in my hair, and he's kissing me. I lose myself in the moment, his firm body pressed up against me, his masculine scent pervading my senses, his soft lips in such contrast to the prickly feel of his beard.

"Oh, my, cousin. Get a room!"

He pulls away with a grin that makes my heart do a somersault. His buxom cousin Megan's standing on the landing above us, her arms laden with folded towels.

"What the fuck are you doing, spying on us?"

"Spying on you? *You're* the ones mugging the face off each other in the damn lobby for God and everyone to see." She shakes her head and walks in the other direction.

"That girl needs someone to keep her in check, goddamn it."

We head upstairs, his hand in mine again as if to remind me I'm not free to go.

I pinch the bridge of my nose. "And I need a moment to just *think*."

"You need more than that," he mutters.

I swallow, my belly swooping at the warning tone he takes. "You've already spanked me. What else do you have in mind?"

His eyes darken, but he doesn't reply. We walk in silence up the stairs toward his room.

When we reach it, he opens the door, and we nearly trip over boxes and bags just inside the door.

"What's all this?" I ask.

"Cormac doesn't want you in borrowed clothing. I don't either. So I had Megan do a little shopping."

"That quick?"

"Aye," he says. "She's got a black belt in shopping."

"Is everyone in your family talented in one way or another?"

But he doesn't respond. He's leading me into his bedroom. While we were gone, housecleaning came. The bed's made, the windows sparkle, and a tray laden with tea and biscuits sits on a little table in the room. It makes me ache a little. I've never had the basic comforts of home like this.

When he turns to face me, his gaze is heated, a look I'm growing to both dread and crave.

"I want a shower," he says. "And I want you with me."

Downstairs, he was every bit the second in line to the throne of the McCarthy Clan, the man who cracks skulls and rules the country. In here, I'm the one he rules.

I fucking love it.

He's grabbing the hem of his shirt and lifting it over his head. I'm still not sure how I'm supposed to feel about him, how I can let go of what I've held onto for so long. A glimmer of excitement pools in my belly when he tugs his shirt up, revealing the hard planes of his stomach sprinkled with a smattering of dark hair.

"I could use a shower, too," I agree.

"Aye, strip."

I yank at my clothes and tug them off, tossing them with his into a pile by the bathroom door. His eyes roam hungrily over me as he reaches for his belt. He unfastens it, folds it over, and gives it a good snap.

My pussy clenches. I've felt that belt before. He knows how to use it. His jeans come next, and soon we're both stripped naked. He snaps his fingers and points to the bathroom.

"Shower," he says. I start walking toward him, but he shakes his head. I freeze. He points to the floor. "Crawl to me, Sheena."

I fall to my knees, excitement lacing through me at his command. I hold his gaze with mine as I move toward him, the carpet soft beneath my knees and hands. I feel graceful as I crawl, moving with ease as he stands and waits. His body's magnificent, muscled and lean, fewer tats than the rest, in sharp contrast against his skin. His eyes follow my every move until I reach him.

I've submitted at the club. I've been with men who commanded and dominated, who've used me for their purposes. I've used my body to get what I want, to get what I need. But I've never been with a man who's delved beneath my tough exterior. I've never been with a man who knows me, the real me, the girl who came from a broken and shameful past, who's done wrong in the name of justice.

I've never been with a man who's seen me cry.

And it fills me with excitement while it terrifies me. Deep down inside, I ache to please him. He's taking care of my family, and there's nothing in the world that matters more to me. He's defended me in front of his brothers. I've been awful to him, and yet he's still here.

When I reach him, he cups the back of my head, drawing me to him. "Good lass. Come here." He reaches for my hands and draws me to my feet, frames my face with his hand, and kisses me. His hard length presses against my naked skin, and I moan when his mouth meets mine.

"Tell me, Sheena," he says. "Why'd you think us responsible for your father's death?"

Is he doing this on purpose? Questioning me when I'm aroused and naked? He's damn clever.

I won't hold the truth back from him. I can't. We have to join together or we'll never do what we need to. So I give it to him, the bald, ugly, shameful truth. "I slept with the Captain of the O'Gregor Clan," I tell him. My voice shakes, but I don't let it deter me. "I wanted answers. He was the one that told me if I gave him what he wanted, he'd tell me what I needed to hear."

Nolan's body tightens, his green eyes narrowing. "And you believed him?"

"At the time, it was the only thing that made sense. My father was dead. I knew it was mafia that killed him, and all signs pointed to the McCarthys."

"All signs or all accusations?"

I sigh. "Accusations. I wanted someone to blame. My mother mentioned names, men that my father interacted with. She mentioned Carson, and Father Finn, and I assumed because he's related to you…" my voice trails off. It sounds so foolish now, so flimsy. "And once I started digging up the truth about all of you, it seemed to make sense. I knew my father had business at the harbor. He went there every night. And once I found out you were the ones that deal with arms, I just… concluded."

"Right," he says. "You know you've been granted an exemption literally *no one* has ever had before, don't you?'

I nod. "I do. And I'm sorry. I'll help make this better, I will."

He nods. "You will. I'll see to it you do." He slams his palm on my backside, and I squeal and trot to the bathroom. "Now get to the shower."

While he turns the shower on, he holds me to him, fondling my breasts almost distractedly while he checks the temperature. My body's on fire, his earlier ministrations making my need flare at his touch.

He drags open the curtain and leads me into the shower. Clouds of hot steam fill the room, taking my breath away. I wonder what he'll do, if he'll master me and dominate me in the bathroom, but he doesn't. He doesn't want to talk either.

Wordlessly, he lathers me up and rinses me off. I like the feel of his hands on my scalp, massaging the shampoo in before he rinses off the suds. I let him wash me, then I turn to him and do the same. Hesitantly, I run my hands over his body. I've longed to do just this, to touch him, to feel his strong, masculine body beneath my fingers and *Jesus,* he feels even better than I imagined. I wonder if what he's done today, both punished and defended me, has affected how I feel toward him. My body comes alive near him.

I watch his eyes as I reach for his cock. He braces, groaning when I stroke the hardened length.

"Not in here," he says. "Shower's foreplay. I want you on my sheets when I fuck you."

I shiver in excitement. I want him. But more than that?

He wants me.

There's no question in my mind it's time. We've been through so much over the years in so short a time. I'm no virgin, but I've never been with a man I really wanted.

That changes *everything*.

We towel off, and he lifts me up in his arms, kissing me as we make our way toward his bed.

"I don't like to fuck gentle," he says in my ear, his words a husky growl that sends molten heat pulsing through my core.

"I know," I whisper. "I've got eyes, you know."

He grins. "I want to claim every inch of your body, and goddamn it, I will."

"Do it."

He flips me around, drops me to the bed on my belly, and slaps my bottom, hard. "Get up on your knees."

I scramble to obey when he slaps my arse again. "I fucking love seeing my handprints on your fair skin. You've still got marks from the spanking you got this morning. *My* marks."

I'm trembling when he arranges my limbs on the bed and fastens my wrists in cuffs he has here for this purpose. The next moment, he's got a gag to my lips. I part my mouth, and he secures it. I freeze when I feel cold lube trickle down my ass cheeks and the cool tip of a plug gliding in and out.

I *knew* he was kinky as fuck.

It fucking thrills me.

I'd have a thing or two to say if I wasn't gagged, and the forced silence heightens my awareness.

"Good girl," he says. Pleasure at his praise warms me. "Relax."

He glides the plug through the lube again, holds me

in place with his hand against the small of my back, then eases it in and out. I'm so full, so aroused. With my wrists fastened, the power of speech taken, I'm at his mercy. The cool metal sends wave after wave of arousal pulsing through me. I'm trembling with need, and it takes me a moment to realize the groans in the room are mine.

He pats the plug approvingly, then glides his fingers through my slick, swollen sex.

"Jesus," he curses. "My God. You're soaked."

Hell yes I am. I'm already ready to come and he's hardly touched me. I shiver when metal grazes my nipples next. I should've expected this. Arousal zings through me when he fastens first one nipple clamp, then the next. He's pushed every arousal button, when he lowers his mouth to my shoulder and sinks his teeth into the tender skin.

Okay, so not *every* arousal button, *my God.*

"Fucking perfection," he growls. I feel him stroke his cock up and down my folds. I hear the crinkle of a condom wrapper, and wish for a moment that we could do this ungloved, that I could feel him in me as closely as possible.

He suckles my shoulder where he bit as he slides his cock in me. I arch my back, welcoming him in. Between the fullness in my arse and the tenderness at my breasts, the only thing I'm missing is his thick cock in my core to make me feel complete.

He holds his cock at my entrance. "You'll do exactly what I say, Sheena." Gagged, I can only nod.

He eases his cock inside me. I don't realize I'm holding my breath until he stops.

"I brought you here to punish you. To question you. But when we're this close… I can see inside you. And you aren't the woman I thought you were. The one I dragged here to be interrogated."

Without further warning, he thrusts into me.

My clit pulses. My body's instantly on fire, igniting as he stretches me.

He bends, his mouth at my ear, brushes my hair off my shoulder and licks my neck. I shiver.

"This isn't what we planned. But we both know this is exactly what we need, isn't it?"

"Mmm." I nod. He thrusts in and out, building a rhythm of perfection that rocks my core, as he continues to talk to me. I'm enjoying this one-sided conversation, because for once my mouth isn't getting in the way. My body's talking for me, and my body says *more.*

With every stroke of his cock and perfect thrust, I'm getting closer and closer to release. He tugs the chain between my nipples, bites my neck, then pulls my hair as he thrusts in me so hard I scream against the gag. His hands dig into my hips as he glides in and out. I try to groan but can't, my moans swallowed with the gag.

"Good girl," he says, his words pitching off in a guttural moan. "I've wanted in you, and you feel even better than I imagined."

I moan and grind against him, until I feel myself on the verge of climax. As he thrusts, I move with him, until the intensity of our movements increase and I'm panting in anticipation. I can tell by the way his own breaths are quickening that he's on the verge as well.

"You'll do what I tell you," he orders with a punishing thrust.

I nod.

"You'll follow my lead," he says, another hard thrust sending spasms of pleasure rippling through me.

I nod again.

"If you disobey me..." another hard thrust... "I'll punish you."

I'm nodding and submitting, something that doesn't come easily to me, but he's pulled the strings of my heart one by one until I've come undone. He thrusts again and again, until his groans fill the room. I'm trembling, on the cusp of orgasm, when he comes. My body ignites, and I'm lost to pleasure. He's so deep, so perfect—this is *bloody perfect*.

He removes the gag and tosses it to the side, presses his forehead to my neck, and sighs.

"I won't let them destroy you, destroy *us*. You understand me, lass?"

I nod. There are so many things I want to say, but I can't seem to gather the right words. So I only nod. "Aye. I do."

"This will be messy, and I need to know you won't fight me. You understand that, too, don't you?"

I nod again. "Aye."

"Good girl," he breathes. "Sweet lass. We'll do this together."

I close my eyes against the flood of emotion at his words. I'm not a good girl. I'm not a sweet lass. And I shudder to think what will happen when he realizes it as truth.

Chapter 13

Nolan

WHEN I TOLD Sheena I'd have her on a tight leash, I meant it. She's on probation, as it were, after what she's done. But hell, keeping her under my control is no hardship. For either of us, really.

I keep her by my side, and make sure she does what she's told. She's feisty as hell and has a temper to match her hair, but I'm up for the challenge. We had a breakthrough, I know we did. I've seen the real Sheena Hurston, and it's an honor and a privilege, one that I don't think many have gotten.

She was angry at us before, so angry it colored every damn interaction we had with her. But now that we know the truth, she's begun to soften, to change.

We expect any moment that there's to be trouble from her mum, but we hear nothing. I watch the video of the execution with Father Finn and Keenan, and there's no doubt the O'Gregors did what Finn says. I don't tell Sheena I did, but somehow she knows. We don't talk of it. I'm glad she didn't see what I did.

We investigate. Carson has connections in Stone City, but no one's heard a thing. The mother hasn't returned since the night we took the children into our custody.

At first, Tiernan didn't trust us at all, but as the days go by, as he sees Sheena interacting with us and he sees we aren't the monsters he thinks we are, he softens a bit. He knows something's up between me and Sheena, but he doesn't ask questions.

And Fiona's adorable. She's got her sister's bright gray eyes and the Hurston family red hair, but she doesn't have the chip on her shoulder like Tiernan and Sheena. Everything's a wonder to her, from the food our staff serves to the gardens we tend.

I haven't given Sheena her phone since the first night she was here, and after several days of investigating and getting her siblings acclimated to life here, she asks for it.

"I'm on holiday at work, Nolan," she says. "But that ends soon. I'll have to go back to work in some capacity, or I won't have a job. And you know how that will impact my ability to do what I need to."

I frown. "Aye. But you'll use it in front of me."

"Do you still not trust me?" There isn't a glimmer of reproach in her question, but curiosity. She knows what she's done and how I have to keep tabs on her. She knows she's got a very long way to go before she can show the men of The Clan she's to be trusted.

"We're getting there," I tell her. And we are. I don't think she's lying in wait, ready to bring us to ruin. I do think she's woven more than one lie, and under the pressure of what she has to do, she could be tempted to snap.

I meant every word of keeping her on a tight leash. She's by my side during the day, even during meetings with my brothers. I've got cameras trained on her in my absence, which is rare, and she's not given freedom like the other girls. We eat every meal together, and sleep beside each other. And we make love, on my terms, every damn day.

Like I said. Not a hardship.

"Alright, lass." I get her phone from the safe and bring it to her. She thanks me, sits on a chair by the window, and swipes it open. Sunlight streams in from the glass doors of the balcony, and for one brief moment in time, she looks like a portrait. Her ankles crossed gracefully, legs clad in dark-washed trousers. She wears a V-neck pale blue top, simple yet elegant, against her pale, freckled skin. Megan knows the kind of clothes that suit her. She did well. Her long, gorgeous hair's swept up into a plait that hangs over her shoulder, making her look even younger than she is.

I walk to her, bend, and kiss her forehead. She blinks and looks up at me.

"I love that," she says, her frankness my reward. I've earned her trust, and it helps bring restoration to us.

"What, doll?" I weave a lock of her hair around my finger and glide my thumb along the silky length.

"A kiss on the forehead. Makes me all soft and melty inside."

I tug the hair. "Good girl. I like you all soft and melty."

I bend and kiss her forehead again. "So that's the ticket, is it? That's your tender spot?"

She shoots me a salacious grin. "I've got several."

Heat flares between us and before we know it, the phone lays forgotten, her clothes are on a pile on the floor, and she's on her hands and knees on the bed.

My need for her's insatiable. She bends to my will, submits to my needs, meets every demand with exquisite perfection. A woman like Sheena doesn't submit easily. Submission from a woman like her is earned, and it's this very knowledge that fuels my desire for her. She's my spoils of war.

I fought a battle of my own once. I wasn't the man I was meant to be when under the influence of alcohol. I tamed that beast, but I fight my demons still.

Sheena has demons of her own she battles. It's probably why we understand each other.

She's panting on the bed after climaxing, her cheeks damp with perspiration, little tendrils of auburn hair stuck to her forehead and the rest a wild, beautiful mess.

"Nolan McCarthy, I'll have you know I spent a full ten minutes taming my hair this morning."

I reach down, wrap it around my fingers, and give it a good tug. Her eyes go half-lidded, and she moans a little. "My God, I love it when you do that."

"I don't care if your hair's tame, lass. And anyway, I'm the one that does the taming around here."

She shoots me a grin over her shoulder. "Is that right, sir?" she asks. I give her arse a good, sharp crack.

"Aye, love. And don't you know it?"

We topple over on the bed, entangled limbs and pounding hearts. She places her hand on my chest, and she's got the soft look in her eyes again, a gentleness she rarely shares. It's the look I've come to crave bringing out of her.

"Today, we need to go to the shops," she says. "Just now I've gotten leave to write a story, and I want to start making amends."

I hold her hand, weaving my fingers through hers, and bring our folded hands to my lips. I kiss her long, beautiful fingers.

"What are you planning?"

She sighs. "Oh, a few things. I need to investigate first. Would you bring me to your finishing school as well?"

"Aye. I have to go there myself."

"Do you?"

I nod. I asked Father Finn for more information about the O'Gregors, but we need to investigate further. Every lead so far has turned up nothing, and in our world, quiet like this is only the calm before the storm.

We head downstairs to the dining room. Mam sits with little Sam on her lap, feeding him his lunch. She looks tired.

"Y'alright?" I ask her. I reach for the little tyke, who lifts his chubby arms up to me.

"He was up a lot last night," she says, running a hand across her brow. "Bit of a tummy ache."

"Oh, I'm sorry, Maeve," Sheena says. "I could—"

I shake my head sharply at her. No, she could not. We're still establishing trust, and Keenan needs to know he can trust her as well. The best way for us to do that is to be sure she stays with me.

"I just… I'm not sure it's the best for them, Nolan," mam says. She looks to Sheena then to me. "All of you are in and out all day, Clan business and the like. They go to the library, they go out to the garden, but Fiona and Tiernan are getting restless.

There isn't much here for them." She looks to Sheena. "They need to see more of you, I think."

"That's my doing, mam," I tell her. "I want Sheena with me for now." I don't even realize I'm sort of swaying back and forth with the baby until I see Sheena's eyes softening as she watches me.

"I know it," mam says. "I'm just saying it can't go on like this for much longer."

"Aye," Sheena says with a sigh.

Good girl.

"Where will you be off to today?" mam asks.

"Heading to the shops," Sheena says. "Maybe we can take them with us, then? Shouldn't be any harm that comes to them there. Might even help our plan. Soften the locals, as it were."

I mull this over and finally nod. Mam needs a break, and something tells me seeing Sheena with the children will give me insight into her as well. Since today's work involves phone calls and questions, no traveling, I concede.

"We can take them to St. Albert's as well, when we go there," I tell mam. "Alright, round them up, then."

Mam smiles at me, stands, and squeezes my arm. "You're a good man, Nolan."

I smile back at her.

She was the one who stood by me when the others

lost faith. She was the one who built me up, encouraged me, and helped me through the darkest time of my life. Leaving behind the vice that helped me cope, I lost my father at the very same time.

In short time, we've got Tiernan, Fiona, and Sam ready to go. We head to the lobby just as Lachlan enters.

"Nolan, a word," he says. I hand baby Sam to Sheena. She looks funny, all feminine and "melty," as she calls it, but I'm not sure why. I walk with Lachlan to the steps.

"What is it, brother?"

"Went to The Craic last night," he says. "Me, Boner, and Tully. Tully ended up with a lass, a girl who's in with the O'Gregors."

Bloody hell.

"Yeah?"

He nods. "Seems the Captain has left quite a line of women in his wake. Hooks up, sleeps with them, has his way, pays them well, sees them off."

Pays them well?

I hope if we battle I get first pick of who we fight. The Captain was the one that touched my woman.

"Alright?"

"The Captain reveals much, it seems. Has a gob he can't keep shut."

"Bloody hell."

"Works in our favor this time. The girl told Tully she was with the Captain last weekend, heard tell of a few things involving the McCarthys. Came to The Craic so she could inform us."

"What's in it for her?"

"Money. Wanted to be paid for the information. Tully took care of her."

"Tell me everything."

"She said a few things you ought to know. First, she told us they're planning retaliation. According to them, we've trespassed on their territory and caused trouble."

"Right."

"Second, she says we've taken one of their runners from them. And *that,* Nolan, is their biggest gripe. Did some digging myself. Seems the prick we beat gets into fights all the time, so much so, they've come to damn near expect it."

"Wait, now. Their runner? What the fuck are you on about?"

Lachlan swallows hard, and his eyes go to Sheena and the others waiting for us in the lobby. He lowers his voice. "Her brother, Nolan. He did paid work for them. And they're *pissed* he's with us now, convinced that we stole him from them and worse still, he was a spy."

"Mother of God," I mutter. This is more complicated than I realized. I have to talk with Tiernan.

And I wonder what Sheena will do when she finds out?

"Perhaps it isn't wise to have Tiernan here after all," Lachlan says. "For all we know, he's been spying all this time."

Keenan would lose his *mind* if he found this out.

"Thanks, Lach."

"Anytime," he says. He looks wistfully over at everyone by the door. "You know I had little brothers and sisters myself at one time."

I know it. He was orphaned young and lost his whole family. A teacher at our school found him. We damn near raised him at our finishing school.

Lachlan continues. "Maybe talk to her brother. Find out what you can."

I nod. "Aye. And I'll get in touch with Tully, too. Have you told anyone else?"

"Not yet."

"Good. Don't."

"Aye," he says. "But you can't keep it from Keenan for long."

"I know it. I'll wait until I've had a chance to talk with her brother, though."

Lachlan leaves. Sheena's watching me curiously. How am I going to tell her what I know? Tiernan watches us as well, and for the first time since I've met him, I think he looks a little guilty.

He and I will have a word. Sheena, too. Did she know about this? Did she willingly bring a runner for the O'Gregors into our home?

I don't know if I've made a mistake, bringing her here, bringing them all here. It's complicated things.

But bloody hell, what's life if it isn't complicated? If you don't take risks now and then? Where's the pay-off in what's easy to do? If there's anything I've learned in my family, it's that life and love are complicated. You have to face what comes at you, and choose to either bow to the demands of the world or let them strengthen you.

Sheena puts the baby in a pram Caitlin's brought out to lend her, and he waves his chubby fists excitedly. Fiona takes the handle of the pram and offers to push it. "Go on, you walk with yer man," she says to Sheena, giving us a coy look.

Yer man. I stifle a snort.

"Oh for pity's sake, Fiona," Sheena mutters.

I beckon to her. "Come here, now, lass. Yer man wants you."

Tiernan watches us apprehensively. I suspect I know why he does. He wants to know his sister's safe with me. What the lad needs to know himself is that I won't allow him to endanger her either, by his own stupidity.

We walk down the path that leads us from the house, past the garden and out to the main road, the ocean behind us as we head into town.

Fiona chatters on about Aileen teaching her to plait her own hair, Caitlin showing her how to play patty-cake with the baby, and mam letting her help in the garden.

"You're a lucky man, Nolan McCarthy," Fiona says. "You've got an amazing family here. One most of us only dream about." She flushes as soon as she says it, and looks to Sheena. "Oh, God, Sheena, I don't mean it like that. It's just—"

"Relax, Fiona," Sheena says gently. Her siblings bring out the softer side of her. I like it. "I know what you mean, sweetheart. It's okay." She looks to me and her eyes grow a bit wistful. "I've thought the same myself, at times."

Tiernan kicks a rock, his face sullen. He isn't buying any of this. Fiona walks ahead when the baby spies a gull, and I intentionally keep Sheena back so Fiona can't hear.

"We need a word with Tiernan," I tell her.

"Oh?"

"Aye." I tell her what Lachlan told me, simply and straightforward.

"You sure?"

"Aye, and I suspect he'll tell us the truth when we ask."

I watch her go from curious to angry. Her beautiful eyes harden, and her jaw firms.

"Mother of God," she mutters. "Of all the—"

I squeeze her hand. *"Sheena."*

When I say her name firmly, she responds to my sharp tone. She pauses, clenching her jaw, but stops talking.

"I know you're angry, lass. What I need to know is the truth from you before we speak to him. Can't let your temper cloud your judgment either. Did you know he worked with them?"

"No," she says. "Nolan, I would've kicked his arse myself. I knew he had jobs, that he did various things, and he was earning money, that much I'll admit. I knew that whatever he did was likely illegal, but I didn't ask questions because I didn't want to know the answers."

She brings her hand to her brow and blows out a breath. "God, this is fucked up."

I shrug. "Eh, nothing we haven't dealt with before. The Clan, I mean. And we'll deal with it again."

Up ahead, the baby turns to us and waves his little dimpled fist. I grin, and wave back. When I look back at her, she's watching me.

"Nolan, I know our relationship is… unconventional, one might say. I mean, I didn't come here on a date. But I…" she pauses. "Do you know how hard it is for me to talk about my… *feelings* and crap like that?"

I squeeze her hand and can't help but laugh. "Aye, lass. I do. And it's one of the things I like best about you."

"What's that?" she says in a whisper, as if she's afraid if she speaks too loudly her voice will crack.

"How *brave* you are. I see the real you. The one whose heart bleeds for those children, the ones you love."

"You're too good, Nolan McCarthy," she whispers.

"Me? Good? Jesus, woman, are you high?"

But still, her praise warms me, and I can't say I don't like it.

"Right, then," she says, changing the subject. "We talk to Tiernan. Now?"

"Aye," I say, my voice hardening. I need this boy to know how serious this is. "*Now*."

"Tiernan." She calls to him. He walks ahead of us with his hands stuffed into his pockets. He looks from me to her, and I swear he already looks guilty. "Come here a moment, will you?"

We're ten minutes from the shops. We may need to talk more later, but I want to get to the bottom of this now.

"Fiona," I call out. "We need to talk to Tiernan for a few moments privately. When we get into town, reckon we'll get a treat at the bakery? They've bought out Lickety Splits and sell ice cream now."

Her eyes go wide. "Oh, aye, thanks!" she says. I take some money out of my wallet and hand it to her. She takes it gratefully.

"Brilliant. Haven't had ice cream in ages. Thank you, Nolan." She pockets the money and goes a few paces ahead of us.

"Is that safe?" Sheena asks.

"Aye, lass. Lachlan and Tully are behind us anyhow."

"Are they?" she swivels around, and her eyes go wide. "Jesus, I'm losing my touch."

Tiernan approaches us as Fiona walks away.

"What is it?" Tiernan asks, and I swear he looks a bit guilty. He watches me apprehensively.

I like this boy. He's on the cusp of breaking into manhood, tall and lanky and thin, with his sister's red hair and freckles. But he's got the look of a boy that's seen too much in his tender years. I feel for him. It's something he shares with the men of The Clan.

Sheena clears her throat. "The time for hiding is over. We can't do this anymore, Tiernan. Can't you see? We've enemies at our back. The hounds of hell, as it were."

He looks at her in confusion, frowning. "I don't know what you mean."

"First off, I was wrong. I thought the McCarthys were responsible for dad's death." I can tell that it costs her to admit this. She's a proud woman who thought her intentions purposeful. "I know now that they weren't. All this time, I was wrong." She stares at him, with a stern expression that would rival mam's. Something stirs and me. She'd make a good mum herself. "So it's time you tell us the truth, Tiernan. We know more than you think we know. Tell us what job you've been doing."

Tiernan's normally guarded expression falls for a moment, and for the first time, I don't see a boy on the verge of manhood, but a boy who's afraid of losing everything.

"What do you know?" he asks.

"No, Tiernan. You tell us." She brooks no argument, and he finally caves.

He swallows before he speaks. "I worked for the O'Gregors for a time. They paid me well to make deliveries. I worked at night mostly... sometimes at school. I didn't ask what they had me deliver and they didn't tell me, but I could imagine."

Sheena winces. "Oh, Tiernan. You're here under the protection of the McCarthys. For God's sake, they're offering us protection, and with your connections to the O'Gregors they could think you a spy."

His eyes narrow on her. "And you're any better? Your job is on the up and up, is it?"

She frowns and looks away before answering him. She clears her throat and speaks without looking at me or Tiernan. "I was. I came here on purpose. I wanted to find out everything I could, you see. I told you I was convinced they were guilty of a crime they didn't commit."

"Now what?" Tiernan asks. He looks sharply at me,

his body tight and rigid with his arms across his chest. "We leave? Go home? We aren't welcome there anymore either, and you know it."

"Who said that, lad?" I ask. "Your sister's got a job here. Part of our promise to her is to keep you safe." I shrug. "It wasn't smart, getting involved with the likes of the O'Gregors. But I did one worse, heading into their territory and causing trouble. But mark me, Tiernan." I frown at him. I want him to feel the full weight of my words as well. "It was dangerous being errand boy for them. You need to know how risky that was, and promise your sister and me you won't do such a thing again."

His eyes flash at me, storm clouds of anger that look just like his sister's. The Hurstons have fire in their blood, that much is true. But I won't be intimidated by him, and I'll have him listen. I won't be put off by his hostility, either.

"You can glare at me all you want. But the fact remains, you did something dangerous and foolish, and if you're going to be a man of integrity, you'll own that."

"Says the man who, what? Runs the mafia on the east coast, is it?" Tiernan says.

Sheena opens her mouth to protest, but I raise my hand to stop her.

"I'll handle this."

The boy needs a fucking lesson. I look ahead to make sure Fiona's a good bit ahead of us, with

Lachlan and Tully nearby. We're by a grove of trees that shades us from her view. I release Sheena's hand and sidestep toward the tree.

I know why he protests, but he needs to know what he's done, how dangerous it is, and I need to prove to Keenan he won't pose a threat to us again.

For once, I imagine I feel the way my older brothers might have when I was horsing around and fucking off, with not a care in the world. Class clown. I remember how they lectured, how they'd try to teach me to grow up and take responsibility. I didn't heed them until it was too late. And I'll be damned if I watch Tiernan do the same.

Under the shade of trees, I beckon him. "Come here."

Every one of the men of The Clan learned *ealaíona comhraic*, Irish martial arts, at St. Albert's, including wrestling, stick fighting, and bare-knuckled boxing. I easily remember what I've been taught. This lad needs a lesson.

I stand casually with my hands on my hips, my eyes on him. He takes one step toward me, looks over his shoulder at Sheena, and when his focus is off me, I make my move. I sweep his leg so he topples over, and in one swift movement, I've got him on the ground, pinned beneath me in the most basic wrestling move I know.

"Get off, motherfucker," Tiernan grunts, but he bears my weight and can't move me.

"You'd rather fight, then?" I ask him. "Trained in boxing, too, have you?"

He blanches when I get off him, and scrambles to his feet. I've spent hours upon hours with my brothers and Malachy learning how to fight. The Irish don't wear gloves but prefer bare fists. My fingers tingle at the memory.

Tiernan heads toward me, his cheeks flaming with anger, but he doesn't assume the stance of a good boxer. I easily duck his blow, and using the flat of my palm, hit him hard on the shoulder. I don't really want to hurt him, I only want to teach him a lesson.

He topples to the ground and comes up raging, and lunges at me. I easily deflect.

"Toe the line, lad."

"What?" he says, shakes his head and attacks again.

I duck his blow, swivel and squat, and when he heads my way I level him with a sharp blow that'll only knock the wind out of him. When he's on the ground, I fall beside him, kneel on his chest, and shake my head.

Sheena doesn't flinch or protest, and that pleases me. She trusts me.

"All you did was take your eyes off me," I say. "You looked away for one second, and it was enough for me to take you down. You call that a fight?" In seconds my knife is in my hand, open, the cold metal against his neck. Sheena gasps but still doesn't move.

I shake my head at him. "One swipe, lad, and the soil's stained with your blood." When he submits with a quiet nod, I release him. He scrambles to his feet, rubbing his neck. He's glaring at me with a look somewhere between fury and admiration.

"You see my point?" I ask.

"Aye," he grunts. "I see your point."

I haven't hurt him, not a bit, only bruised his pride.

I get to my feet and brush the stray bits of grass from my legs.

"Now, walk over to your sister," I order.

This time, he eyes me warily. He's no fool, he's gotten my point. He expects my next move. So when he starts to walk over to her, and I shoot my leg out to trip him, he's ready. He dodges my leg, but still, he's no match for me. I was trained heavily at St. Albert's. Malachy worked us until our eyes blurred with sweat, our bodies were pushed to exhaustion, our muscles ached. We learned to adapt to the pain and sting of bruises, to use open palms to avoid breaking the bones in our hands.

So when he moves to deflect, I easily grab his wrist and pin it to his lower back. He hisses out a breath, but still, I don't hurt him. It's uncomfortable, no doubt, but I have a point to make. This time, it's the cold metal of my gun I press to his temple.

"And that easily again," I say quietly. "You're fucking dead."

"Fine," he says. "Get off me!"

"This is just me, Tiernan," I tell him. "I'm just one man. But you see, up ahead of me? I've got brothers, also armed and trained. Willing to sacrifice their lives for me, bound by honor to do so. One word from me, and you're surrounded." I let my words sink in. "Can you say the same?"

I know he can't. He's alone in this world, one untrained lad against an army. He doesn't stand a chance.

"No," he says, and now his voice is more subdued. I'm afraid he might cry, but he clears his throat and composes himself. "I can't. Now let me go before Fiona loses her damn mind."

I can't help but grin at that. I release him and reach a hand out to him. He takes it and gets to his feet.

"Made my point, then?" I ask him.

He watches me for a moment, then nods his head and runs his fingers through his hair. "Aye," he says. "One question for you, though."

"Yeah?"

"Teach me how you did that?"

Chapter 14

Sheena

FALLING in love with someone is a bit like being mired in quicksand. The harder you pull against it, the more you get sucked in.

My job, my very purpose on this earth, is to find out truth and bring it to light. I've used methods that weren't exactly kosher to do just that, but it doesn't mean that I haven't trained myself to observe things, to note what's important and what isn't. To find what's actually happening versus what appears to be.

And goddamn it, I know. I know in my heart that I'm falling in love with Nolan McCarthy.

I've been lying to myself when I've said that I've hated him. Hell, maybe I did, a little. But love and hate are so closely entwined, both friends on the spectrum of passion. Sometimes all it takes is one tiny action to make the two collide.

Or many actions, as it were.

Beautiful, ardent love-making. The exhilarating, erotic pull of being dominated with a man who does it well. Watching him with my brothers and sister, the way he opens his heart and home. A pair of green eyes that see into my very soul.

I'm falling so deeply in love with Nolan, I'm not sure I'll ever surface. I'm not sure how.

Just now, the way he was with Tiernan… my *heart*.

At first, he lectured the boy with the sternness of an older brother, and he made his point well. I feared he'd hurt him when he first beckoned him over, but I trust him. He didn't. He was careful not to, while he made his point. And the truth is, the lesson he gave my brother was a mercy, given how Tiernan could've fared with what he's done.

Afterward, Tiernan is humbled, and he should be. I can't imagine how I'd have dealt with what he's done if I had to manage him alone. But Nolan did it just right. Tiernan learns best with experience, and being overpowered in seconds by an older, stronger man who didn't even lose his breath, was a humbling experience. After, Nolan reached a hand out to Tiernan, helped him get to his feet, and they talked. I'm not sure what was said, but when they were done, Tiernan was grinning.

"He's fine," Nolan says when he joins me again as we take our last steps to the bakery.

"I know it," I tell him. "I could tell you didn't hurt him."

"Aye. I wouldn't, he's just a lad."

"What did he ask you?"

"Wants to learn *ealaíona comhraic*."

"All of it?" I ask, a bit surprised. The martial arts in Ireland encompasses everything from bare-knuckled fighting to stick fighting.

"Aye."

We enter the bakery, and Nolan walks ahead of me.

I stand a bit away from them, observing the bakery. He smiles, bends to the pram, and wipes whipped cream off baby Sam's nose.

I hated the man I thought he was.

I'm in love with the man he really is.

And hell, where does that leave me? I've done wrong against his family. And I may have many flaws, flaws I know so well they plague me. But if there's anything I am, it's determined. I persevere. And when I resolve to do something, I don't waver.

I should've known better than to trust a *feckin'* O'Gregor. It was more than word of mouth, though. Everything they told me aligned with what I saw, what I believed to be true. But I see now, that I was only looking for a scapegoat. I needed someone to blame, and the McCarthys fit that bill well. And hell, they're not exactly model citizens, so they gave me plenty to work with.

I *hate* that Tiernan's been involved in such dangerous exploits. I'm glad Nolan took him to task for it. A week ago, it would've infuriated me, but I'm starting to trust Nolan. The O'Gregors are nobody to fool around with, damn it. I wonder what else we'll have to deal with because of this.

"Sheena, have some ice cream," Fiona says. She's got a large cone with chocolate, and her eyes are bright and shining. Nolan watches her and the baby, smiling, but he's having a word with his men as well. They're speaking in hushed tones when I approach them.

"Fancy a cone?" Nolan asks me.

I shake my head. "No, thanks. You tell them what we found out?"

"Aye," Nolan says. "They were the ones that told me, doll."

He reaches for my hand, and it feels nice, holding his hand like this.

"And he told me *you're* to be making amends," Lachlan says. Though he's younger than the rest, he carries himself with the air of a much older man. Wise beyond his years, I'd guess. The boy's seen and experienced much. I can't help but wonder what his story is.

"Aye," I tell him. "I will. And when I say I'll do something, I mean it."

"Good," Lachlan says.

"How?" The man with the glasses, the one they call Carson, watches me with his arms crossed on his chest. I hate that none of them trust me, but I hope that I can fix that. He looks familiar to me, and I can't quite place him. I need to investigate, I think.

"First, my job is to vindicate you with the locals," I tell him. "And I will."

"Right," Carson says, his jaw tight as if he doesn't believe me.

Just then, the owner of the shop comes round from the counter and approaches us. She looks a bit like Mrs. Claus with her white hair twisted in a bun at the top of her head and round spectacles perched on her nose.

"I know you," she says looking at me. "You look familiar to me." She screws her face up as if trying to place me.

"Miss Isobel, this is Sheena Hurston." Nolan introduces us, and it's not lost on me how others in the shop watch him. "You probably know her from—"

"Ahh, the reporter." Her eyes grow cold at the realization. It's hard to imagine a jovial, friendly woman like her shooting daggers at someone, yet she manages to pull it off. "I have no use for people who drag the McCarthys through the dirt," she says, turning away, but Nolan reaches for her hand.

"Tell her, Sheena," he says, warning laced in his voice as he looks to me. This is my chance, to prove to him I mean what I say. I swallow, lace my fingers together, and face her. "I've come here to have a little chat with you. I was wrong, before, and I'd like to interview you next week. The purpose is to redeem your friends here. May I?"

She stares at me with wide-eyed surprise, but as my words sink in, she flushes pink. "Oh, well, now," she says. "*Me*? Why would a big news reporter like you interview a woman like me?"

I flash her my most charming smile. I'm aware of Nolan watching me, of Lachlan and Carson as well. I have to prove myself to them.

"I'm sure you've much to tell me," I say. "You've a thriving business in Ballyhock, and I'm told you're good friends with the McCarthys."

She nods, and she grows sober. "Aye, lass. I am. And you ought to know, they keep the people here safe. We've no crime to speak of—"

I stop her. This isn't a good place for us to talk. "Why don't we speak of this privately next week and you can tell me all?"

"Of course," she says with a smile. It's not often people smile at me like that, but I'm starting to like it. No, crave it. It's much nicer to feel welcomed than hated.

My old doubt plagues me. How can I prove myself to be someone that's trustworthy? I've been so mired in revenge that I've lost sight of the good and the light in this world. I've no friends to speak of, and the only people I care about are right here in front of me, sitting at little round tables eating ice cream and scones.

But I will. I will prove they can trust me, goddamn it.

We leave the shop and head into town. I've never really been here before, though I've known of the quaint little places to go in Ballyhock. The coastal village draws tourists from around the world, and thrives on the business they do. I walk with Fiona on my left and Nolan my right, as we walk the cobblestoned streets until Sam's head falls to the side in the pram, and he naps.

Tiernan's much more subdued after Nolan had a word. To be honest, it's the first time since dad passed I've seen anything that resembles a boyish look about him as he chatters away to Nolan.

"Best place to go would be the school," Nolan says. "We've the tools, the studio, and the teachers there."

"Wait, what's this?" I ask.

"I've asked Nolan to teach me ealaíona comhraic," Tiernan says. "He's a feckin' master at it, I want to learn."

"He said that. Are you sure, Tiernan?"

They've been kind, yes. But kindness aside, this troubles me. If Tiernan gets involved with them…

227

"I've some concerns, Nolan," I say to him. "We've borrowed your home and taken up your time. I can't ask that you spend even more time teaching Tiernan."

Not only that, it scares me to think of my brother being involved in anything dangerous.

Nolan shrugs. "He's got a good head, Sheena. He's brave and strong, and would do well to learn the skills we can teach him."

"You have time?"

"We can make it."

"Right," I tell him. "But…" I don't know how else to state my concerns.

We don't belong here. They owe us nothing. I have to do my job, then we'll be on our way. *Somehow.*

He tugs me closer to him, and I'm overwhelmed with his strong, clean smell, woodsmoke and leather. He laces his fingers around the back of my neck and smiles, though he has a glint in his eyes I know too well.

"What are you afraid of, doll?" he asks. "There's fear in your eyes you can't hide. Are you afraid he'll get hurt?"

"Well, no," I tell him. "But yes. Yes, I am."

He smiles. "He might, but it'll only make him stronger. We've all been trained, and it was for the best."

"I just… it concerns me to see that my brothers and sister are… are growing attached, as it were. But we can't do that, can't form these attachments, you see."

Nolan's jaw firms. "And why's that?"

"Because we don't belong here," I tell him. "You know it, Nolan. You have a family. There's no room for us here. I have to do my job then get out of your hair. And that means taking them with me."

I watch as his jaw grows rigid. I know that look. "And that's your decision, then, is it?"

I shake my head. I'm not sure what to say, how to argue my point. "I didn't say it was, Nolan. But we've brought trouble here. Between my mother and my brother and *me*. And… the sooner we get out of your hair, the better."

We're back at the house. Lachlan and Carson go their way, and Maeve is waiting for us in the entryway. I wonder if she waited for us. If she did, that's admittedly sort of cute. I wish I hadn't let myself grow to hate her, when it seems she's done nothing wrong at all.

If Nolan loves her… can I?

"Dinner's ready," she says. "Will you be joining us, then?"

A newly awake Sam reaches his arms for her, and she smiles, bends, and lifts him up.

"No," Nolan says. "Not tonight. Have them fed and

see what they need," he says. "Tiernan, you'll go with me to St. Albert's at the weekend. Aye?"

Tiernan's eyes brighten and he grins, actually *grins* at Nolan. My heart… *God*, my heart. I'm so used to steeling myself against this type of thing, of not letting myself become vulnerable, but Nolan does every single thing to rip down every damn barricade I've put up.

"Sheena and I need some time alone, to talk of a few things," he says. He draws himself up to his full height, and I swear it seems he fills the whole damn room. His eyes cut to mine, sharp and stern, and his jaw firms. "Don't we, lass?"

Do we?

When he looks at me like that, his voice hard, the power he holds emanating from his very pores, I'm done for.

I'm not Sheena Hurston the investigative reporter, or the girl who fought her way out of misery and made a life for herself.

I'm a melty, boneless, puddle of goo.

"Aye," I say, my voice husky, betraying the excitement and nerves that pulse through my body.

"Right, then," Maeve says. "Off we go."

Heated voices rise in the direction of the dining room. Nolan looks that way, then shakes his head and looks back to me.

"Something you need to tend to?"

"Oh, there's something I need to tend to," he says with meaning. He tugs me by the hand to the stairs.

"I mean in the other room. Is everything okay?"

He snorts. "Course it is. Haven't you been around these men of The Clan long enough to know? We're brothers. Hardly a few days go by without one or two of them having a tussle. Just the way it goes."

But he's lying. He does want to find out what's going on.

"Still, I can tell you want to investigate."

"Aye," he says, when we reach the landing. "I do, and I will, but by the time I've got *you* sorted, they likely will have sorted themselves out anyway."

"I'm not so sure I need sorting out," I begin to protest. With a shake of his head, he gives me a tug so I'm in front of him, then slams his palm against my backside, a firm but teasing smack I feel straight to my sex.

"Oh, but you do."

"Not sure what I've done," I say. "And what do you mean by—"

He's pinned me up against the wall before I can finish my sentence, the hard length of his cock rigid against my belly. I can't breathe, I can't speak, my heart taps a crazy beat in my chest. His large, rough hand cups my jaw, and he holds my eyes with his.

"Quiet, lass," he says. "I've given you freedom. I've

let you do what you need to. But you'll be wise to remember that here, you belong to me."

I swallow and take a deep breath in, then nod. "Aye, sir."

He lowers his hand from my jaw to my neck. His rough, callused palm makes me shiver when he grips my neck and tightens his hold. "Good answer," he breathes in my ear. "No more questions, Sheena. We'll have dinner in my room tonight. You won't leave my room without permission. In fact, you'll do nothing else this evening without my permission."

"Yes, sir," I repeat, a little dizzy and lightheaded.

He's either impatient, or feels like he needs to prove his point, for he bends and lifts me straight up into his arms.

"My shoe!" I protest, reaching fruitlessly for the little flat that fell straight off my foot.

"Leave it," he says. "We'll get it later."

My arms encircle his neck as he marches with purposeful strides.

"You should drag a club," I mutter, and the next thing I know I'm over his *shoulder,* kicking my legs and scrambling for purchase. He slams his palm on my backside again.

"Should drag *you,*" he says. "By the goddamn hair."

"And pound your chest and call me *woman*? Monosyllabic grunts might make communication easier to—ow!"

Another hard and punishing smack. I squirm, and I also shut up.

I'm not exactly sure what's in his mind, or what he's planning, but I think I'm about to be punished, and I'm not exactly broken up about that.

He opens the door to his room, slams it behind him, and still, I'm over his shoulder. When we reach the bedroom, he slides me down his body and plants me on the floor in front of him, while he drags a chair over and sits heavily on it.

I know what he's doing a split second before I land belly-down over his knee.

"Now, wait a minute," I protest.

"Quiet."

He's no longer teasing, all traces of humor gone.

I'm quiet. I'm turned on. I'm curious and also a little... humbled.

I've never been with a man who handles me like he does, with uncompromising sternness. But it isn't just his unapologetic dominant ways that undo me. There's so much more.

He drags down the top of my leggings, grabs the elastic of my knickers, then peels them down my legs until he gets to my feet. My sex pulses, my body heating at his touch, at the anticipation of the loss of control and measured pain. One shoe remains, and that's easily dealt with. He bends, removes first one foot from my leggings, then the other, until I'm stripped from the waist down and dangling over his lap.

He pats my arse, then grips one cheek in his massive hand and gives it a hard squeeze.

"Ohh, ouch!" I protest. That only spurs him on to grab the second cheek and give that a good squeeze as well.

"Now," he says. "We talk."

My sex throbs with need, but even as my body responds to his mastery over me, crazy emotions rise to the surface.

"Okay, then," I say, trying to hold onto a shred of dignity. Spoiler alert? It doesn't work. I'm half naked, dangling over his knee, clearly about to get my arse spanked.

"So let me get this clear," he says. You came here because you thought us responsible for your father's death."

Well, that ones's easy. "Yes."

He pats my arse. "Good. And let's get *this* clear. You have it in your head that you're a nuisance to us, that you're in our hair, and you have to pack up and go."

"Also, yes."

"And that, lass, is where you're wrong."

I squeal when his large palm crashes against my upturned backside. "Ow!"

"Furthermore," he continues. "You think I've taken you from the club, brought you here to interrogate and question, and that you'll just waltz your way right back out of my life, do you?"

There's no right answer to this question, and I'm determined to tell the truth, so with my eyes squeezed tight, I nod. "Aye."

He gives me three more uncompromising spanks before he speaks again.

"Can't you see what's happening? What's *happened*?" he asks.

I answer honestly. "No."

He spanks me again.

"Hey! I told you the truth."

"I spanked you for not seeing it."

"You can't do that!"

I scissor my legs when he gives me another three hard, searing spanks. "Clearly, lass, I *can*."

He rests his palm on my flaming hot arse. "Now, Sheena, I do believe I've got your attention. Don't I?"

I squirm but nod my head. "Aye, clearly." My entire body's at full attention.

"Good. Now listen to me," he says. "You've brought your brothers and sister to my home. We brought them here for protection. There were misunderstandings, and we've much to sort out. But they like it here, and we like having them here. And if you think I'll let you waltz into my life, then take those children and yourself and waltz right back out again? Then you deserve this."

That's when the spanking he gives me begins in earnest. I can't breathe or speak, as his hand falls. He slows down, adjusts me, and lets me have it.

It hurts, but nothing worse than I've had before. There's more to it than that, though. I thought he broke down my walls before, but this... this is something else altogether.

He cares about me. He cares about us. Against all odds, he's forgiven my transgressions against his family, and won't let me run.

I've run all my life. It's what I do. I run from anything that hurts, and letting someone care about me... goddamn it, letting someone *love* me... it could bring the very worst pain of all.

I'm sniffing and resigned, draped over his knee, when he finally stops and lifts me to his lap. My spanked bottom burns against the rough fabric of his trousers as he holds me, drags me to his chest, and kisses me so fiercely I can't breathe. The salty taste of my tears invades the kiss, as he holds the back of my head. Then we're up and I'm in his arms, and we're heading to the bed.

He lays me down on my back, and watches my eyes.

"Will you run, Sheena?"

I shake my head from side to side. "No, sir. No, I won't."

"Good lass," he says with approval, his words like salve to my wounded soul.

He's taking off his clothes, but his eyes don't leave mine.

"Will you hold yourself back from me?"

A part of me wants to run and hide, to bury the parts of me I show no one. But I can be brave. I *can*.

I shake my head. "No, sir. I won't, I promise, even if it kills me."

He bends and tangles his fingers through my hair. "Lass, I won't ever lie to you. You're a hard woman to love, Sheena Hurston. You need someone willing to break down the fortress you keep yourself in. This is no rescue, doll." He strips while he talks, and I watch him grip my hips as he lines his thick, swollen cock at my entrance. "This is plundering. Ravaging. Taking home the spoils of war."

It's a battle of hearts in which there are two victors.

Without preamble, he thrusts into me. I moan. I love that he knows I need him right now, to fill me, to take me, to unite us together. He builds a rhythm that sends spasms of pleasure rippling through me, my heart pounding harder with every perfect, powerful thrust.

"And you, Sheena, are worth it." He thrusts again,

as he claims me, takes me. "I'll fight for you. I'll take you on. I'll make you mine."

That does it, goddamn it. I'm no more able to stop my heart from joining his than I am to stop the tide. I'm swept under, swallowed by waves of longing.

"I love you," he says with a grin, like he needs to say this as badly as I need to hear it. "You're impossible and headstrong and you've got a smart mouth to boot."

I do, I don't deny any of it.

"Is that right?" I ask on a moan. "And *you,* sir, are bossy as fuck and sexy as hell."

He thrusts so hard I might split in two. "And that's exactly what you need," he counters.

"Aye," I say, my voice cracking from the need that suffuses me as my heart threatens to burst. "'Tis. I'll give my everything to you, Nolan McCarthy. There's no other man in the world who knows me like you do." He bends and his forehead meets mine. My voice wavers but I don't stop. Now that I've started, I can't. "There's no other man who's seen the ugliest side of me and still... and still..." I can't finish. I close my eyes and moan, as he comes inside me, and I explode with pleasure. I'm at his mercy as spasms of ecstasy wash over me.

We join our release as one. I entwine my arms around him as our movements slow.

"Finish the sentence, Sheena," he pants. "And still..."

I close my eyes because it's too much. I can't hold him and surrender to him, and look him in the eyes all at once.

At least I don't think I can, not at first.

But I'm tired of hiding behind my anger and vengeance. With effort, I open my eyes and look at him. "And still loves me," I finish.

He grins, that heart-stopping, panty-soaking grin that melts me, every time. "Aye, doll," he says. "And still loves you."

Chapter 15

Nolan

I'VE NEVER BEEN the brother that follows the rules like everyone else. I've never been the one who does what's expected, what's tradition.

Keenan brought home a woman, a captive, as it were, but he was heir to the throne and needed a wife.

Cormac bowed to the will of The Clan, the expectations and code we adhere to. As such, he agreed to an arranged marriage.

They did things the way they were expected to.

Figures, then, that I'd fall in love with our enemy. The men of The Clan don't do this, not even close. Anyone who threatens the livelihood of The Clan faces certain and severe punishment. I've known this since I was little, still clinging to my mother's skirts. Though she sheltered me from some, I knew even then that we've laws we abide by.

But I can't help but love Sheena. Hell, I think I've been attracted to her since the first time I met her, years ago at The Craic. I can still remember how she looked, her gorgeous hair all twisted in some sort of up-do, dangling silver earrings hanging at her ears, dressed in a shiny black dress that could've been painted on her.

It seems so long ago.

I watched her from a distance at the club, unable to take my eyes off her. A man came up to her, said something in her ear, and she turned her back to him. He reached for her shoulder and yanked her over to him. I was on my feet, ready to break his neck, before any of the security officers even knew what was happening.

She shoved him off, and I could see it happening before it did. Pricks like him get angrier when women get aggressive. He came at her again. Before I even knew what I was doing, I'd decked him so hard he flew backward onto the bar, glasses crashing to the floor.

"Come at *me*, motherfucker," I told him, taking the stance I was taught, prepared for the attack. He did. We fucking brawled, but my brothers were there, bore witness. He was hauled away, and Sheena bought me a drink.

We made small talk, and I liked her at once. Witty and intelligent, beautiful and intriguing. Then she saw my ink, something hidden under my shirt sleeve until I reached for the bar tab.

"I know who you are," she said, and everything changed.

And so it began, years of her pursuing us and my keeping her at bay. Years of her angering me so much it felt like an answer to my prayers when I finally got my hands on her. Years of sexual tension that throbbed between us like the beating of a heart.

But I knew… somehow, I knew that if I got behind that tough exterior of hers, I'd strike gold. And I have. Christ, but I have.

The days pass quicker than I expect. I watch her with Tiernan, giving him the guidance he needs and the space to be himself. She was angry with him for his involvement with the O'Gregors, but also real-ized that he only did what she did herself—compro-mised her values to protect her family.

I watch her with Fiona and Sam, the doting sister who loves them so much she'd give all of herself to them if she could. And she tries. I pull her back some, under the guise of her being my prisoner. We both know it's only an excuse.

I call her to me because I like when she submits, not because I expect it. I keep her by my side not only to protect her, but because it's where she belongs. It feels right. And any man who's won a woman over knows that when a brilliant, feisty, headstrong woman relinquishes any part of herself to you,

you've earned it. The gift of submission from a woman like Sheena is the crowning fucking victory.

We've been watching for news of the O'Gregors uprising, and until recently, we've heard nothing. It's not a good silence, though, and it doesn't put us at ease. We're all skilled enough to know that it's only the calm before the storm.

We keep as close an eye on the most vulnerable among us as we can. The women and the little ones are kept under constant guard. No one goes to the shops or beyond the cliffs that overlook the sea right outside our windows. A solid week's gone by without a word from the O'Gregors when Keenan calls a meeting.

I leave Sheena with Fiona and mam in the garden. Sheena's taking a call from her employer. She's eager to get back to work, and has been doing her research just like she promised us, but she's extended her leave for a bit while she prepares.

The inner circle assembles inside the meeting room. Boner meets me at the door, bouncing on the balls of his feet with pent-up energy. He grins when he sees me.

"Haven't seen you at The Craic, lately, brother." he says, while the others enter.

Tully lumbers in behind him, so much larger than Boner he dwarfs him. He pounds him on the back with a grin and Boner nearly topples over. "You got eyes in your head, lad? Why would he go to the club when he's got sweet pussy tied to his bed of an evening?"

My hands clench into fists, and I don't realize I'm stepping toward Tully until Lachlan grabs me from behind and holds me to his chest to keep me from killing Tully.

"Easy, brother," Lachlan says in my ear. "Keenan's coming in. He'll kick both yer arses if you fight before a meeting like this."

Tully's eyes widen in surprise. "Jesus, Nolan, didn't mean to piss you off like that. I'm sorry. Just giving you crap."

I shake Lachlan off and step toward Tully. "You'll watch your fucking mouth. You talk about Sheena like that again, I'll knock your fucking teeth out." And I mean it. My hands shake with rage, and I swear to God my vision's blurry and hazy with it.

"Nolan." Keenan's sharp voice comes from the door. I bite my tongue, keeping myself in check with effort. All the men stare at us, likely prepared to interfere if we come to blows.

"My bad, Keenan," Tully says. "Made an offhand comment about his girl."

His girl.

Keenan shakes his head. "Are you that tone deaf, Tully?" he says, as he enters the room and heads for his desk. "You say anything about Sheena to Nolan again, I'll give leave for Nolan to beat your arse right here, right now."

Cormac snorts, kicks back in a chair, and laces his hands behind his head, his muscles bulging as he stares down Tully. "And I'll hold you down while he does."

Tully holds his hands up in surrender, "Alright lads, alright, you'll hear nothing but respect out of my mouth when it comes to her." He mutters under his breath. *"Mother of God."*

"Take a seat, lads," Keenan says, giving us all a look that's so much like my father it's almost eerie. He likely knows it's harder to get into a knock-down fight if we're sitting.

"Tell me this, though," Tully says. He crosses his arms on his chest and addresses Keenan. "Since when did the girl who tried to destroy us become off limits?"

I regret not decking him.

Keenan eyes him levelly, leaning forward with his fists on the desk.

"Since my brother took her as his own."

They hold each other's gazes for a moment. I've had enough.

"You all know that Sheena Hurston thought us guilty of the death of her father. Think on it, boys. You know as well as I do we'd have done the same," I say.

Tully looks away and doesn't respond, but Carson

245

nods his head. He's a quiet sort, but when he speaks, we pay attention.

"Aye," he says. "It's clear, isn't it?"

The overhead light glints on his glasses. He pushes them up on his nose and eyes the room. "If she thought us responsible for her father's death, she wouldn't handle things the way we would. One woman, against a whole clan of men? 'Tisn't physical methods of retaliation she'd seek, but another way."

"Aye," Lachlan says. "Can't say it doesn't piss me off some even now, but I've watched her since the meeting with Father Finn. And the woman's stood by her word. She's interviewed the locals and contacted her friends in the media. Haven't you all seen the various articles that've come out?."

"I have," I say quietly. I want to hear what they all have to say before I speak my mind. It's telling.

"Same," Cormac says. "Aileen was pleased as fucking punch reading the article about the donations to the schools. Says the articles almost made us seem like celebrities."

Keenan smirks. "Going to pay the school a visit for a celebrity reading, then, Cormac?"

"Feck off," Cormac says with a grin.

Keenan looks to me. "Nolan, any word on when she'll return to work? I haven't heard anything about her reporting lately. You?"

"Aye," I tell him. "She was on leave, as it were, doing her investigation. And she was supposed to return this week, but I asked her not to."

Keenan raises a brow but doesn't speak.

"Too risky," I tell him. "Not when we don't have a handle on the O'Gregors."

"Right," Keenan says.

"So her boss has given her permission to report from where she is. They're in regular contact. She hasn't shown her face, but she's given him stories. They work closely with the paper as well."

Keenan nods. "Very good. Aye, even Caitlin, who doesn't like attention, was pleased with some of the more recent articles and news coverage. So what do we know about the status of their mother?"

I shake my head. "Nothing. We've tried to find out what we could, but there's nothing at all."

"She been killed, then?" Lachlan asks.

I cringe at his words, though I know it likely true. I wonder how her mother's death would impact Sheena. Sheena hates her, and I don't blame her based on what I've heard myself, but the woman's still her mother. And her loss will impact... well, damn near all of us.

"I don't know," I tell him. "But it wouldn't surprise me."

"Anyone been in touch with the police?"

"Aye," Lachlan says. "Just this morning. Walsh says he's heard nothing from the O'Gregors at all. Thinks it isn't good news, though, that they're planning something big."

Cormac groans. "Fucking figures."

Keenan shrugs. "Nothing new, though, brothers. They've been on us for years. So now they have an excuse to retaliate? They've wanted a piece of what we have since we buried dad."

"Aye," Tully says. "'Tis true."

Alright, then, so I forgive both of them. They had a chance to throw me under the bus, and they didn't.

"Nolan," Keenan says. "Tell us what you've planned to do with the lot of them, then. Have you thought about this?"

I take in a deep breath, my chest rising, then falling as I exhale. I nod, meeting Keenan straight in the eye. "Aye," I tell him. "To be honest, I like having them here. Brings a certain softness about things, doesn't it, having children around?"

"Aye," Cormac says. He's changed since he's become a father himself. "They aren't family, though," he says, and he isn't wrong. "Is it safe for us?"

"That's the problem, isn't it?" Keenan asks. "It's one thing to have a flat right here on our property, to be part of the clan by blood. But it's another to be brought here as guests. You know we're safe here, all of us. With our location, the safety measurements in place, aye… we're as safe as can be. But with them not being family…"

"And we know now that her brother was involved with the O'Gregors, don't we?"

Keenan knew this. I told him first thing, after I found out. Not everyone else did, though. There's murmurs and curses as the others realize our predicament.

"Yes, we do," I tell them. "I've questioned him at length. He's had no contact since he came here, and Lachlan and I are confident he's no spy."

"Sure he isn't," Lachlan says. "Hell, truth be told, I think he'd be a fine asset for us to have. If we enrolled him at St. Albert's like you did me, the lad's got what it takes to be a brother of The Clan."

Keenan raises his brows heavenward. "Really, Lachlan?"

Lachlan doesn't back down. "Aye."

"I've thought so myself," I tell them. "I've been teaching him at the weekend. Boxing, fighting, wrestling, and damn, he's a quick study. He's got a temper like his sister's, but you know… well, tempers can be sorted. Can't they, Lachlan?"

Lachlan gives me a sheepish grin. It took time for us to help him learn to control his temper, but he's mastered it now.

Boner snorts, and Cormac shakes his head, rolling his eyes to the ceiling.

"Honestly, though, I trust him. He isn't with them anymore."

Keenan nods. "Aye. Agreed. But you know, Nolan."

He's got that look in his eyes I've seen before. The one I've learned to heed, because he's hatching some sort of plan.

"We *could* move things along with the O'Gregors, couldn't we?"

Foreboding roots in my belly at his words. I'm no fool. I know how these things go. Any plan at all that would "move things along" with the O'Gregors would likely endanger Sheena.

"How so?" I ask, my voice tight with apprehension.

The room stills as Keenan strokes his chin. "The O'Gregors were responsible for the death of Sheena's father. We know that now."

"Aye," I say.

"We further know that they're planning retaliation, because we've set foot on their territory and assaulted one of theirs. And, the complication with Tiernan."

"Aye," I repeat.

"We know they're likely suspicious because her brother's on our property now. Think of the danger that puts him in. If they think he was a spy for us, the second he sets foot off our property, he's endangered as well."

I nod. I don't like where this is going, not one bit.

"There's not a doubt in my mind that they're planning something. Are you men in agreement?"

Murmurs of assent go up around us. Even I find myself nodding. Yes. Yes, of course they will.

"I don't like this game," Keenan says. "Lying in wait, as it were, waiting for the rattler to strike. Anxious for the sound of his rattle."

"I agree," I tell him. He's right, and hell, Tiernan and Sheena are made of sterner stuff than the others even know. I hate the idea of leaving this property and going somewhere else, but it has to be done. "We need to bring them out of hiding, then."

Keenan looks to me, and his eyes are sympathetic. He knows what it's like to love someone, how you want to wrap them up and keep them safe, and protect them from the dangers that lurk outside your door. How you want to shield them from anyone and anything that could bring them harm.

But it doesn't work that way. Love isn't about control, or capture, and can never be brought about by force. Love is about letting them go, so they can spread their wings... and fly back to you. Freely.

"Do you have a plan, Nolan?" Cormac asks quietly. His eyes meet mine, and like Keenan's, I see sympathy behind his gaze. My heart squeezes. I know then, like I've known before but now I *feel* down to my bones, these men would lay down their lives for me. They'd follow me through fire, would give up everything out of loyalty, integrity, and the love of the brotherhood.

I swallow, and my voice is a little husky when I nod my head. "Haven't worked out the details, yet, but I have an idea." I face Keenan but address the room. "Help me do this."

"I'll do whatever you need me to," Keenan says. "You have my word, Nolan."

"And mine," Boner says.

"And mine," Tully grunts.

"Goes without saying, mine, too. He's my brother, you pricks. Don't one-up me," Cormac mutters.

"Mine, too," Carson says with a smile, and Lachlan shakes his head.

"Always making me look like the twat, eh? Mine, too, but it'll cost you."

I punch his shoulder but he easily deflects.

"A fucking *pint,* brother, not your little redheaded firstborn," he says.

We settle down, talk out our options. And we make our plan.

Chapter 16

Sheena

WE'RE out in the garden, surrounded by a sea of green leaves and grass, the sun beating down overhead, and for one brief moment in time, I try to hold onto this.

I've gotten to a place in my life where I don't expect good things, like family, and peace, laughter and joy. The comforts of home and a good meal prepared for me and served amidst the companionship of others. And here, at the McCarthy household, they have that, every damn day.

And I want that so badly it makes me ache inside. But it isn't just me I'm thinking about.

When I see baby Sam smile at Maeve, the way his dimpled arms reach for her and he toddles her way… she smiles at him and bends to lift him, tucks him against her chest and kisses the curls on his head, swaying back and forth as if he brings joy to her heart… I want that for him. He's had me and Fiona and Tiernan, and for that I'm grateful. But he's a burden to mum. She doesn't delight in him the way Maeve does, and dammit… little babies ought to have someone who delights in them.

When I see Fiona's eyes light up at dinner, when she speaks animatedly to anyone and everyone who'll listen, when she walks the grounds of the compound and tucks wildflowers in her hair… I want this for her. The safety and security of a family that will protect her, so she's free to grow with grace from childhood to womanhood.

When I see Tiernan learning the skills the men teach him, sparring with Nolan or Lachlan, I see the man he's going to become. He takes pride in a job well done, and I haven't seen that light in his eyes since… well, since dad died, really. And being around these men, who treat him like a brother, has been good for him. The hardened edges to his jaw and eyes soften when he's in their company. He's learning loyalty and friendship, self-confidence, and bravery.

I want this for them. Family and friends. Security and comfort.

But I can't expect that it's the McCarthy family that can give them any of that permanently.

"Penny for your thoughts?"

Damn, it's hard to doubt things when Nolan comes up behind me. He slips a hand to the small of my back, his touch at once warm and possessive.

"Oh, nothing," I lie, but my words stick in my throat. I've built a fortress of protection with my lies, and I hate that I've let that happen. No matter what it takes, I have to stop it. I have to speak the truth to get the future I want.

"Not *nothing*, Sheena," he says, a hard edge to his voice that tells me he knows I'm hiding something. Why is it that he can see straight through me? "Something's on your mind, doll."

"Many things are on my mind, Nolan," I tell him truthfully, though I know I'm being evasive.

He nods, accepting the answer. I exhale in relief. I don't want him to know how badly my heart breaks for the children in front of us. How much I long to give them comfort and security and the home they need when this eventually ends.

Even if I could bring them all home… I wouldn't be able to give them *this*.

"How did your interview go?" he asks, but his eyes are distant, and he doesn't look at me when he speaks, like he's hiding something. He's turned away from me, a distant look in his eyes that tells me he's troubled. I look at him curiously. I've learned to read his body language well.

"Went well," I tell him. Several of the local towns-people had nothing but good things to say about the McCarthys. My campaign to vindicate their name's gone so well, better than I could have hoped. "Article will come over the weekend, and my boss wants me to return to work the following week."

He nods. "Good," he says, but it's again a distant sort of comment. He isn't really here, but some-where else.

And then he drops a bomb.

"It's time we move them off the property, Sheena," he says.

I don't respond at first.

Did he just say what I think he did?

I swallow hard. "Who?" I ask stupidly.

He sighs and jerks his chin to the children before us. "Things have changed. We're going to have to move them somewhere else."

His voice is tight, and he won't meet my eyes when he says it.

Even though logically I know what he says is true, my head goes to a place it shouldn't. I should trust him more, but I'm immediately rejected, cast out, and it hurts so badly I can't breathe at first.

I knew this, that we can't stay here forever… I know it still… and yet I can't bear to think about it.

"I know they can't," I say, my voice taking on the

hardened edge I can't help when I'm hurt. "But I'm not sure where to take them."

And the question that plagues me… if I take them away…will that be the end for the two of us?

I never even let myself give voice to my fears. That I'm not good enough. That he can't possibly love someone who's treated him the way I have. That no man in his right mind would want anything to do with a woman saddled with *three* children, no less. And that even if none of those factors were at play… he's the pillar of the Irish mob.

We can't be together. The logical part of my brain knows this, even as my heart breaks.

I nod, because I can't trust my voice.

I step away from him, because I don't want him to touch me right now. I can't. I won't.

"Sheena—"

He's calling me, but I ignore him. I don't want him to see me cry. I don't want any of them to. Maeve looks up as I walk by, and her eyes meet mine. I look away too quickly. She's too empathic, too sensitive… I don't want to see my pain mirrored in her eyes.

Wordlessly, I reach for Sam, who's now toddling on the ground beside her. I lift him and bring him to my chest, holding him as tightly as I can without hurting him.

"Sheena?"

Fiona stands a bit away. When I don't respond, she jogs up to me.

"We have to go," I say to her.

Nolan comes up on my left.

"Sheena, would you stop a minute. Honest to God," he mutters. *"Stop."*

My heartbeat spikes. I've learned to obey that tone of voice. With a sigh, I stop, take in a deep breath, and look to him. His green eyes flash beneath drawn brows, and his hands are anchored on his hips.

"Where are you going to?"

I stare at him dumbly. I don't answer, because I don't know what to say. I have no answer, because I don't know *where* I'm going.

"What do you mean? Where are we going?" Fiona asks. She looks from me to him, and her lower lip quivers. I can't look at her.

"We can't stay here," I tell her. "The McCarthys were nice enough to take us in, to make us feel welcome, but we can't stay here, Fiona."

"We're going back to your home in Stone City until we can find a place to stay," Nolan says.

Wait. We?

I turn to him. "Ah, no. I have no interest in going back to that place. You know it isn't safe there, Nolan. And anyway, they can stay with me."

He said we.

He raises a brow. "We need to talk privately, Sheena. You didn't give me a chance to tell you everything."

I'm still fired up, still nervous about where all this is going, so I almost tell him no. That we've got this, thank you very much. But instead, I nod. I'll at least let him talk to me. We walk ahead to a clump of trees, shading us from the overhead sun.

"First of all, calm down," he says, which does literally nothing to calm me down. "Second of all, *listen*."

"Why do you think I came over here? Of course I'm listening."

His eyes narrow on me before he leans in and growls in my ear. "I've got half a mind to toss you over my knee right here in the garden to make you hear reason. You're infuriating sometimes, you know that?"

"Takes one to know one," I mutter. "You're no walk in the park, Nolan McCarthy!"

"Impossible woman!" Baby Sam clings to me, and Nolan looks instantly remorseful.

He inhales, then exhales slowly before he speaks. "We won't lie in wait for the O'Gregors anymore. We want to bring them out of hiding, fight them head on."

I frown, but nod. What does this have to do with us leaving?

"They won't come here on our property. We're too heavily guarded here, and they know they don't stand a chance. They will, however, attack if they think we're vulnerable."

I really should listen more before I jump to conclusions, but sometimes I can't help the way I react. It's self-defense, really.

"I'll go with you," he says.

"Do we have to go back to that home, though, Nolan? It damn near gives me anxiety attacks being back there, I hate it so."

"We do, but you won't be alone. I'll be with you. Carson found a nearby home that's unoccupied, only a few doors down. My brothers will be there, prepared to help us. We just have to be discreet about it and it shouldn't take long. We've planted the news that you'll be coming back. We don't want them knowing we're lying in wait."

I think over this plan. "We won't draw them out as easily if we were at my place, then?"

He shakes his head. "No."

He steps a little closer to me and places his hand on my arm. His touch is warm and reassuring. "You can do this, Sheena. And after this... after we've ended this threat to my family and yours... you and I will talk about the next step we take together."

Reluctant hope blooms in my heart as I listen to what he has to say. But I've been through too much to really believe there are happily-ever-afters for a girl like me. So I don't think of it. I only nod. "Okay, then. Let's do it. But Fiona and Tiernan are old enough to know why we're doing this."

"Aye," he says. "But so help me, Sheena, I'm not going to fight you every step of the way and drag you along with me."

Sam starts to fuss a little, so I sway with him on my hip. "Shhh," I whisper to him, while I nod to Nolan. "I know it. You're like your brothers. Remember, my job is to observe details, isn't it?"

He gives me a crooked grin that melts my heart. "Aye."

"And I'm well aware that you won't fight me. You'd just as soon manhandle me into submission."

He shrugs.

I clear my throat and gather up my courage. "But that won't be necessary."

He gives me a wary look. "Right." He doesn't believe me.

"What?"

"You want me to believe that you won't fight me, then?"

"Well…" my voice trails off because I'm not exactly sure how to tell him the truth. *Can* I? "I'll try my best," I finally say. There must be something about my expression that amuses him, for he laughs out loud and shakes his head.

"Let's take this one step at a time, then. First, we

move them to your mother's home. We get things set up. Then we take step two. No step two until step one is complete. Listen, Sheena. We need to draw the O'Gregors out. The plan is for us to set up in the family home in Stone City, but once we've sorted everything with the O'Gregors, we'll move them to your place, or…" his voice trails off and he works his jaw.

"Or what?"

His eyes come back to mine. "Or, we find a place together."

"We?" I ask. "We who?"

"All of us," he says. "You, Tiernan, Fiona, Sam. And me."

He isn't saying this. Is he? But I mask the hope that rises in me, because I'm afraid if I move too quickly, this dream will vanish.

"What about my mother?" I ask

He hesitates before he responds. "I don't think she'll prove a threat."

I breathe out in relief. "Right, then. Aye. I can do this, yes."

"Good," he says, reaching for baby Sam. Sam leans over and lets Nolan take him, then nestles against his hip. I wonder if taking the baby is a power move, because my body responds of its own accord whenever he's got the baby. I can't help but swoon a little. I can't think of any of this now, because

Fiona's gone off to find Tiernan and both of them are approaching us now.

We've got to sort this out.

But move back to the family home?

The very thought makes me nauseous.

Chapter 17

Nolan

I EXPECTED Sheena to fight me. I had a plan in place, and was prepared for her to balk, to resist going back to the childhood home she despises.

But I never expected *mam* to put up such a fuss.

"I don't know about this, Nolan," she says, following us into the house when we go to pack their things. She's heard the plan from someone, and now she's following after me and Sheena on a mission.

"It's the only way," I tell her, not meeting her eyes. Keenan's just coming out of the office when he sees us enter. He looks from her to me and watches in silence.

"The only way?" she says. Her eyes flash at me, and

she throws her hands up in the air. "The only *way*?" Her voice cracks a little. She's gone full on mama bear. "The problem is, it isn't safe for them there. You know it isn't."

I sigh. "I'll be with them," I say. "They won't be alone."

"Doesn't matter," she protests. "You against those ruthless men? I know how they are. Don't forget, I grew up among the likes of those men. I know what they're capable of."

I try to be patient, but I don't have time for this. "I know that. But listen, we have our reasons for what we have to do."

"You always do," she says, her voice shaking. "Every decision we make comes down to this, doesn't it?"

"Down to what?" I ask with a sigh. Keenan watches me from the door but still says nothing.

"The good of *The Clan*," she says. "Always. It doesn't matter if it's good for anyone else, does it?"

I think before I answer her. Her heart is the very life of our brotherhood, our home, our family. I have a job to do and I'm tempted to dismiss her protests, but I can't do that, not when she's given so much to all of us. So I take in a deep breath, then let it out slowly, to calm myself before I speak to her.

"Mam," I say, as gently as I can. "Yes. It does, and you know it. It doesn't mean that others have to suffer for our sakes. It does mean we have to make decisions that will solidify and strengthen the brotherhood. If The Clan is attacked, or weakened in any way, you know the devastation that brings to countless others."

She scoffs, but I know her resolve is weakening when she turns away from me and won't meet my eyes.

"He's right, Maeve." Sheena's says. "I ought to know. I once thought, not so long ago, mind, that all of you McCarthys were as guilty as the others. And I won't argue they're the Robin Hoods of Ballyhock. But I do know that without the McCarthy Clan's strength, the other Clans in Ireland may come to power. And we can't have that."

Mam sighs and looks away. She bites her lip, but nods. "I know it," she finally says sadly. "But you don't know what it's like, Sheena. To see the ones you love put themselves in harm's way, every damn day. 'Tis like seeing my sons go to war on the frontline with no hope of it coming to an end."

Sheena nods with sympathy. "I can imagine. Knowing how it felt to walk away from my brothers and sister and leave them in the state I did."

Lachlan steps forward from behind Keenan and clears his throat. "Now that we've had our little family chat about feelings and all, perhaps we can move on to more pressing things?" He scrubs a hand across his brow. "Haven't been to the gym in a few days, and goddamn I'd love to kick some O'Gregor arse already."

Mam shakes her head. "Impossible, the lot of you," she says, heading for the stairs. She speaks over her shoulder to Sheena. "I'll pack up baby Sam's things and make sure he's got his special blankie and toys." She turns to Lachlan. "And *you*. Watch that mouth of yours in front of the baby."

He looks suitably abashed. "Sorry 'bout that."

She trots up the stairs. When she's gone, Keenan looks my way. "Nolan, a word before you go?"

"Aye." I hand baby Sam to Sheena. "Go. Pack. We leave within the hour." I kiss her cheek and lean in to whisper in her ear. "I love you."

I walk to Keenan before she even has a chance to reply. He and Lachlan follow me into the office and shut the door behind them.

"Well done, Nolan," Keenan says. "You know I'm not above admitting when I'm wrong."

I nod. A good leader shows meekness, and Keenan demonstrates this well. "Aye?"

"I was wrong about your ability to be a strong leader in our Clan," he says. "What you said out there... would've made dad proud."

His praise warms me through, but I only nod. "Thanks, Keenan. You'd have made him proud as well." And goddamn, but he would have.

"Let's not get all gushy again," Lachlan says with a grimace. "On to business before we start holding hands and singing fucking *Kum Ba Yah* by the campfire."

I cuff him upside the head, and he looks relieved, but it's fleeting when Keenan speaks. He leans against the edge of his desk when he addresses him.

"Tell him what you found today, Lach."

Lachlan turns to face me, and his boyish face looks older. His brows draw together, and there are lines around his mouth he didn't have before. Being an active member of The Clan ages you.

"Went to scout out the family home," he says. "Carson and I went. Fixed the locks, installed a few more. Carson knows his way around there better. Would've gone with Cormac, but you can't go anywhere discreetly with a guy like him."

I can't help but smile. Cormac's enormous size makes it impossible for him not to be noticed.

"Aye."

"Evidence of a struggle. Carson and I found a few locals, did some digging, asked some questions." He pauses. "Found something that matters."

The skin on the back of my neck prickles with awareness. I know what he's about to tell me will hold weight, might even impact everything else we're doing.

"The body of Aine Hurston."

Mother of God.

"Haven't told anyone else yet," Keenan says. "We have a plan, and I don't want to fuck that up. Not now. And it doesn't impact much of what we have to do right now."

What is he talking about? It impacts fucking everything.

Without her mother around, Sheena will have to do something about custody of her siblings, and if she means to me what I think she does…

"You alright, Nolan?"

"Aye," I say, shaking my head. "You think the O'Gregors had anything to do with it, then?"

"No doubt," Lachlan says. "She was into them for money for the drugs."

I turn to Keenan. "You know what this means."

He nods. "It means you'll do whatever you have to. Whatever you decide, you've got the backing of the brotherhood."

"Where does it end?" Lachlan asks. "If they want vengeance on us, and we draw them out of hiding… if we fight them, where does this end?"

"Doesn't have to be an all-out brawl between us," Keenan says. "Their gripe was because they think we took Tiernan. We ventured onto their territory, ruffled their feathers, but that's more easily forgiven."

"They killed his mother," I say.

"Aye," Keenan says. "And according to Clan code? That means he owes them nothing."

"What do we owe them?"

Keenan clenches his jaw and looks out the window. "We didn't harm them. We don't owe them a tribute, we don't even owe them money."

"Of course not."

"We draw them out," I say to Keenan. "Make them meet us, and tell us what they demand. Then we'll have counsel and decide if we can meet their demands."

He thinks over what I've said, and nods. "Right. It's the only way. Who's going with you, Lachlan?"

"Carson, Tully."

"And Cormac and the rest stay here in case the O'Gregors go momentarily insane and decide to attack us here at our house."

I can't help but chuckle. "They *are* the drug dealers around here. Could be high."

"Good stuff they carry. Could lead them to believe they might actually defeat us."

"Hallucinogens, then," Keenan says with a smile.

We can't help but joke about this, but we know the threat is very real.

I meet Sheena upstairs. She needs to know about her mother, but not now. Not when she's already on edge about where we're going and what we need to do. In silence, we prepare, packing only what's necessary. Her hand trembles as she zips up a bag with clothes. A little bag sits by the door.

"What's that?"

"Sam's things," she says in a little voice. I turn to her, but she turns away. I reach for her, but she deflects my hand. I don't pursue her, not now. We have a job to do.

In short time, Tiernan, Fiona, and Sam are ready to go. We give Sheena a car, but I don't join her, not yet.

"You go ahead," I tell her. "It's best if they think you're alone."

She nods, swallowing hard. A strange look crosses her face, but I don't really understand it.

"Y'alright?" I ask.

She nods. "Aye," she says, her voice hoarse.

"Wish you weren't going alone?"

Her eyes fly to me. "Of course, Nolan," she says. "Don't you know?"

I shake my head. Goddamn, I don't know anything for certain anymore.

Her eyes soften, and she reaches a hand out to me and squeezes.

"I don't want to do this alone." For some strange reason, her words hold a note of finality. "But I will. I have to."

"Do what alone?" I ask.

She only shakes her head and walks away.

We'll talk more about that later.

I track her on my phone and watch as the cars behind her leave. The plan is for me to follow behind in short time. I can't follow too closely, or people in Stone City will get suspicious.

It kills me, though, to watch her drive away, to know that she's taking herself and those children into a dangerous situation.

"Fuck it, give me the keys," I tell the driver who stands next to me.

"Sir?"

"Give me the fucking keys," I repeat.

He hands them to me, watching me warily, but my decision's made. I sit in the driver's side, slam the door and put the keys in the ignition. I drive toward them, but at a distance so no one notices. I took nothing with me, but all I need is right ahead of me, only two cars up.

The ride is slow and arduous, with my instinct to step on the gas and drive faster. But I let her go. Just ahead of me. Still, it feels weirdly symbolic. Am I getting sentimental in my old age? Everything feels symbolic and poignant.

Her goodbye kiss. The way she drives away from me. I can't shake the feeling that something terrible's going to happen.

But we pull up to her house, and I'm parked a good bit behind. I wait, while she takes the kids out of the car and heads inside. She shuts and locks the door behind her, and still I wait. I watch to be sure no one followed them, that they're alone. I wait just until I see the son of a bitch she calls her ex lurking in the shadows.

I'm tempted to get out and call to him, to draw the gun I've got tucked in the harness around my waist, and point it at his scrawny head. If I fucking knew he ever put his hands on Sheena before...

"You motherfucker," I mutter to myself. "Didn't wait long, did you?"

Didn't think he would, though. We had a few locals spread the word they were returning. He's been lying in wait.

I watch what he does. He isn't alone. He nods to one man, then another. These fucking douchebags think they're not so transparent but I can see right through them.

I tug a hat on my head and drape a jacket around me, all black so I blend in with the surroundings, when a text comes in from Lachlan.

We're here. O'Gregors are about. Didn't see us, we came in one by one. You see anything?

I text back.

Aye. Fucking douchebag ex hovering outside.

Lachlan: Don't kill him. Not yet. You'll fuck things up.

I mutter to myself but don't reply just yet. It's time for me to go in though.

I'm going in.

I open the car door when I feel someone behind me and cool metal pushed up to my neck. "Make a fucking sound, I kill you."

Chapter 18

Sheena

I DESPISE BEING BACK HERE. The trash bin's overflowing, the sink still filled with dirty dishes, and it smells like garbage and weed. I hate that Nolan's plan involves us being here, but I know he has reasons. We can't lie in hiding from the O'Gregors any longer. It's time we draw them out, make it clear where our loyalties lie.

I hate that my family's been dragged through this. I feel responsible, somehow, even though their very presence in Stone City puts them in contact with the O'Gregors. Reason doesn't matter at times like these, though. My instinct to gather my family to me and run is stronger than ever.

"I hate it here," Fiona says, echoing my own thoughts. "Why are we back? I don't understand why the McCarthys kicked us out like that."

"Right," Tiernan says, shaking his head. "I actually thought for a while they were friends of ours. Bloody hell."

My heart squeezes. I can't believe it didn't even dawn on me to explain anything to them.

"Listen," I say. "I can't speak freely here. I don't know who's watching or what the plan is, but you have to trust me. Can you trust me?"

Fiona nods first. "Of course. Yes, of course I can trust you."

Tiernan finally nods, too. "Of course is right," he says. His jaw hardens. "And we don't need the McCarthys. We can get by on our own."

His words make a lump form in my throat. I want to tell them that it'll be okay, that we can trust them. Instead, I gather up my courage, draw myself up to my full height, and nod. "Aye," I tell them. "We will get through this. Once we know for sure the O'Gregors aren't going to hurt us… we'll regroup. This is part of the plan, though." I'm afraid if I tell them the plan, we could be overheard.

"What about mum?" Fiona asks. Her normally pretty eyes grow hard when she speaks of her.

"We'll deal with her. Don't you worry about her, now, sweetheart."

She sighs. "I'm going to get Sam's toys."

I reach over and ruffle her hair when I get a buzz on my phone.

I see Nolan's name come up and go to swipe it on.

"I'm getting this stinking trash out," Tiernan says. He ties up the bag as I open the text.

It isn't a text but a video. I blink in surprise at first. I can't comprehend what I'm seeing. It's Nolan, but he's tied up and gagged, his head hanging as if he's passed out, or worse.

The door shuts as Tiernan steps outside.

The words below Nolan's picture are even worse than the image. Chilling.

Give us your brother or the boyfriend dies.

"Tiernan!" I scream. "No!"

But Tiernan doesn't come back.

Fiona comes into the kitchen with the baby on her hip, her eyes wide. Her face pales when I show her the text. She looks to the window, but I tell her not to. "Go to your room," I tell her in a hoarse whisper. "Take the baby and hide in the closet. Go!"

She runs.

I look out the window and my heart pounds.

They were sending out word we'd be back, but I never expected they'd act so soon. Where's Tiernan?

Why didn't he come when I called him?

A knock comes at the door. My heart pounds so fast it nearly hurts, the blood rushing to my head making me dizzy. I have to face this problem head on. I can't run from my fears any longer. The lives of literally everyone in the world who matter to me at all are at stake. I open the door to find Cian standing at the door, his hands shoved in his pockets. It's odd. Why didn't he just barge in? Why knock and then enter like this?

"Fancy a visit?" he says, his beady eyes focused on me.

He isn't alone. Half a dozen other men come in with him.

Where are the others? Nolan said we wouldn't be alone, that we'd have protection. Are they letting us be taken for a reason? Why did Nolan himself get captured?

"What do you want with me, Cian?" I ask, backing away as if I'm afraid, when what I'm really trying to do is not poke his fucking eyes out.

"Just you," he says. "You here alone?"

"Of course."

He rears back and slaps me across the face. Pain explodes across my cheek and my eyes blur with tears. "You fucking lying bitch," he says. He grabs the back of my head and drags me out, followed by the others. "Your brother came, too, didn't he?"

If they get Fiona and the baby... my God... what will happen to them?

They have to be safe. I have to trust the McCarthys. Nolan told me they'd be safe.

I'm dragged out of the house and shoved into a car beside Tiernan. I wait for someone to come and help, but no one does. Tiernan's gagged, so he can't speak to me. A moment later, I face the same fate. We careen through the streets, my thoughts on Nolan, Fiona, and baby Sam. Would the O'Gregors stoop so low as to take them, too?

It's a damn good thing I'm gagged. Otherwise, I'd curse these men out and my mouth would get us in trouble again. I recognize where they're going, where they're taking us, to the abandoned church I used to visit when I was younger. This feels like a nightmare I can't wake up from. I want this to end.

We're taken out roughly, dragged along, and brought into the side door of the old church. This isn't the place it was in its heyday, long since abandoned and left to ruin. The stained glass windows are brilliant against the streams of moonlight, even as the rest of the church has fallen into a state of disrepair. And somehow, some way, the colors that fall on the ground before us give me hope, like the stripes of a rainbow after a rainstorm.

I can do this.

I have to trust the McCarthys.

They promised me protection and now I have to trust they'll give us just that.

But I've never trusted anyone in my life before. I

don't know *how* to trust. The only way I've ever brought myself out of my misery was with my own two hands, and now… now I'm being forced to do something I've never done before.

But I can do this.

I think of Fiona and baby Sam, smiling and laughing in the garden with Maeve. The way Tiernan came alive with the men of The Clan, how he took up the challenges they presented him and gave it his all. They did it, damn it. They faced their fears and trusted. So now, I have to do the same.

We're brought into a room, and few words are spoken. Cian looks like he's lowest on the totem pole here, *thank fucking God,* because he takes orders from all the others. He jeers at me when I'm dragged forward and placed on a burgundy carpet before an old, dusty altar.

"Take her gag off," a cold voice says. I look up to see a man I don't recognize. He's tall and thin like Cian, so close in resemblance it's uncanny, but much older. They're related, then?

They take my gag off and shove me to the floor so I can't get up.

"Bring him in, then?" Cian asks.

"Aye."

The older man with the cold black eyes lights up a smoke and eyes me. "So you're the pretty little bitch who likes to interfere with mafia, eh?"

Cian brings in Nolan. Relief and pain flood me at the sight of him.

I look at Nolan, and I'm grateful to see there's no serious signs of assault. His jaw is tight and his body rigid as they drag him in, as if he's prepared to spring from these snares at the very first chance he can. He hasn't been weakened at all. They've under-estimated him. His eyes meet mine across the wooden benches between us and he gives me a smile and a wink, so quick I wonder at first if I imagined it.

"Answer me, woman," the older man says.

"I'm the reporter, yes," I tell him. "Thought that much was clear."

"You watch your tongue, or the boyfriend gets hurt." To demonstrate, he turns to the side and kicks Nolan's shin. To Nolan's credit, he only hisses and winces, but he doesn't cry out. I can't hold it together though. Inside, I'm screaming.

I love that man. I love that fierce, loyal, beautiful man, and it kills me to see him at their mercy.

"Take off his gag as well." He nods to Tiernan.

When Tiernan's gag lies on the floor, he glares at Cian. "I gave you what you want," he says. "You have no quarrel with me. What have we done to you?"

The old man shrugs. "Your sister doesn't know to leave well enough alone," he says. "Brings her arse-hole boyfriend in here to show off his muscles, mmm? Beats up one of my own. Takes the lot of you away? Our best runner, traitor to the McCarthys?"

Nolan looks to Tiernan. "Ignore him, Tiernan," he says. "And remember what we talked about. Remember what we practiced."

What the hell?

Tiernan and Nolan look at each other. Tiernan nods, and Nolan begins to count. I decide to distract the others.

"You know you're a fool to be doing this to us," I say to the man in charge. "And you also know that Cian's a lying sneak, don't you?" My words might get me injured, but I'll survive.

"You bitch," Cian says, raising a hand to strike me at the very same time Nolan yells to Tiernan.

"Three!"

Tiernan knifes up and grabs Cian around the neck. He drags him to the ground and incapacitates him in seconds, using the skills he's learned from Nolan and Lachlan to defend himself and overpower Cian. Nolan kicks his foot out, and the man beside him trips. Others arrive, Carson and Lachlan. Nolan's ropes are cut, gun shots ring out, but they've planned this.

I feel like I need to fight, as if I should defend myself, but I'm mesmerized by the way they orchestrate this. The way they move as one is like a well-oiled machine.

Cian reaches for me, but Tiernan's got him. Another one of his cronies tries to get me, but I roll to avoid him, get to my feet, and give him a swift, hard kick between the legs. I nail him straight in the bollox. He howls with rage and comes after me again, but Nolan's got him. I cringe as he grabs him by the shoulders, drags him down, and knees his belly before he shoves him to the ground and grabs a gun. He points it at his head. Carson's got the older man in the same position.

"We don't want war, lads," Nolan says, panting from the exertion. The Clan has the others subdued, Cian still in Tiernan's grip. "We *do* want your undivided attention."

The older man glares but he can't move. Carson's got a gun trained on him and Tiernan's beside him, ready to throw down if he needs to.

"The Hurston family is under our protection," Nolan begins. "We're aware Tiernan was a runner for you. We've questioned him at length, and believe what he says is true. He has proof he cut ties with you a week ago, told you he wouldn't be working for you anymore, and he's under no obligation to fulfill any more contracted work."

"Aye," the older man says. "'Tis true. Now prove to us he isn't a spy."

"Can't do that," Nolan says. "Though it should be noted we didn't even know he worked for you until we'd already taken him into our protection."

The man shakes his head, and my belly clenches

with apprehension. "Doesn't matter. You know what Clan law states. If we have reason to believe he's a spy, his life is forfeit."

A chill runs down my spine as I watch, first one then the other.

"They're both spies," the man says. "And you know it. The lass does nothing but dig up dirt on the mob and publicize it. She demonizes you. We're next."

Nolan stands to his full height and glares. "And you're responsible for the death of both of her parents. You've left four children orphaned. And you know what clan law says about *that*."

Wait. What?

Orphaned?

Does Nolan know something I don't?

It's hard to breathe, suddenly, like someone's pulled the plug on the air in my lungs and it's all whooshing out of me. I'm not sad. I'm not angry. I think I might be in a state of shock.

The O'Gregors look at each other, and the leader nods. "Aye," he says with a sigh. "I'll have it on record I did not authorize the death of their mother."

"Doesn't matter," Nolan counters. "You know the law. You orphaned the boy with no proof. You have nothing on him that says he was a spy, nothing at all. You killed his father when he worked for you, never informed him, then your men killed his mother."

The man's jaw tightens but he nods. "I know what happened."

"Then tell them," Nolan says. "Tell them what Clan law states."

"Bloody hell," Cian mutters, but the older man curses.

"Shut it, Cian. Was your fault their mum died and you know it."

Tiernan meets my eyes across the rows of benches.

If she's gone... we're free.

Where does this leave us? Where do we go next? I have no idea.

"Means we let you go," the man says. "We can't hold you in any way. Under normal circumstances, Clan law states we owe you restitution." He faces Nolan. "But this isn't free and clear," he says. "Normally, a wrongful death means restitution in full, but with the mitigating circumstances we can cut a deal. Their father deserved the death he had. We've no proof Tiernan betrayed us, and their mother's death was on us."

He stands to his full height, and he's intimidating as hell. "But I want them gone. Their entire fucking family. We'll pay minimum restitution for the death of their mother, under the condition that not a fucking one of them ever comes back here."

Nolan's eyes narrow. "They leave," the man says. "Their entire family gets off this land. They never return to Stone City. If they do, our vows not to hurt them are null and void."

"Done," Nolan says.

I open my mouth to protest, because I don't think it fair they make this deal without any consent from me or Tiernan, but Nolan shoots me a look so fierce I immediately clam up.

Right now, maybe it's best I stay *out* of Clan business for once.

Nolan holds Cian up by the shirt. "It's a deal, under one condition of my own," he says. He gives Cian a shake, like he's a naughty boy and he's caught him stealing from his candy shop. "This man ever comes near my woman again, his life is mine."

The older man's eyes zone in on Cian. "Done."

Nolan drops Cian to the ground. He hangs his head and doesn't protest. He knows he's lost this battle.

"You know you've got a spy among you, McCarthy?" the old man says.

Nolan looks at him sharply.

"Watch your back, son," he says.

Nolan looks at me, Tiernan, and his brothers. "Let's go."

"You have one hour," the old man says.

"Won't need more than ten minutes," Nolan

mutters. He reaches for my hand. I don't know how to respond.

Where do we go now? I have to pack their things up and leave. Where will we go? Do I even want to take his hand?

I don't know what he thinks of me, what he thinks of *us*. My family. Does he trust us? Does he think we're spies?

There's too much to process, too much on my mind.

Tiernan's talking to the men behind us, and Nolan's got my hand.

"Keep your head down," he says. "And I'm sorry."

I blink. Why's he apologizing?

"No talking right now, Sheena. Let's get you home so you can leave."

You.

Not us. Not we. *You.*

Me, Tiernan, Fiona, and Sam.

Why does that make me feel bereft?

I walk in a stupor beside him. I feel like I need a stiff drink, followed by several days of uninterrupted sleep.

"Fiona," I say, my heart leaping into my throat. "Where is she? Is she okay?"

"Lach's with her," Nolan says. "She's fine."

When we get back to the house, Lachlan's at the door, standing sentry. His weapon's drawn, and the look in his eyes is so intimidating, it makes me momentarily pleased he's on my side.

Nolan fills him in, talking all kinds of guy speak that I don't even understand. I catch words like, "restitution," "code," "blowback," and "amnesty." And for the first time... after literal years of watching them, of observing and spying and gathering intel, I understand.

They live and die by a code that bears them up, a code deeply embedded in centuries of tradition in the land of the Irish. Though their mob has only been around for half a century, their family hearkens back to the days of Vikings and Celts. I've seen how they behave. I've seen how they treat each other, and I know now.

They aren't just reckless criminals who wreak havoc. They don't just think they're above the law. They're a brotherhood of loyal men who'll do anything for each other and for the ones they love.

The ones they love.

How I wish I knew we were in that category.

I take Fiona and Sam, one in each arm, and hug them to me.

"We'll say goodbye to this home," I tell them. "And we'll do our best to make our own."

Chapter 19

Nolan

I KNOW the lass is traumatized. Hell, I don't fucking blame her. She's been through hell and back, and no one deserves to find out their mother's been killed in the middle of a battle for their own life.

We can't talk now, though. We're moving as quickly as we can. We've been given an hour to get them out of here, and goddammit, I'm doing my best to ensure that's exactly what happens.

Being told to leave here is the best possible solution.

We pack them up, but take hardly anything. I'm glad to leave this fucking house, and I imagine they feel the same.

Sheena won't look at me, but I don't give it a second

thought. Not at first, anyway. She's got to be under enormous stress and after what just happened. I imagine she's just doing what she has to, like I am.

Tiernan takes baby Sam and fills a flimsy plastic grocery sack with a few things.

"Anything else you need?" I ask him.

He shakes his head. It saddens me that the boy has nothing of importance at all to him, nothing that matters. I don't own many things myself, but I've a few items that do matter to me.

Lachlan helps Fiona. She's taken a liking to him from the beginning, I've noted, and guess she must trust him. Could be because he's the youngest of all, the one with the most boyish temperament. She has a few more things than Tiernan does, but still, her items are few, a little notebook, and a box tied with string she tucks under her arm. Lachlan takes the rest of her things and helps her carry them.

Sheena takes nothing. She scowls at the house as we go to leave and mutters under her breath, "Good fucking riddance."

I can't talk to her now. We're moving them out of here and back to our home temporarily until we find another place for them to live. I have to fill Keenan and the rest of the men in, and we need to ensure that everything we've recorded tonight with the O'Gregors will be fulfilled.

We drive back to Ballyhock in silence. Sheena and

me, that is. Sam coos and fusses a bit until Tiernan finally snaps, "Will you be quiet already?"

No one bothers to contradict or correct him. Tension's high, and we've hardly gotten out of danger.

Fiona and Sam quiet.

We get back to Ballyhock well past midnight. Seems every fucking light's on in the mansion. With a sigh, I turn to Sheena.

"You stay with them tonight," I tell her. "It's important to have you with them. I'll be up with Keenan for a good long while, and we'll make plans to move you in the morning."

She doesn't meet my eyes but looks somewhere past me. For the first time tonight, I wonder what she sees. What she feels.

"Aye," she says. "Thanks very much."

Thanks very much.

It's like we've come to the end of something and are making polite talk, planning to send cards at the holidays, shake hands, and that's about it. I feel as if something's off between us, but I don't really know what. I chalk it up to my preoccupation and her trauma from the night.

"Do they need to see Sebastian?" Lachlan says when we get out of the car.

I shake my head. "I don't think so. Everyone needs a good night's sleep."

"And a strong drink," Sheena mutters. That makes me smile.

"Aye, doll. I'll have something sent up to you."

She smiles sadly. "Thanks—"

I put up my hand to stop her from speaking. She gives me a strange look.

If she says *thanks very much* again I might take her across my knee and give her a good spanking.

I'm pleased to see both mam and Megan waiting for us when we arrive.

"Take care of them," I tell them. "I've got to meet with Keenan straight away, and it's been a difficult night for them."

"Aye," mam says. She reaches for Sam, who goes to her eagerly and tucks his little head against her neck. She closes her eyes when she embraces him, swallows hard, then nods.

Megan takes both of Fiona's hands and gives her a squeeze. "Oh, it's good to have you back."

"They won't stay long, Megan," I tell her. "Just for the night, most like."

I don't miss the way Sheena's body tightens. I reach for her, but she steps away from me and marches up the stairs. Did she see me reaching? Or did she step away on purpose? I frown after her, confused about exactly what just happened, but I have no time to think anything over. We'll deal in the morning.

Keenan's waiting for me in his office. Lachlan and Carson join me as we go in to tell him everything that happened.

He scrubs a hand across his brow when we enter. "Didn't expect you boys to deal that quickly," he says. "Efficient, aren't you?"

"Didn't have much of a chance," Lachlan says. "They were waiting for us."

"Aye," I tell him. I fill him in on all that happened, what was said, and how we negotiated restitution.

"Told us we had a spy among us," Lachlan says with a frown. "Think he was pulling the mickey, Keenan?"

Keenan looks sharply at Lachlan, then me.

"What do you think, Nolan?"

"No idea," I tell him.

"We'll have to see," he says. "In the past, a warning from the O'Gregors hasn't been something to heed, has it?"

"I agree. He's no friend of ours, Keenan," Lachlan says. "Could've just been stirring up trouble among us."

"Aye," Keenan says. "No doubt. For now, we make sure that we're safe and secure. I'll follow up with Father Finn to ensure he's heard nothing more about stirrings at the O'Gregors. Nolan?"

I nod. "Where's Sheena tonight?"

I tell him. He nods. "Seems like the right decision. And your plans after tonight?"

"Don't know," I mutter with a sigh. "I'll deal in the morning."

Keenan nods, then pushes to his feet. "It's late, lads. Get some rest. We'll have another meeting in the morning." He holds up a finger in warning. "But see to it that no one else hears about this talk of a rat, understood?"

"Aye," I agree.

"Aye," Lachlan repeats.

We leave Keenan's office, and a part of me wants to go to Sheena. Hell, no. *All* of me wants to go to Sheena. But something's off, and I know it. I tell myself she's upset about tonight, she can't deal with whatever's happened. That whatever's made her pull away from me has nothing to do with us.

Now that her mother's gone... now that they've left Stone City... I should feel free.

But I don't. It feels like a great weight hangs on my chest, and I'm helpless to push it off.

So I go to my room alone.

I tell myself she needs space.

She needs time.

I want to pour myself a few fingers of the best damn Jameson I have and swig it. I haven't been tempted to drink this badly since I gave it up. It's a damn good thing I have none nearby. Not sure I'd be able to stop myself tonight.

I stare out the window to the sea, dark and barely visible but for the moonlight that filters from above. I yank open the balcony door. The sea's tumultuous and vicious tonight, so powerful it could pull a grown man beneath the surface, never to return again. We used to have a lighthouse here but it burnt down a few years ago. I wonder idly if we should build a new one.

Why do I feel as if I'm grieving a loss? As if tonight marks the end to something powerful? I stare at the sea and breathe in the salt air until I shiver with cold. I've got a big day ahead tomorrow and need to get to bed.

I hate going to bed alone.

Chapter 20

Sheena

I SHOULD FEEL RELIEF. I should be happy about all that's happened. We're free.

Free.

And yet it doesn't feel that way.

I'm grateful that Maeve and Megan go back to the room with us. I don't want to be alone with my brothers and sister tonight. The weight of responsibility falls heavily on me with my mother's passing. I'm not sure how to process my feelings toward her death, and am even less sure how to help them as well.

"What happened tonight?" Maeve asks me, as Megan walks ahead with Fiona. Tiernan joins us and fills her in.

She listens with patience, never interrupting, with no outward show of emotion until he gets to the part of mum's passing.

Maeve gasps and covers her mouth. "Oh, I'm sorry."

"Don't be," Tiernan says. "Honestly, it's the best thing that could've happened."

"I agree with him," I say.

Maeve shakes her head sadly. "It's a sad day when children don't grieve the loss of their mother. She must not have appreciated all of you the way she should have."

Tiernan and I look at each other briefly, one moment of grief we share. Not for the loss of a woman who didn't deserve our love, but for the loss of a life we should have had.

"No," he says, shaking his head. "She didn't."

Megan watches us in silence, her wide eyes taking it all in. She isn't usually so quiet, and it makes the night feel somber. I wonder what her story is.

"Well," Maeve says. "We'll get some rest for tonight, and tomorrow, I'm sure the boys will help us come up with a plan for all of you."

"Aye," Megan says. "Those boys are good at that type of thing." Her twinkling eyes look teasingly at Maeve, who swats at her with affection. Megan laughs and runs ahead, opens the door to the room where they've been staying, and ushers us all in.

I get the kids situated finally. Maeve and Megan offer to stay, and at first I tell them I'm fine.

"You've been through a lot," Maeve says gently. The three of us sit in a small dining area, drinking steaming cups of tea while the others sleep soundly. "Let me stay tonight and help if Sam wakes? You need your rest."

I look at her kind, gentle gray eyes, and to my shock and horror, find my own filling with tears. She notices and reaches her hand to mine.

"Oh, Sheena," she says softly. "Don't cry, lass. It'll be alright."

But she doesn't know why I'm crying.

"I hated you, though. And I'll never forgive myself for it."

She blinks in surprise and Megan places her cup on the table, then stills.

I tell her everything. How I was told Seamus McCarthy was to blame for my father's death, and how I set out to right the wrongs done to me in pursuit of the wrong family. How I nursed my hatred and let it fester until I wanted every one of the McCarthys to pay.

"All of you," I say, crying freely now, not even bothering to check my tears. "I hated all of you and wanted you all to suffer for what I thought he did."

Megan lifts her cup of tea and takes a long pull before she responds with a roll of her eyes. "Well," she finally says. "They aren't exactly saints, now, are they?"

And for some reason, her response amuses me. I can't contain the maniacal laugh that bubbles up inside me. I place my mug down and cover my mouth. My whole body shakes with laughter.

"Mother of God, child, you've lost yer mind, haven't you?" Maeve says, rubbing her hand across my back, but Megan loves any chance to laugh, so she quickly joins in. We silently snicker until finally Maeve laughs, too, and the three of us silently laugh and cry until Maeve gets up, walks to a sideboard, unlocks it and withdraws a bottle of whiskey. She comes back to us and douses each of our mugs.

"Jesus, have a drink, girls," she mutters, which makes me and Megan laugh even harder. And somehow, right then, with the dim light above us and the soft sounds of gentle snores coming from the other room, on the night I lost my mother, I found a friend. Megan reaches for my hand and squeezes it.

"No one blames you now, Sheena. Won't say you were anyone's favorite for a while, I won't lie. But something tells me that cousin of mine would rather cut off his right bollox than see you come to harm."

"Megan," Maeve hisses. "He's my *son*."

"Aye, and he's got a pair like the rest, doesn't he, now?"

Maeve rolls her eyes, sighs, and sits back down next

to us. But instead of drinking her tea, she lifts the slim bottle of amber whiskey to her lips and swigs straight from the bottle. She doesn't even wince, but chugs the fiery liquid straight, plunks it back down on the table, and sighs with satisfaction.

"Megan's right," Maeve says. "I don't blame you for hating me. I'd have hated me, too, if I thought what you did."

I shake my head. "I don't deserve your forgiveness, though."

She leans in and smiles. The woman's old enough to be my mother, dressed in a simple pair of faded trousers and a slim-fitting white tee, but right then, I've never seen anyone more beautiful.

"There's something I've learned, having lived my entire life surrounded by these men," she says. "You can't hold onto anger, Sheena. You have to forgive. If you don't, it eats you up inside like acid, burning away the good bits until there's nothing left but rot. It isn't your *enemies* that bear the brunt of your anger. It's *you*."

I look away, because I have to think about this. A part of me knows she's right, because I've experienced just this. My anger and hatred didn't bring justice to those I thought wronged me. Instead, it left me bitter. It ate me up inside to the point where I could barely bring myself to even think of the well-being of another.

"You're right," I tell her. "I felt that. I did."

She nods. "I know you did. That kind of hatred can't be hidden. But the vengeance in your eyes, lass... it's gone now. Those children in the other room have given you so much, haven't they? If not for them, you wouldn't be where you are today."

I nod with a sigh. "Aye."

Megan yawns wildly. "I wish I could stay up, but I've got a shift at the hospital in the morning and need to get some rest. Will you be here tomorrow, Sheena?"

I answer her honestly. "I don't know."

"Well, if I know my cousin, he'll reach out to me for help moving, so I'm sure we'll be in touch." She leans in and kisses my cheek before turning to leave. A lump rises in my throat again.

Maeve sees her to the door, then comes back to me. Wordlessly, she bends down, and wraps her arms around me. She holds me, and the damn tears I fought back surface again. I close my eyes to them, grateful she doesn't expect me to talk. Nolan's held me, and the children have embraced me, too. But I haven't had this, the touch of a mother, in so long I forgot what it's like.

"You're a good girl," she whispers in my ear. "And my son will do well by you. Now get some rest. The sun will rise on another day, and we'll put this all behind us."

And then she's gone into Sam's room where there's

a little bed set up next to his crib. She shuts the door.

The whiskey's warmed me through and made me sleepy. I rise, walk to the window, and look outside. From here I can see a dim light by the greenhouse, but everything's at rest. I miss the view of the sea from Nolan's balcony. It soothed me before I went to bed. We're on the other side of the house here, not facing the ocean, and though it's lovely and quaint here, clean and secure, it isn't the same. I tell myself it's the view that I miss, that's all. But it's the first night apart from Nolan since I came here.

My son will do well by you.

Will he, though? Or are Nolan and I through?

Were we even together to begin with?

Why doesn't he come to me? Why has he sent me away? He had us leave his home, then brought us here. I wonder what he'll do in the morning.

I wonder what I will.

I don't ask for things and never have. I'm not that girl. I'm the independent one, who does things on her own. I'm the girl who finds her own way. I don't depend on others. But now I've been thrust into a situation where I'm left with only two choices.

Leave and begin again, without the help of the McCarthys.

Or take their help.

I finally get ready for bed and sleep on the sofa. It's

a wild, restless sleep. I dream of guns and babies crying, and the places I traverse in my dreams is an odd conglomeration of the McCarthy mansion and the hovel back in Stone City. I wake when the sun rises, my eyes so tired they hurt. I try to get some sleep, but I can't.

I want Nolan.

I want to see him. To feel him. I want to lay my head on his chest and be strengthened by his warm, firm hand on the small of my back. I want to kiss him and tell him thank you. I want to make slow, passionate love to him until we're sated. I want him to take me, own me, dominate me in the way that brings peace and freedom to my mind.

But I can't have those things.

I know now that I love him, and loving him means I have to let him live his life unencumbered with a woman like me.

Realizing this makes me ache, but at the same time I feel almost… free. I tell myself this is what selfless love is.

Maeve's words from the night before echo in my thoughts, until it's all I can think of. But it isn't fair, to foist the troubles of my family on theirs. I don't know how I can ask that of them.

A soft knock comes at the door. I'm dressed in joggers and a faded t-shirt Megan lent me. I toss the blanket aside and walk quickly to the door, so I don't wake anyone else. Maeve opens the door, dressed in a robe, baby Sam against her hip. She smiles and mouths, "Good morning." I smile back and whisper the same.

I go to the door. There's a peep hole here, and when I look through I see not one but four men outside. There's only one I have eyes for. He stands in jeans and a t-shirt as well, rumpled as if he slept in them.

I open the door quickly, and Nolan steps in.

"Are you all coming in, then?" I say, looking in surprise at the others.

"No," he says. "This is the guard I left here for you last night. They'll stay right here."

I can't let myself get all swoony over this, I can't. It's just standard, what they do for everyone under their protection. This is what I tell myself, anyway.

He slams the door, turns to me, and reaches for me. Before I can protest, his hands are wrapped in my hair and he's kissing me, his body pressed up to mine as if he can't take another breath without touching me. I pull away with effort.

"Nolan!" I say in a hissed whisper. "Your mother is *right there.*"

He holds the back of my head, his eyes burning into mine while he looks behind me.

"Ah, hi, mam," he says. "I need to talk to Sheena alone for a bit."

She smiles. "Of course," she says. "Go on with you.

Sheena, go pack the things you've got in his place and I'll get the children ready and fed."

"Thank you—" I start to say, but my voice pitches into a squeal. He's yanking me straight out of the door.

"If anyone sees me…" I try to protest but naturally he doesn't heed me.

"Don't care," he says. "One night apart was enough. I was an idiot for letting even that happen."

"Nolan," I begin. I have to tell him everything I've decided, that I can't let his family suffer for mine any longer. "You have to let me go. I can't go with you. You need to listen—"

"I'll listen," he half-growls, crossing the landing by the stairs and bringing me down the hallway that leads to his room. "When I'm balls-deep in you and your eyes are locked with mine."

"My God," I whisper. "Are you out of your *mind*?"

"Nope. The most honest answers I get out of you are when you're being properly, soundly fucked. So that's how we'll talk."

Right, then, my ovaries twitch again and I think I just got struck with lightning, for my body's sizzling right about now. A tiny, little voice inside is telling me to protest harder, not to let him seduce me, that I have to stand my ground and do what's right. He yanks open his door, drags me in, and pushes me up against it.

Suddenly, the little voices in my head stop talking.

He wraps his hand around my throat, not harshly, but enough that I'm pinned against the wall and can't get away. He bends, brushes his lips against mine, then plunders my mouth. His tongue sweeps against mine, and I feel as if he's swallowing me whole. For every sigh I release, he breathes in deeper. I'm boneless, unable to stop this, when his hands reach for my waist and he strips my clothes off. First, the t-shirt, balled in his fist and whipped over his shoulders to land on the floor behind him. Next, the joggers, yanked down my hips until I'm standing before him stark naked.

"Bloody hell," he mutters. "Jesus, you're a picture."

I whimper when he brings his mouth to my neck and suckles the delicate skin while he pinches my nipple between his thumb and forefinger. I'm dwarfed by him, and not just physically. His energy and need to possess me clears my mind as it makes my heart dance a crazy rhythm.

"It was a mistake," he groans, releasing me just long enough to strip off his own clothes.

"What was?"

His forehead falls to mine. "Letting you go for even that one night."

Chapter 21

Nolan

WE LAY in the stillness of early morning. I left the balcony door open, and a chilly, salty breeze rustles the bedsheets. Sheena draws closer to me, her head on my chest. She grips me so hard I feel she may never let me go.

And Jesus, I hope she doesn't. I hope she never lets me go.

"I've always left when things get difficult," she says. "But I won't, Nolan. I won't."

"Good. I won't let you. I'd track you down and drag you home by the hair."

She shivers and smiles. "Mmmm, I love it when you talk dirty to me."

I grin.

I love this woman.

"Mam is going to lose her mind," I tell her. "Three more to call her Granny? Well, one. I think Fiona and Tiernan may not go for the granny thing."

"Fair enough," I say around a grin.

Keenan may lose his mind, too, when I'm telling him I'm moving away from here. My plan isn't to move far, though, but right by the Church. There's a little cottage there, big enough for all of us. For now. I don't tell Sheena it's likely Tiernan will board at St. Albert's soon.

We'll work the details out later.

We shower and dress, and when we go to meet her family for breakfast, we tell them the news. Neither of us sees the point in holding back any longer.

"Where's the ring?" Fiona asks with a little dance.

Sheena rolls her eyes. "Give us *time*, Fiona. My God, but you're a little matchmaker, aren't you?"

Lachlan walks in the room and Fiona clams up so quickly, it's amusing. I look from him to her, then back again.

He smiles warmly at her, before he takes a plate and loads it up with food. He doesn't eat it, though, but walks over to Fiona and places the plate in front of her. "You love the currant scones," he says. "Have to get them before Cormac comes in."

She smiles and flushes even deeper.

Sheena narrows her eyes, having watched this exchange. "Mother of God," she says to me through gritted teeth. "If that brother of yours thinks for one goddamn minute that my *child of a sister—*"

"Is no more than a child who's here under the protection of the brotherhood? A friend, as it were? Aye," I tell her. "Trust me, Sheena. He wouldn't think of it. And if for some ridiculous reason he ever *did* get the notion in his mind? I'd kill him with my bare hands before you got a chance yourself."

"I'd help you," she begins.

I take her hand in mine and give her a little squeeze. "Down, girl. He gave her a plate of scones. It's harmless."

She sighs, then shakes her head. "If you say so."

"I *do,*" I tell her. "Now come, today's a celebratory day, isn't it?"

She finally gives me her winsome smile, the one that lights up her whole face. I bend and kiss her forehead, my hand cupped at the back of her neck. She sighs into me and places a gentle hand on my arm.

"You're too good to me," she whispers.

"Nah," I tell her. "Don't worry, doll, I'll make you pay up later."

She winks. She's game.

Tiernan is understandably hesitant at first, then

finally gives us a sheepish grin. "Means you'll be my brother, Nolan?" he says with a shy smile.

I grin at him. "Aye, brother."

He swells with pride. It's the first time I've given him the Clan title of brother. Sheena may have issues with our recruiting him, but she'll learn to deal with it. He's meant to be part of the brotherhood as much as I am, or Carson, or Lachlan, or any of the other brothers who aren't related by blood but heart. They are every bit as much my brothers as Keenan and Cormac.

"What's this?" Keenan walks in the room, Cormac behind him. I stand with Sheena to greet them.

"They're moving in together!" Fiona says, and when Lachlan laughs out loud, Fiona hides her face in her napkin.

Keenan swings his gaze to mine, his brows lifting upward. "What's this, Nolan?"

I meet his gaze squarely and don't look away. I stand by my decision.

"We'll have to talk about this," he says. "In the history of The Clan, no blood relation has ever lived off the premises."

"Aye," I tell him. "But sometimes it may be time to break tradition."

"Break tradition?" Carson enters, his hair still damp from a post-run shower, most like. He saunters up to the table and grabs the last scone just before

Cormac does. Cormac growls at him, but Carson ignores him. "What's Nolan doing now?"

"Why'd you assume it was *me*, you motherf—"

I pause when Sheena smacks my arm.

"Course it's you," Carson says. "Fess up."

Keenan fills him in, and Carson heads to the table with a plateful of food. "Aye," he says. "Smart. The O'Gregors might have told Sheena they'll leave off, and they may have made a bargain because of Tiernan. But I don't trust them. If you show them you two have a solidified relationship, there's no way they'll touch you."

Sheena's brows raise, and she looks at me with her mouth slightly parted. "What's he talking about?" she says.

"Marriage!" Fiona says. Keenan groans and pours himself a cup of tea. Cormac grins around a mouthful of scone. Mam pretends she's just buttering a scone, but it looks like she isn't even breathing, and Fiona once more flushes a shade that matches her hair. Poor lass.

I blink, as what Fiona just said makes sense to me.

Marriage.

"Aye," Carson says. "You know Clan law, Nolan. If you're married to her, no rivals can touch her without certain and severe consequences. It's the safest thing to do. And if you marry her, Tiernan becomes like family. Also subject to the protection of The Clan."

"We need to talk about this later," Cormac says.

"Sure," Carson says, ever pragmatic and logical.

"If later means right after breakfast, yes," Keenan says sternly, giving me a serious look that once more rivals dad's.

I grin at him.

"I'm done eating. You?"

He puts the rest of his scone in his mouth, a mammoth bite, then chases it down with a cup of tea.

"Animals, every one of them, like I never taught them a day's worth of manners," mam mutters to herself. It's the first she's spoken since Sheena and I came down. I wonder what's on her mind, what she thinks of all this.

Our meeting is brief, all the members of The Clan who were at breakfast joining us.

I tell them why I made my decision and hold Sheena's hand and look Keenan in the eye when I tell him, "And this is what's best for us. Think on it, Keenan. You know we planned this from the beginning."

"We did not," Keenan says, eyeing Sheena thoughtfully. "We planned on Sheena and her family leaving, yes. We did not plan on you going with them."

Sheena bristles, but I place my palm on her lap to settle her.

"And now I think it's the right decision," I tell him. "It doesn't mean I'm any less devoted to The Clan than I am now."

He works his jaw but doesn't respond at first.

"Yes and no," Cormac says. He leans back in his chair, stroking his chin thoughtfully. "Truth is, when you take a family of your own, your duty is to them above all. And even though you're still dedicated to The Clan, it's impossible to be as dedicated as you were when you were single."

"That may be true," Lachlan says, his eyes serious. He's leaning back in a chair perched precariously on two legs. "But think of all the time he *won't* spend chasing pussy now?"

I punch his arm so hard he topples over. "Not in front of Sheena, you—"

Keenan raises his eyes heavenward. Lachlan's laughing even as he rubs his arm and adjusts his chair.

"It's my job, Sheena," he says. "I don't mean anything by it. Nolan has no younger brother, see."

She shakes her head and cracks a smile. "He can still chase pussy," she says. "Around the dining room table, then?"

Even Keenan chuckles. I only shake my head.

"Alright," I say out of the side of my mouth. "Behave yourself."

"Or what?" she breathes in my ear.

My God, the little brat.

I bend my mouth to her ear and make a promise that makes her flush as deeply as Fiona.

Keenan clears his throat. "Since something like this is unprecedented, I thought it prudent to discuss it as brothers. But you have your mind made up, Nolan. And I understand why." He draws in a deep breath, and once more the heaviness of leadership rests heavily in the lines of his forehead. "So tell us how we can help, and we'll do what we can."

Sheena blinks rapidly, as if she's trying to hold back tears. I squeeze her hand.

"Aye, brother. I will."

We stand together and leave the room. It feels symbolic, leaving a meeting of The Clan together like this, like I've made my choice. We did it once before, but the circumstances were very different.

I won't choose. I refuse. I love Sheena, and I love The Clan. And if Cormac and Keenan can raise a family in The Clan, so can I. Hell, I've already recruited a new brother.

Still, as the days pass and nothing comes of the run-in with the O'Gregors, we pack our bags and prepare to move, a part of me grieves this. It's what anyone would, I suppose, like the loss of a childhood innocence.

We move to the vacant cottage that overlooks the Irish Sea, just like the mansion. It's only a stone's throw from the home where I grew up, which pleases mam immensely. She can go for a bit of a walk and come visit anytime she wishes. It pleases Keenan, too, to have me so close he can call a meeting whenever he needs. Carson says the location is perfect for safety purposes and shows me how we can surround our new home on all sides with the protection we need.

On the day we move, I find myself standing at the edge of the cliffs, just like I did the day I was instructed to find Sheena. I look out at the sea and take a drag from a cigarette. I don't smoke much, but there are times it helps.

"Didn't you know you smoked, Nolan." I look over my shoulder to see Tiernan and Fiona approaching me.

I toss the cigarette to the ground and grind it beneath my heel. "I'm quitting," I tell them. "That was my last one. It's a terrible, nasty habit." I'm suddenly aware of the fact that I'm responsible for these two now, to help Sheena raise them right. I cross my arms on my chest and give them a serious look. "And if I ever catch the two of you smoking—"

"Wait, now, how did catching *you* with a smoke become a lecture to *us*?" Fiona asks, her eyes dancing with amusement.

I stroke my chin thoughtfully. "Well, since I'll... sort of be your brother now."

She grins. "Sort of. But be warned, I already have an older brother, and I don't let him boss me around either."

Tiernan growls, and I feel an instant kinship with the lad. He rolls his eyes as he looks to me, then clears his throat. "Anyway, Nolan, we're here for a reason," he says. "Can we have a word?"

"Of course." Mam and dad were always good about being available for us, never turning us away. They never made it feel like an inconvenience. I feel the weight of responsibility for these two. And if I'm honest?

I like that.

I wasted years of my life before I got my head on straight, with no one to care for, no responsibilities. And now that I have them... even if by choice... I feel more fulfilled.

Fiona crosses her arms over her chest, and though she looks at me kindly, her voice holds an edge of steel that reminds me of her sister.

"We've seen what Sheena's gone through the past few years. And if you have any intentions at all about leaving her, know this. It will break her heart."

Tiernan nods. "Aye. And we won't allow it, Nolan. We won't let anyone lead her around, you see. We saw her waste herself on men who didn't deserve her in the past. And let's be honest. A connection to your family brings added complications."

"Aye," I tell him. "I know it. But on the other side of that coin, Tiernan? If I claim your sister and make her mine, she'll have more than a connection to The Clan. She'll have their protection and guidance. Financial and physical security all the days of her life."

"And family," Fiona says softly. "She'll have family. More than the dysfunctional crew she currently has."

Tiernan frowns. "Speak for yourself."

"Lad, you're most definitely a dysfunctional crew," I tell him affectionately. He playfully punches me, and I lose my footing, stumbling toward the cliff's edge. Large rocks loosen and drop downward and rain into the ocean below. Tiernan grabs me by the arm, and though I'm in no real danger of falling, yanks me back to firmer footing.

"Mother of God," he mutters. "I could've killed my sister's man."

I shake him off and punch him back. He takes it unflinchingly. Likely thinks he deserves it.

"Don't flatter yourself," I tell him. "Gotta try harder than *that* to kill me. Anyway, welcome to the brotherhood. It's what we do. Threaten the lives of each other one minute, then save the very lives we threatened the next."

Fiona shakes her head. "I will literally never under-stand men."

Tiernan glares. "*Good.*"

"Neither will I," Sheena says, walking toward us with baby Sam on her hip and mam by her side. "But do you *have* to do this right at the edge of the cliff? *Really?* As if my heart can take anything else?"

"Honest to goodness," mam says, shaking her head. "Get back here, will you? Lord but I'm thankful the new house has a fenced-in yard for the likes of you."

I walk from the edge and take baby Sam in my arms. He jabbers on about something in baby speak. "Really?" I ask him. "You've got an opinion, too, hmm?"

Sheena's eyes shine at me. "He adores you."

"Good," I tell her. "Maybe then he'll sleep for me tonight, after we move everything?"

She grins and kisses my cheek. "Don't count on it."

I give her a wink. "That's fine," I lean in and whisper in her ear. "Because I already fully planned on keeping you up all night."

She gives me a coy smile, and my heart warms.

This feels right. Sheena. Her family… *our* family. I'm still firmly established in the brotherhood, but now I'm moving in a direction that's all mine. Taking on the responsibility of a family and soon, I'll take Sheena as my wife.

Mam stays back when the others go ahead and squeezes my hand.

"Your dad would be proud of you, Nolan McCarthy. *I'm* proud of you," she says. She kisses my cheek, and we go meet up with the others.

Sheena smiles at me.

"It's a different world, isn't it?" I say. "Facing the same things today as we did yesterday, only now we do it together."

She takes my hand in hers and gives me that beautiful smile that lights up her eyes and makes my heart squeeze. "Aye," she says. "Together."

EPILOGUE

SHEENA

I love our new home.

Love it.

It's nowhere near as elaborate as the McCarthy mansion on the cliffs, but it overlooks the sea, the view of the ocean right outside our living room windows as gorgeous as a painting. There's a little swing set in the backyard, a little play center, a picnic table, and it's fenced in for privacy. Nolan took with him a security detail, men that are as faithful as guard dogs. Lachlan occasionally joins them.

The inside of the house is well-lit and well-furnished, simple but modern. The kitchen is airy and spacious with tiled floors and stainless-steel appliances. Honestly, I've never had anything like it. Fiona and Tiernan each have their own room, and baby Sam has a little nursery right off our room. It's peaceful here. Calm. It isn't perfect. There are growing pains when merging a family, trials and errors and tears and confusion, at times. But we manage to make it work.

Some days, it doesn't seem real. But it isn't in the moments of vivid, utter perfection, that I want to pinch myself.

Not when we sit around the enormous table in the McCarthy dining room, joined together as one while the brothers regale us with tales of their childhood. Not when we celebrate together, my brothers and sister feasting on decadent foods and being spoiled for the first times in their lives. The bonds of family are a blessing, but those aren't the times that feel surreal. I cherish those moments. I hold them in my heart like they're closely guarded buried treasure, and maybe they are, those sweet moments of perfection that fill my heart.

But no, those aren't the times I feel this is almost too good to be true. It's in the trying times I sometimes struggle to accept this. To embrace this. To own it.

When baby Sam wakes in the night with an upset stomach, crying while standing in his crib, fat tears rolling down his chubby cheeks, and Nolan stumbles out of bed in pajama bottoms and a wrinkled t-shirt.

"Sleep, doll," he tells me. "You got him last night. I'll get him tonight." And he does.

When Fiona goes and pulls an all-nighter with her friends, never coming home for curfew. We have to find her, bring her home, and make sure she understands the importance of safety and honesty.

When Tiernan is accepted into St. Albert's, and we drop him off at the door, and he walks away with a grin on his face and a duffel bag in his hand. I collapse in the car when he's gone and cry as if my heart will break.

Those are the moments that I give thanks with all my heart that I'm no longer alone. A lesser man would've bowed under the weight of this responsibility. Raising a family, while devoting himself to the demands of his Clan. But not Nolan. And every day that we face as one brings me closer to him.

He's gone during the day on Clan business, and I've hung up my job as reporter. Instead of the investigative reporting I once did, I now write for the media, though I've been assigned a travel column instead.

It's a lot less dangerous, and a lot more exciting.

Though Nolan doesn't hide who he is from me, I chose to be ignorant of what he does. It's a challenge at first, but I adapt. And eventually, I come to accept this. All of this. That the work of The Clan isn't legal but necessary, the backbone of Ballyhock in more ways than one. Crime is nearly nonexistent, the church thrives, and law enforcement work with them like a well-oiled machine. I don't even pretend to know what they do. I don't pretend this is all okay. What I do is mind my own damn business.

We don't have the privacy we crave, though. Between the children underfoot and the men of The

Clan always about, we sneak in our private moments in stolen bits and pieces.

The first day mam comes to take Sam for an outing and Fiona is in school, I'm working in the bedroom. I have a deadline at noon to submit an editorial on inexpensive family travel destinations in South America, when I hear the door open.

"Hello?" I call out. No answer. I open the drawer next to my desk where I keep my tools for self-defense that Nolan gave me. I look outside the window briefly and note my bodyguards in place. So whoever's entered hasn't gotten their notice.

"Hello?" I say again, my heart beginning to pound. I hold the pepper spray in my hand, ready to use it, my cell phone programmed to call the guard if necessary.

The door to the room flings open, and I throw the pepper spray at him with a blood-curdling scream. I gasp when I see it's Nolan.

He ducks just in time to avoid it, and the items he carries in his hands go flying.

"Bloody hell, Sheena!" he bellows. "What the fuck are you doing?"

"Oh, Nolan! Oh my goodness, are you okay? Did I get you?"

I fall to my knees beside him.

"I'm fine," he growls, reaching for me. "But I'll teach you to attack me in the middle of the day when I've come for good reason!" Though he's growling at me, his eyes are twinkling. He's been looking for a good reason to toss me over his knee, the kinky bastard.

And the next thing I know he's kneeling on the floor and dragging me across his lap. I haven't been spanked in ages, and even though I wriggle and squirm in protest, I know he's not really punishing me. He misses this as well as I do.

He slams his palm against the fullest part of my arse.

"That, woman, is for trying to burn the eyes out of my head! And for future reference, you spray the damn thing, not throw it!"

I squeal, my yelps buried in laughter while he continues the torrent of hard smacks.

"You didn't answer me!" I protest. "Twice I said *hello* and you said nothing in return!"

"Had headphones on," he says pleasantly, gripping my waist and continuing the sound spanking he set out to give me.

"Doesn't matter," I say, panting, when his hand rests in between smacks. "You still scared me."

He sets me upright on the carpet, and plants me sitting on my scorched backside. It's then that I notice what tumbled from his hands. I cover my mouth with my hand in surprise, not sure how to respond.

"Nolan," I whisper. There's a bouquet of wild-flowers wrapped in cellophane and a black velvet box.

"Oh, don't get all excited, now," he says with mock severity. "Not gonna propose to the girl who tried to blind me."

"Tried to blind you?" I say, giving it right back. "One could argue, sir, that *I'm* the one who was blinded." I mutter to myself. "Falling head-over-heels, help-lessly, madly, *irrevocably* in love with *mafia*."

He raises a brow questioningly. "Mafia? Is that plural? I swear you get more verbose on writing days."

"Verbose? Did you have to look that one up?"

He shakes his head. "Careful, doll, or I'll put you back over my knee and you'll lose the trousers and knickers."

A trill of excitement weaves through me. "Mmmm," I moan.

He's kneeling in front of me, grinning, when he reaches for the little box. His hand shakes a little. I blink in surprise. He never shakes.

"Since you didn't succeed in blinding me, we will commence," Nolan says, with the air of a judge and a grin that melts my heart.

"Will we?" I ask in a husky whisper, all humor now gone.

"Aye," he says, mirroring my whisper. "Because it's

time. We work well together, you and I. We know each other, Sheena." He holds my gaze as he continues. "And I love you. Let me claim you, lass. Let me make you a McCarthy. It will keep you safe, and it will…" He swallows hard. "It will make me a happy man."

He opens the box. I give him a coy look. "Megan helped you pick that out, didn't she?" I tease.

He grins. "Of course. Now answer the damn question."

"Is there really a question, Nolan?" I ask him, and my nose tingles when I answer. "I love you. And you love me. And every day I spend with you makes me even more grateful that we're together now. Yes. Yes, of course I'll marry you, if you'll have me."

He slides the ring on my finger, drags me to my feet, and pulls me into his chest in a hug so tightly, I can't breathe for a few seconds. Then he whips his phone out of his pocket and makes a call. Squeezing my hand so tightly it hurts, he shouts into the phone, "She said yes!"

The door bursts open, and suddenly, our entire home is filled with people. Megan runs in first, gives me a massive hug, then opens a bottle of champagne. Maeve comes in with Sam, and Carson comes in with Tiernan. I run to him and embrace him as I haven't seen him in weeks. Keenan's there with Caitlin and the children, and Cormac and Aileen as well. Tully and Boner arrive, and even Father Finn comes, bearing cakes and scones from the bakery. He gives us his blessing, and we party long into the night.

Finally, after the kids have gone to bed and Tiernan back with Lachlan and Carson, Nolan and I collapse into bed ourselves.

"I want to pinch myself," I whisper to him.

Nolan reaches to my arse and gives it a good pinch. "Happy to do it for you."

"Of course you are." I sigh.

His phone rings and he answers it on the first ring.

"Hello?"

His brows knit together, and he frowns. "Aye. I'll be there shortly."

He gets out of bed and hangs up the phone.

"Nolan? Can you tell me what it is tonight?" Some nights he has to keep his calls secret, and I honor that. "

He nods. "Aye. Carson's Eve's gone missing."

"Missing?" I ask.

He sighs. "Aye. Went off with some friends back in her hometown and hasn't come back. We need to go searching."

"Why would she do that?" I ask, mulling it over.

"He should've married her," Nolan says.

"Why?"

"You know why, Sheena. Think about it."

I do. I feel my mouth part when I look at him, my eyes widening. "You think someone took her?"

He shrugs. "Don't know. He hasn't wed her, could be anything. But honestly, she probably just lost track of time with friends. He can be a little over-protective."

"Oh, right, I don't know anyone like *that*. And you're going with him to find out."

"Of course. He's gone with Megan already. Megan says she thinks she knows where she might've gone. But Lach and I will go in as back up."

It's a stark reminder that no matter how much we love each other, no matter how perfect this all seems, he's still deeply entrenched with whatever happens to the McCarthys. But I'm okay with that. I accept it now. Life is messy, and there is no escaping that. You can't really.

But I've got family on my side and friends who love me.

"Y'alright, doll?" he asks, running his fingers through my hair. I sigh again, but this time it's in contentment. I love how he does that.

"Aye," I tell him. "I am. I'm fantastic, honestly. And so thankful, Nolan. Some days I ask myself how to thank you. How I can possibly give back what you've given me. How you could've forgiven me for what I've done. And I vow that I will be devoted to you." I smile and use the words of his brothers. "You have my word."

He smiles and pulls me to him in a warm, firm embrace before he shrugs on his shoulder holster and slides two handguns in place.

"And I love you," he says. "There's no need for you to ask for forgiveness or to prove your worth anymore, Sheena." A lump forms in my throat. He holds me harder. "I've already claimed you. I've already made you mine. And you're already *everything*."

Already everything.

The words echo in my mind and heart while he kisses me.

Already everything.

Everything I have. Everything I need.

Everything we'll become… together.

FROM THE AUTHOR: I hope you've enjoyed reading Nolan: A Dark Irish Mafia Romance.

I AM SO grateful for your support! Please read on for a preview of the next in the Dangerous Doms series: Carson: A Dark Irish Mafia Romance. *I've also included previous of other books you may enjoy.*

PREVIEW

Carson: A Dark Irish Mafia Romance

Coming soon

🐍

Two years later

PROLOGUE

Carson

THE PHONE CALL wakes me out of a dead sleep. I roll over and look at the time. Two o'clock in the morning. I blink, bleary-eyed, when the phone rings again, and stare at the empty bed beside me. Eve's gone on holiday with a friend of hers, and I've been watching the baby on my own. I just got her back to sleep.

The phone rings again.

Keenan.

"Hello?"

"Carson."

His voice is tight and laced with pain, as if he's braced himself to make this call. Something's wrong.

I sit up, my heart racing, and I glance again at the empty bed beside me.

"What is it?"

"There was an accident," he begins. "The police called me first. They didn't have your number."

Cold dread shivers down my spine. I'm fully awake now, and this moment feels surreal, as if frozen in time, suspended in ice, a moment I already know I'll never eviscerate from my memory.

"What kind of an accident?" I ask. My voice isn't my own, like it's borrowed from an alien life form.

He gives me the news that shatters my world.

Rain.

Car accident.

She didn't make it.

It's like an invisible hand draws down a shade over my life.

My heart.

My mind.

I slither down into darkness.

Previews

KEENAN

Chapter one

I watch from where I sit on the craggy cliffs of Bally-hock to the waves crashing on the beach. Strong. Powerful. Deadly. A combination so familiar to me it brings me comfort. It's two hours before my alarm goes off, but when Seamus McCarthy calls a meeting, it doesn't matter where you are or what you're doing, the men of The Clan answer.

I suspect I know why he's calling a meeting today, but I also know my father well enough not to presume. One of our largest shipments of illegal arms will arrive in our secured port next week, and over the next month, we'll oversee distribution from the home that sits on the cliff behind me. Last week, we also sealed a multi-million-dollar deal that will put us in good stead until my father retires, when I assume the throne. But something isn't right with our upcoming transactions. Then again, when dealing with the illicit trade we orchestrate, it rarely is. As a high-ranking man of The Clan, I've learned to pivot and react. My instincts are primed.

The sun rises in early May at precisely 5:52 a.m.,

and it's rare I get to watch it. So this morning, in the small quiet interim before daybreak and our meeting, I came to the cliff's edge. I've traveled the world for my family's business, from the highest ranges of the Alps to the depths of the shores of the Dead Sea, the vast expanse of the Serengeti, and the top of the Eiffel Tower. But here, right here atop the cliffs of Ballyhock, paces from the door to my childhood home, overlooking the Irish Sea, is where I like to be. They say the souls of our ancestors pace these shores, and sometimes, early in the morning, I almost imagine I can see them, the beautiful, brutal Celts and Vikings, fearless and brave.

A brisk wind picks up, and I wrap my jacket closer to my body. I've put on my gym clothes to hit the workout room after our meeting if time permits. We'll see. My father may have other ideas.

I hear footsteps approach before I see the owner.

"What's the story, Keenan?"

Boner sits on the flat rock beside me, rests his arms on his bent knees, and takes a swig from a flask. Tall and lanky, his lean body never stills, even in sleep. Always tapping, rocking, moving from side to side, Boner has the energy of an eight-week-old golden retriever. My younger cousin, we've known each other since birth, both raised in The Clan. He's like a brother to me.

"Eh, nothing," I tell him, waving off an offer from the flask. "You out of your mind? He'll knock you upside the head, and you know it."

If my father catches him drinking this early in the day, when he's got a full day of work ahead of him, heads will roll.

"Ah, that's right," he says, grinning at me and flashing perfect white teeth, his words exaggerated and barely intelligible. "You drink that energy shite before you go work on yer manly *physique*. And anyway, get off your high horse. Nolan's more banjaxed than I am."

I clench my jaw and grunt to myself. *Fuck*. Nolan, the youngest in The Clan and my baby brother, bewitched my mother with his blond hair and green eyes straight outta the womb. Shielded by my mother's protective arms, the boy's never felt my father's belt nor mine, and it shows. I regret not making him toe the line more when he was younger.

"Course he is," I mutter. "Both of you ought to know better."

"Ah, come off it, Keenan," Boner says good-naturedly. "You know better than I the Irish do best with a bit of drink no matter the time of day."

I can toss them back with the best of them, but there's a time and place to get plastered, and minutes before we find out the latest update of the status of our very livelihood, isn't it. I get to my feet, scowling. "Let's go."

Though he's my cousin, and I'm only a little older than I am, Boner nods and gets to his feet. As heir to the throne and Clan Captain, I'm above him in rank. He and the others defer to me.

He mutters something that sounds a lot like "needs to get laid" under his breath as we walk up the stone pathway to the house.

"What's that?" I ask.

"Eh, nothing," he says, grinning at me.

"Wasn't nothing."

"You heard me."

"Say it to my face, motherfucker," I suggest good-naturedly. He's a pain in the arse, but I love the son of a bitch.

"I *said*," he says loudly. "You need to get fuckin' *laid*. How long's it been since the bitch left you?"

I feel my eyes narrow as we continue to walk to the house. "Left *me?* You know's well as I do, I broke up with her." I won't even say her name. She's dead to me. I can abide many things, but lying and cheating are two things I won't.

"How long?" he presses.

It's been three months, two weeks, and five fucking days.

"Few months," I say.

He shakes his head. "Christ, Keenan," he mutters. "Come with me to the club tonight, and we'll get you right fixed."

I snort. "All set there."

I've no interest in visiting the seedy club Nolan and

Boner frequent. I went once, and it was enough for me.

Boner shakes his head. "You've only been to the anteroom, Keenan," he says with a knowing waggle of his eyebrows. "You've never been *past* there. Not to where the *real* crowd gathers."

"All set," I repeat, though I don't admit my curiosity's piqued.

The rocky pathway leading to the family estate is paved with large, roughly hewn granite, the steep incline part of our design to keep our home and headquarters private. Thirty-five stones in the pathway, which I count every time I walk to the cliffs that overlook the bay, lead to a thick, wrought-iron gate, the entrance to our house. With twelve bedrooms, five reception rooms, one massive kitchen, a finished basement with our workout rooms, library, and private interrogation rooms, the estate my father inherited from his father is worth an estimated eleven million euros. The men in The Clan outside our family tree live within a mile of our estate, all property owned by the brotherhood, but my brothers and I reside here.

When I marry—a requirement before I assume the throne as Clan Chief—I'll inherit the entire third floor, and my mother and father will retire to the east wing, as my father's parents did before them.

When I marry. For fuck's *sake*. The requirement hangs over my head like the sharpened edge of an executioner's blade. No wedding, no rightful inheritance. And I can't even think of such a thing, not when my ex-girlfriend's betrayal's still fresh on my mind.

I wave my I.D. at the large, heavy black gate that borders our house, and with a click and whirr, the gates open. When my great grandfather bought this house, he kept the original Tuscan structure in place. The millionaire who had it built hailed from Tuscany, Italy, and to this day, the original Tuscan-inspired garden is kept in perfect shape. Lined with willow trees and bordered with well-trimmed hedges, benches and archways made from stone lend a majestic, age-old air. In May, the flowers are in full bloom, lilacs, irises, and the exotic violet hawthorn, the combined fragrances enchanting. The low murmur of the fountain my mother had built soothes me when I'm riled up or troubled. I've washed blood-soaked hands in that fountain, and I laid my head on the cold stones that surround it when Riley, my father's youngest brother and my favorite uncle, was buried.

We walk past the garden, and I listen to Boner yammer on about the club and the pretty little Welsh blonde he spanked, tied up, and banged last night, but when he reaches for his flask again, I yank it out of his hand and decidedly shove it in my pocket.

"Keenan, for fuck's—"

"You can have it after the meeting," I tell him. "No more fucking around, Boner. This is serious business, and you aren't going into this half-arsed, you hear?"

Though he clenches his jaw, he doesn't respond, and finally reluctantly nods. I'm saving him from punishment ordered by my father and saving myself from having to administer it. We trot up the large stairs to the front door, but before we can open it, the massive entryway door swings open, and Nolan stands in the doorway, grinning.

"Fancy meetin' you two here," he says in a high-pitched falsetto. "We won't be needin' any of yer wares today."

He pretends to shut the door, but I shove past him and enter the house. He says something under his breath to Boner, and I swear Boner says something about me getting laid again. For once in my life, I fucking hope my father assigns me to issue a beating after this meeting. I'm so wound up. I could use a good fucking fight.

"Keenan." I'm so in my head, I don't notice Father Finn standing in the darkened doorway to our meeting room. He's wearing his collar, and his black priest's clothes are neatly pressed, the overhead light gleaming on his shiny black shoes. Though he's dressed for the day, his eyes are tired. It seems Boner isn't the only one who's pulled an all-nighter.

"Father."

Though Father Finn's my father's younger brother, I've never called him uncle. My mother taught me at a young age that a man of the cloth, even kin, is to be addressed as Father. It doesn't surprise me to see him here. He's as much a part of the McCarthy family as my father is, and he's privy to much, though not all, of what we do. It troubles him, though, as he's never reconciled his loyalty to the church and to our family.

Shorter than I am, he's balding, with curls of gray at his temples and in his beard. The only resemblance between the two of us are the McCarthy family green eyes.

Vicar of Holy Family, the church that stands behind my family's estate, Father Finn's association with the McCarthy Clan is only referenced by the locals in hushed conversation. Officially, he's only my uncle. Privately, he's our most trusted advisor. If Father Finn's come to this meeting, he's got news for us.

He holds the door open to my father's office, and when I enter I see my father's already sitting at the table. He's only called the inner circle this morning, those related by blood: Nolan and Cormac, my brothers, Boner, Father Finn, and me. If necessary, we'll call the rest of The Clan to council after our first meeting.

"Boys," my father says, nodding to Nolan, Boner, and me in greeting.

My father sits at the head of the table, his back ramrod straight, the tips of his fingers pressed together as if in prayer. At sixty-three years old, he's only two years away from retirement as Chief, though he keeps himself in prime physical shape. With salt and pepper hair at his temples, he hasn't gone quite as gray as his younger brother. He jokes it's mam that keeps him young, and I think there's a note of truth in it. My mother ten years his junior, they've been wed since their arranged marriage thirty-three years ago. I was their firstborn, Cormac the second, and Nolan the third, though my father's made mention of several girls born before me that never made it past infancy. My mother won't talk of them, though. I wonder if the little graves that lie in the graveyard at Holy Family are the reason for the lines around my mother's bright gray eyes. I may never know.

I take my seat beside my father, and pierce Nolan and Boner with stern looks. Boner's fucking right. Nolan's eyes are bloodshot and glassy, and I notice he wobbles a little when he sits at the table. Irishmen are no strangers to drink, and we're no exception, but I worry Nolan's gone to the extreme. I make a mental note to talk to him about this later. I won't tolerate him fucking up our jobs because he can't stay sober. I watch him slump to the table and clear my throat. His eyes come to mine. I shake my head and straighten my shoulders. Nodding, he sits up straighter.

Cormac, the middle brother, sits to my left and notices everything. Six foot five, he's the giant of our group, and, appropriately, our head Bone-breaker. With a mop of curly, dark brown hair and a heavy beard, he looks older than his twenty-five years.

He nods to me and I to him. We'll talk about our concerns about Nolan later, not in the presence of our father. Or any of the others, really.

"Thank you for coming so early, boys," my father begins, scrubbing a hand across his forehead. I notice a tremor in his hand I've never noticed before and stifle a sigh. He's getting older.

"It came to my attention early this morning that Father Finn has something to relay to us of importance." He fixes Boner and Nolan with an unwavering look. "And since some of you haven't gone to bed yet, I figured we should strike while the iron's hot, so to speak."

I can't help but smirk when Nolan and Boner squirm. When Boner's father passed, one of the few gone rogue in our company, my father took Boner under his wing and treated him as one of his own. I love the motherfucker like a brother myself. Though he's got a touch of the class clown in him, he's as loyal as they come and as quick with a knife draw as any I've seen, his aim at the shooting range spot-on. He's an asset to The Clan in every way. When he's fucking sober, anyway.

Now, under both my gaze and my father's, he squirms a little. My father keeps tabs on everyone here, Boner no exception.

"I think it best I let the Father speak for himself, since he needs to leave early to celebrate mass." None of us so much as blink, the Father's duties as commonplace as a shopping list. We're used to the juxtaposition of his duties to God's people and to us. We have long since accepted it as a way of life. He has a certain code he doesn't break, though, and out of respect for him, we keep many of the inner workings of The Clan from him. We give generously to the church, and though God himself may not see our donations as any sort of indulgence, the people of Holy Family and Ballyhock certainly do.

Father Finn sits on my father's left, his heavy gray brows drawn together.

"Thank you, Seamus." He and my mother are the only ones who call my dad his Christian name. Finn speaks in a soft, gentle tone laced with steel: a man of God tied by blood to the Irish mob.

My father nods and sits back, his gaze fixed on his younger brother.

Father clears his throat. "I have news regarding the... arms deal you've been working on for some time."

My father doesn't blink, and I don't make eye contact with any of my brothers. We've never discussed our occupations with Father so out in the open like this, but like our father, he sees all. The church he oversees is sandwiched between our mansion that overlooks the bay to the east, and Ballyhock's armory to the west. Still, his blatant naming of our most lucrative endeavor is unprecedented.

Though we dabble in many things, we have two main sources of income in The McCarthy Clan:

arms trafficking and loansharking. Though neither are legal, Father Finn's insisted we keep out of the heavier sources of income our rival clan, the Martins from the south, dabble in. They're known for extortion, heroin imports and far more contracted hits than we've ever done. Rivals since before my parents married, we've held truce ever since my father took the throne. Both his father and our rival's former chief were murdered by the American mafia; the dual murders formed a truce we've upheld since then.

"Go on," my father says.

Father Finn clears his throat a second time. "There's no need to pretend I don't know where you're planning to get your bread and butter," he says in his soft voice. "Especially since I've advised you from the beginning."

My father nods, and a muscle ticks in his jaw. His brother takes his time when relaying information, and my father's not a patient man. "Go on," my father repeats, his tone harder this time.

"The Martins are behind the theft of your most recent acquisitions," he says sadly, as he knows theft from The Clan is an act of war. "Their theft is only the beginning, however. It was a plot to undermine you. They fully plan on sub-contracting your arms trafficking by summer. They have a connection nearby that's given them inside information, and I know where that inside information came from."

Boner cracks his knuckles, ready to fight. Nolan's

suddenly sober, and I can feel Cormac's large, muscled body tense beside me. My own stomach clenches in anticipation. They're preparing to throw the gauntlet, which would bring our decades-long truce to a decided and violent end.

"Where would that be?" I ask.

Finn clears his throat again. "I'm not at liberty to give you all the details I know," he begins.

Boner glares at him. "Why the fuck not? Are you fucking kidding me?"

The Father holds up a hand, begging patience.

"Enough, Boner," I order. There's an unwritten rule in my family that we don't press the Father for information he doesn't offer. I suspect he occasionally relays information granted him in the privacy of the confessional, something he'd consider gravely sinful. Father Finn is a complex man. We take the information he gives us and piece the rest together ourselves.

"I can give you some, however," the Father continues. "I believe you'll find what you need at the lighthouse."

I feel my own brows pull together in confusion.

"The lighthouse?" Nolan asks. "Home of the old mentaller who kicked it?"

"Jack Anderson," the Father says tightly.

The eccentric old man, the lighthouse keeper, took a heart attack last month, leaving Ballyhock without a keeper. Someone spotted his body on the front green of the lighthouse and went to investigate. He was already dead.

Since the lighthouses are now operated digitally, no longer in need of a keeper, the town hasn't hired a replacement. Most lighthouse keepers around these parts are kept on more for the sake of nostalgia than necessity.

The man we're talking of, who lived in the lighthouse to the north of our estate, *was* out of his mind. He would come into town only a few times a year to buy his stores, then live off the dry goods he kept at his place. He had no contact with the outside world except for this foray into town and the library, and when he came, he reminded one of a mad scientist. Hailing from America, he looked a bit like an older, heavier version of Einstein with his wild, unkempt white hair and tattered clothing. He muttered curse words under his breath, walked with a manky old walking stick, and little children would scatter away from him when he came near. He always carried a large bag over his shoulder, filled with books he'd replenish at the library.

Father Finn doesn't reply to Nolan at first, holding his gaze. "Aren't we all a little mental, then, Nolan?" he asks quietly. Nolan looks away uncomfortably.

"Suppose," he finally mutters.

The Father sighs. "That's all I can tell you, lads. It's enough to go on. If you're to secure your arms deals, and solidify the financial wellbeing of The

Clan, and most importantly, keep the peace here in Ballyhock, then I advise you to go at once to the lighthouse." He gets to his feet, and my father shakes his hand. I get to my feet, too, but it isn't to shake his hand. I've got questions.

"Was the lighthouse keeper involved?" I ask. "Was he mates with our rivals? What can we possibly find at the lighthouse?"

Inside the lighthouse? I've never even thought of there being anything inside the small lighthouse. There had to be, though. The old man lived there for as long as I can remember. There's no house on property save a tiny shed that couldn't hold more than a hedge trimmer.

My father holds a hand up to me, and Cormac mutters beside me, "Easy, Keenan."

Father Finn's just dropped the biggest bomb he's given us yet, and they expect me just to sit and nod obediently?

"You know more, Father," I say to him. "So much more."

Father Finn won't meet my eyes, but as he goes to leave, he speaks over his shoulder. "Go to the lighthouse, Keenan. You'll find what you need there."

READ MORE

THE BRATVA'S Baby (Wicked Doms)

Kazimir

THE WROUGHT IRON park bench I sit on is ice cold, but I hardly feel it. I'm too intent on waiting for the girl to arrive. The Americans think this weather is freezing, but I grew up in the bitter cold of northern Russia. The cold doesn't touch me. The ill-prepared people around me pull their coats tighter around their bodies and tighten their scarves around their necks. For a minute, I wonder if they're shielding themselves from me, and not the icy wind.

If they knew what I've done... what I'm capable of... what I'm planning to do... they'd do more than cover their necks with scarves.

I scowl into the wind. I hate cowardice.

But this girl... this girl I've been commissioned to take as mine. Despite outward appearances, she's no coward. And that intrigues me.

Sadie Ann Warren. Twenty-one years old. Fine brown hair, plain and mousy but fetching in the way it hangs in haphazard waves around her round face. Light brown eyes, pink cheeks, and full lips.

I wonder what she looks like when she cries. When she smiles. I've never seen her smile.

She's five-foot-one and curvy, though you wouldn't know it from the way she dresses in thick, bulky, black and gray muted clothing. I know her dress size, her shoe size, her bra size, and I've already ordered the type of clothing she'll wear for me. I smile to myself, and a woman passing by catches the smile. It must look predatory, for her step quickens.

Sadie's nondescript appearance makes her easily meld into the masses as a nobody, which is perhaps exactly what she wants.

She has no friends. No relatives. And she has no idea that she's worth millions.

Her boss, the ancient and somewhat senile head librarian of the small-town library where she works won't even realize she hasn't shown up for work for several days. My men will make sure her boss is well distracted yet unharmed. Sadie's abduction, unlike the ones I've orchestrated in the past, will be an easy one. If trouble arises eventually, we'll fake her death.

It's almost as if it was meant to be. No one will know she's gone. No one will miss her. She's the perfect target.

I sip my bitter, steaming black coffee and watch as she makes her way up to the entrance of the library. It's eight-thirty a.m. precisely, as it is every other day she goes to work. She arrives half an hour early, prepares for the day, then opens the doors at nine. Sadie is predictable and routinized, and I like that. The trademark of a woman who responds well to structure and expectations. She'll easily conform to my standards... eventually.

To my left, a small cluster of girls giggles but quiets when they draw closer to me. They're college-aged, or so. I normally like women much younger than I am. They're more easily influenced, less jaded to the ways of men. These women, though, are barely women. Compared to Sadie's maturity, they're barely more than girls. I look away, but can feel their eyes taking me in, as if they think I'm stupid enough to not know they're staring. I'm wearing a tan work jacket, worn jeans, and boots, the ones I let stay scuffed and marked as if I'm a construction worker taking a break. With my large stature, I attract attention of the female variety wherever I go. It's better I look like a worker, an easy role to assume. No one would ever suspect what my real work entails.

The girls pass me and it grates on my nerves how they resume their giggling. Brats. Their fathers shouldn't let them out of the house dressed the way they are, especially with the likes of me and my brothers prowling the streets. It's freezing cold and yet they're dressed in thin skirts, their legs bare, open jackets revealing cleavage and tight little nipples showing straight through the thin fabric of their slutty tops. My palm itches to spank some sense into their little asses. I flex my hand.

It's been way, way too long since I've had a woman to punish.

Control.

Master.

These girls are too young and silly for a man like me.

Sadie is perfect.

My cock hardens with anticipation, and I shift on my seat.

I know everything about her. She pays her meager bills on time, and despite her paltry wage, contributes to the local food pantry with items bought with coupons she clips and sale items she purchases. Money will never be a concern for her again, but I like that she's fastidious. She reads books during every free moment of time she has, some non-fiction, but most historical romance books. That amuses me about her. She dresses like an amateur nun, but her heroines dress in swaths of silk and jewels. She carries a hard-covered book with her in the bag she holds by her side, and guards it with her life. During her break time, before bed, and when she first wakes up in the morning, she writes in it. I don't know yet what she writes, but I will. She does something with needles and yarn, knitting or something. I enjoy watching her weave fabric with the vibrant threads.

She fidgets when she's near a man, especially attractive, powerful men. Men like me.

I've never seen her pick up a cell phone or talk to a friend. She's a loner in every sense of the word.

I went over the plan again this morning with Dimitri.

Capture the girl.

Marry her.

Take her inheritance.

Get rid of her.

I swallow another sip of coffee and watch Sadie through the sliding glass doors of the library. Today she's wearing an ankle-length navy skirt that hits the tops of her shoes, and she's wrapped in a bulky gray cardigan the color of dirty dishwater. I imagine stripping the clothes off of her and revealing her creamy, bare, unblemished skin. My dick gets hard when I imagine marking her pretty pale skin. Teeth marks. Rope marks. Reddened skin and puckered flesh, christened with hot wax and my palm. I'll punish her for the sin of hiding a body like hers. She won't be allowed to with me.

She's so little. So virginal. An unsullied canvas.

"Enjoy your last taste of freedom, little girl," I whisper to myself before I finish my coffee. I push myself to my feet and cross the street.

It's time she met her future master.

READ MORE

ABOUT THE AUTHOR

USA Today bestselling author Jane Henry pens stern but loving alpha heroes, feisty heroines, and emotion-driven happily-ever-afters. She writes what she loves to read: kink with a tender touch. Jane is a hopeless romantic who lives on the East Coast with a houseful of children and her very own Prince Charming.

Would you like to read *Island Captive: A Dark Romance* totally free? Sign up HERE for my newsletter, and grab your freebie!

What to read next? Here are some other titles by Jane you may enjoy.

DARK ROMANCE

Dangerous Doms

Keenan: A Dark Irish Mafia Romance

Cormac: A Dark Irish Mafia Romance

Ruthless Doms

King's Ransom

Priceless

Beyond Measure

Wicked Doms

The Bratva's Baby

The Bratva's Bride

The Bratva's Captive

Undercover Doms standalones

Criminal by Jane Henry and Loki Renard

Hard Time by Jane Henry and Loki Renard

The Savage Island Duet

Savage Dom

Savage Love

Standalone

Island Captive: A Dark Romance

CONTEMPORARY ROMANCE

NYC Doms standalones

Deliverance

Safeguard

Conviction

Salvation

Schooled

Opposition

NYC Doms boxset

The Billionaire Daddies

Beauty's Daddy: A Beauty and the Beast Adult Fairy Tale

Mafia Daddy: A Cinderella Adult Fairy Tale

Dungeon Daddy: A Rapunzel Adult Fairy Tale

The Billionaire Daddies boxset

The Boston Doms

My Dom (Boston Doms Book 1)

His Submissive (Boston Doms Book 2)

Her Protector (Boston Doms Book 3)

His Babygirl (Boston Doms Book 4)

His Lady (Boston Doms Book 5)

Her Hero (Boston Doms Book 6)

My Redemption (Boston Doms Book 7)

And more! Check out my Amazon author page.

You can find Jane here!

Reader group, The Club (on Facebook)

Website

Made in the USA
Columbia, SC
14 June 2020